The Most Unlikely
Beginnings

Signet

Volume 1

The Most Unlikely Beginnings

K. Merriweather

MAJESTIK MULTIMEDIA • ST. LOUIS

Signet: The Most Unlikely Beginnings
Published by Majestik Multimedia
A subsidiary of Create Space Independent Publishing Platform
Copyright © 2012 Kimberly Merriweather and Katherine Merriweather
All rights reserved. This book, or parts thereof, may not be reproduced or transmitted by any means in any form without permission from the publisher; exceptions are made for brief excerpts used in published reviews.

First Edition

This book is set in Georgia Type Text.

Printed in the United States of America

First Edition: July 2013
First Printing: July 2013

ISBN-13: 978-0615734507
ISBN-10: 0615734502

Cover Art by Kita Parnell

For more awesomeness, visit *Majestik Multimedia*!
www.majestikmultimedia.com

Beyond the edge of imagination begins a new universe. Where, at the edge of space, a war has been raging between those who rule with fear, and those who protect life; both are seeking the most powerful weapon ever existed.

*This weapon has more power than all the stars could ever provide! It is the most coveted, feared, or hated object that could ever be possessed, whom only a fool, or a madman, or the **right** man would dare harness and control the power of THE SIGNET!*

PART ONE

THE SIGNET

Late September in Petoria felt as if it were the middle of August, with unusually hot weather. The frigid air on the bus put James Russell in better spirits during his short twenty-minute commute to Downtown Petoria until he had to make the five-minute walk to Parsons and Parker's Shipping and Receiving Services.

James sighed once he stepped off the bus and winced from the sudden scorching heat and sun. It was only a quarter to nine in the morning and was already another one of those sweltering and muggy days.

James felt crummy, still sore and stiff from dancing at the discotheque last night. Break dancing was still the newest craze that he couldn't command his formerly gymnastic body before his growth spurt into doing. At least the clothes, with its bright, stretchy, form-fitting fabrics amid crazy patterned leggings and leg-warmers, looked great on the women.

James made his way to the brick building with solid cherry Windsor doors and whitewashed oak Monticello windows, finding it easily among the drab gray, tan, or red brick warehouses on the waterfront. Entering through the double glass doors, he gave halfhearted waves to his coworkers who bypassed him.

Heading for his gray cubicle at the end of the corridor, James dreaded his usual duty of answering telephone inquiries for some product getting sent to another part of the world. When the questions over the phone didn't keep him biting the ends of his already pitted pencils, James fielded mail to other departments on his floor. He also typed documents on his trusty word processor, readying them for processing sent downstairs to the mail sorting section.

James didn't mind his job as it was easy, yet it gave him time to mull about working for Pome Computers. He enjoyed crafting code for the newest machine, the Orichide system. James socked away as much as he could from his paltry desk jockey paycheck hoping to buy the computer to tinker on in the near future. The Orichide had the fastest processor, displayed the most colors, and had an integrated synthesizer chip for sound. It was top of the line compared to other computers currently on the market.

James frowned, remembering his dashed take on acceptance at Worldwide Computing Machines as he typed another report. He considered the hard slap he received from the secretary and watched her shred his application. James had dated her for a time then stopped calling, not bothering breaking up with her properly.

"Come on," he had pleaded. "Just forward it to Human Resources! I won't even work on the same floor with you!"

"No," she snapped. "All you blonds are the same. I'm getting sick of this crap."

"Maybe you're with the wrong ones--"

"Yeah," she said and glared. "Get out of my office before I call security!"

When James left WCM, he caught his reflection on the glass doors. He thought himself average in looks, with short blond hair and narrow blue eyes that occasionally roved for the ladies, but at six feet tall and weighing at an athletic one-hundred eighty pounds, he stood out.

"*If that harpy hadn't sabotaged me*," James said to himself and his word processor chirped at him, bringing him out of his thoughts. A message on-screen stated the program needed a new floppy disk so it could automatically save. The floppies constantly stuck inside the machine and the program faulted from its unable to read it properly. He banged the side of the word processor.

"Great!" James grumbled when the screen suddenly went black, "A power failure!" He forcibly pulled the power cord out the wall. "Damn machine has been giving me problems all day!"

"Yo, incoming!" called Robinson, the office mail clerk.

James reached out blindly and captured a small box tossed to him. Looking down at it, he noted the new company desk calendars for the following year had come in and set the daybook aside on his desk. James sighed and looked up at the overhead clock, noting he only wasted two hours after starting his job that morning.

"Gonna catch the last ball game of the season, Russell?" asked Mitchell, another coworker.

"I'll try," James called back.

"I heard the Series is supposed to be matched up good."

"Really now?"

Taking a break from the machine, James grabbed a problem ticket from his desk drawer and wrote his complaint to send to the Information Systems department.

"Like they'd get anything done!" he muttered, "Those party animals only come to work on Tuesdays after getting over their hangovers!" James blew a hard sigh and slipped the report into his 'out' box at the end of his desk.

Getting code for the Orichide during one of their shindigs was never easy from the reliable tech crew. Despite being clearly ripped from pills, booze, and lots of herb, James wished he could party with them, however his work came first no matter how soul-destroying. Now trying to get an actual machine to test it on was something else entirely...

At five minutes to twelve, James loosened his blazer, left his desk, and made a mad dash for the door.

"Hey," called Simmons, "where ya going?"

"I'm taking off," James called over his shoulder. "*My brain needs it*," he thought and threw open the glass doors. "*Parsons and Parker keep me so busy; it's no wonder they have a high turnover rate because of suicide!*"

James pulled out of his blazer and draped it over his shoulder, finding the morning heat worsened once it became noon. He saw across the yard that it didn't stop the exercisers from doing their thing. They took part in the martial arts program provided as part of the Employee Assistance Division. Officially, it was for employees who felt they were going mad from their job and to help them blow off steam as a preventive measure before the required 'three day think-over'.

Making his way to the nearby office park where other workers did slow-moving martial art exercises, James stopped nearby, staring at the women who did the delayed movements with the men.

"*Down, Jim, cool it,*" he said to himself as his face flushed. "*You'll get yourself into trouble again!*"

Walking away, James recalled times he received complaints about his wandering hands and his comments to the female workers at Parsons and Parker. He didn't consider himself sexist. Women going out and doing whatever empowered them, he agreed with. James needed no help from a woman. He thought himself a decent cook and knew how to do his own laundry without turning his white work shirts pink, but always turned into a raving drooling Neanderthal when a beautiful woman caught his eye.

Parsons and Parker wanted to keep James since he lasted beyond the two-year mark without becoming depressed or suicidal and thought better to put him into the all-male secretarial department who handled heavy-duty typing and filing duties.

James bristled at the mere thought of working in that part of the cube farm. He found one specific coworker exceptionally unsettling. The man's unwarranted attention always creeped James out to the point it nearly unnerved him and made him anxious about coming to work. He figured it had to be some kind of karmic backlash for treating women badly for so long.

Taking in a deep breath of fresh air, James headed to the rear of the office park commissioned by Parsons and Parker. It was rumored around the water cooler that the park, used as a time-out area for company workers from the office, gave those unable take it anymore enough space to shoot themselves in solitude.

His thoughts about the backbreaking company silenced once he took in the sight of downed charred trees and burnt grassland.

"Did a fire happen just here?" James wondered, dropping his blazer in surprise. He scanned the area that appeared scorched and flattened, with many broken-down trees. *"Or was it a bomb?"*

James found it odd there were no police or fire personnel around the area. Ignoring the nagging thought of what could have caused the strange incident, he checked his watch. James only had about a half hour to investigate, but his stomach told him otherwise. He picked up his blazer, figuring grabbing lunch at the food court and eating at his desk again would be a better idea as there would be plenty of time to look around later.

"Hey, wait!" an accented voice called to James as he turned to head back to the office. James paused then stepped back in mild alarm when a harried figure advanced, panting for breath. It wore a form-fitting uniform, having rips on the leg and chest. On its feet were heavy calf-high black leather boots long red leather gloves cuffed at the elbow covered its hands. A silver visor obstructed its face, but the lower half appeared human and had dried blood and many cuts on its lip, jaw, and chin.

Noticing a glowing golden pistol strapped to the stranger's thigh and an illuminated green staff on its back, James swallowed his fear and drew what little courage he had to back away.

"Please, wait," said the uniformed stranger, reaching for James. "I have an important message; it is a life-or-death matter!"

"I can't help you," James replied nervously, pulling out of the fighter's grasp. "I'm not getting involved!" He gave the stranger a critical glance, noticing from the sound of its voice, the stranger was seemingly a young male around his age. "What's with the weird clothes? You a fan of *Space Wreck* or *Space Junk* or something?" James scoffed and waved him away. "You missed the convention back in August!"

"*Space Junk*? *Space Wreck*?" The young man shook his head and gestured to himself. "These clothes aid me in my travels, good Sir!"

"Um, okay."

"I have been searching for so long; I think I found it now!"

James took another step away. "*Great, a lunatic,*" he thought and asked warily, "So, how does this include me? What *are* you searching for, exactly?" The young man grinned brightly and James quickly pulled into his suit jacket, immediately growing anxious. "If you tell me you're looking for me, forget it. I've already got one guy in the office lusting after me."

"But--!"

James stormed away. "I don't want to know!"

"Please!"

James paused for a moment, considering the strange uniformed man disoriented after getting banged up. He grunted and turned around, ignoring the nagging feeling that he was betraying his instincts to leave. "Anyway," James demanded, "who are you and *why* are you here?"

"*How* did I get here is a better question!" the young man replied, smiling faintly. "I almost did not make it. I was followed." He hustled up to James. "The kind who followed me would not have been much trouble usually if my equipment had not failed on me!"

"So you want me to *fix* it, right?" James snorted. "Look, man, I'm just a hobby programmer, got it? I'm doing the pencil pusher thing until I can break into Pome. I'm not fixing some crapola BUCOL machine."

"So, you *are* interested! Good," said the young man. "I hope to give you something before those guys returned--"

"If it's enough to fight over, then no thanks!" James waved him off and glanced at his watch, noting the time. "Anyway, I'm running late. My lunch break is long over!" James began walking away.

"At least take a look," the young man called after him.

James stopped and sighed heavily. "Alright," he said. "I guess it doesn't hurt to at least try..." James turned to face the stranger and froze in stark fear when the young man removed his visor. "Your eyes--!"

The faint crept up came quickly, blotting out James's surroundings.

"Ugh," James moaned once his mind returned to reality. He squinted and groaned as bright light seared his eyes. "Morning?" he muttered, "What the hell?" James sat up, holding his head. "This had better be a dream!" He found his clothing roughly rearranged, with his shirt unbuttoned, tie loosened, and his suit jacket halfway on his arm. "Did I get into a fight?" He heard a minute chirp in the distance.

"What's that sound?" James thought as he straightened his clothing and glanced at his watch, noting the time. *"No matter; Parsons and Parker will open in a few minutes if I don't hurry!"* He gasped as everything suddenly hit him at once and he recalled the strange meeting.

James saw himself sitting on the ground across from the mysterious young man who had blank white eyes. The stranger spoke to him candidly, yet did not open his mouth. In his free hand, he held the silver visor.

"Now listen carefully," said the young man. *"I was originally sent here to obtain information about the 'Supernova' program of your planet."*

"Who sent you?" James asked. "Why do you want to know so much about this?"

"It is because of the streaming data emitted from your satellites which had brought the attention of my home world's scientists."

"Who are your people and why is it I can only hear you in my head?"

"We are a peaceful race and our intentions are to ask you to halt your program and join our federation of peaceful

worlds. I thought Terra was more advanced, but I see it is not so."

"You didn't answer my question!" James snapped. "Besides, the Supernova program is just a missile defense system."

"Before I could report my findings, I was attacked by Corpii," the young man continued. "They are also searching for this planet's purported 'Supernova' program, especially something called the 'Death Ray'. I can not let them destroy this planet searching in vain for technology that has yet to exist!"

"Do you realize that the 'Death Ray' thing is in a movie?"

"However, I sustained numerous injuries in that one-sided battle. My scanners reported there was a restore point near here."

"Restore point? You mean like a computer repair shop, right?"

"My scanner is failing and I need you to fix it. I know you are capable of such advanced machinery."

"I have a good friend, Allen Jontei who works at WCM and builds machines."

"You will need a Signet to access this particular machine, and your friend Allen is not strong enough." The stranger took off his glove, revealing a mark on the back of his hand. "Think of this brand as a sort of tattoo. Just touch my hand and I will do the rest! Do not worry; I will leave my GEARS unit for more information."

James reached out with a shaky hand, clasping it over the back of the mysterious fighter's hand and felt warmth wash through his body. A sudden crash came behind them and the young man quickly stood, hand over the hilt of his glowing pistol.

"What was that?" James cried.

"*They have brought reinforcements!*"

"Holy shit!"

"*I will keep them at bay! Guard the weapon well!*"

Suddenly everything brightened before descending into darkness.

"It's no dream!" James blurted as he shook his head, clearing the fog of the past. "It's real and the mark--!" He looked at his hand, noticing the tattoo on the palm. James scratched at his hand and rubbed his palm on the grass. Panicked, he realized it wouldn't rub off. Immediately rising to his feet, James searched around for the strange visitor.

"Hey, Space Guy!" he called. "We gotta talk, man! Where are you?" Hearing another chirp, James whirled around, spotting a small palm-sized machine on the ground. "*What's this?*" he wondered as he approached and perched down, picking it up. James turned it over in his hand.

On the face was a dark screen, with several buttons and an arrow pad. To James, it looked like a portable television unlike others crafted from manufacturers overseas. Glancing up, James noticed footprints on the ground.

Following the tracks to the edge of a cliff, he paused when he noticed a small charred object in the far distance. Pocketing the small device, James made his way along the cliff side, jumping down onto the small ledge below and approached two smoking bodies of the strange young man and another who wore heavy armor.

"He's dead," James muttered to himself, "and so is his killer. I can't believe this is happening; he's dead and it's because of this damn *thing*!" He glared with revulsion at his branded left hand that had the strange sigil of a single circle with a cross in its center "Why me?"

"In your language," the haunting voice of the mysterious young man said to James, *"it would be called 'The Signet'. You are the perfect choice and I am relieved! Hopefully you will not regret it later..."*

"I already regret it!" James thought and walked away from the smoldering crater.

Leaving the park and heading back for the offices, James greeted no one who passed him.

"Hey, Russell," called Mitchell as he entered his cubicle, "had a hard night?"

"Yeah," James called over his shoulder, "a real doozy!"

"Too bad we missed it!"

Slouching at his desk, James worked in relative silence, dreading the rest of the day and fretting about the mark on his hand.

CHAPTER TWO

When evening came, James burst outdoors before the courtyard clock struck five and caught the next bus that rumbled up.

"I gotta go home and think about this," he thought, showing his bus pass to the driver. James draped his blazer over his arm and held onto the holding strap above his head with his free hand. He ignored the other passengers on the very full bus who grew familiar to his presence.

"So, not talking today, huh?" the driver quipped.

James said nothing, wanting to get home, shower, and think. He arrived a half-hour later at the Verde Court Apartments in North Petoria County, a quiet suburb where he lived. After getting off the bus with heavy steps, James went to his apartment, number nine.

Fumbling for his keys from his pocket, James found it and with some difficulty, managed to open the door. He didn't bother turning on the lights, though out of habit, James chucked aside his blazer in the nearby chair and leaned against the doorframe, sighing as he took in the empty space fit for a bachelor.

"It needs a girl in here," he reflected as he loosened his tie. *"Maybe she can brighten the place a little."*

James kicked shut the door then pulled out the portable device from his rear pocket and placed it on the end table as he passed it, heading into his bedroom.

Later, after showering and changing into a T-shirt, jeans, and running shoes, James grabbed a can of cola from the kitchen, turned on the main lamp in the parlor and dropped onto the couch. He stared at his marked hand in disbelief once in better light.

Popping the top on the soda, James noticed faint golden light surrounding his hand as iridescent orange flames traveled down his arm. Concentrating harder, he felt warmth spreading throughout his body.

Taking a long drink of cola, James leaned back into the couch and closed his eyes, feeling the warmth becoming him. Hearing a small chirp, James opened his eyes and sat up, reaching for the machine he left on the end table.

"This weird thing, all it does is *beep* at me!" he grumbled. "Why did he leave it behind?" The machine suddenly turned on once the power in his flaring hand abruptly died, forcing the screen glowing lime green. James gasped, dropping his soda. "What the hell?" he cried as information in cyan digital text appeared on the screen.

SIGNET IDENTITY: CONFIRMED
SIGNET NAME: LUMINIS
SIGNET PRIMARY ELEMENT: FIRE

"The machine is going nuts!" he muttered as more information scrolled across the small screen. "Is it because I *touched* it?" After the data stopped scrolling, another message appeared.

SIGNET BASIC ABILITIES:
BASE SPEED X2
BASE STRENGTH X2
FLIGHT
BARRIER
PRESS 'O' TO CONTINUE...

"So nothing can hurt me and there's no limit to my strength?" James wondered in astonishment. *"Insane!"* He tossed aside the small machine, feeling confident. *"Let's see if this flight thing really works!"* Concentrating on the meaning of flying, James felt himself levitate several feet. *"This is awesome; I think 'up' and off I go!"* Stumbling forward once his feet touched the ground, he hurried to his patio door. *"Good thing it's dark out..."* James opened the door and bounded out, took a leap, and felt his body soar upwards several feet from the ground. *"This is almost too easy!"*

Landing back down, James stumbled over his steps and hurried inside, grabbing for the electronic device. Pocketing it, he raced outdoors and a leap, hovering near the roof of the complex.

Contemplating on what to do next, an idea occurred to James and he broke out grinning then took off for his friend's house, miles away in the upscale uptown suburb of Cedarwood in greater Petoria.

Touching down behind a large two-storey home that had several pane windows and surrounded by large elms and pines, James grunted when he struck the ground with force and tumbled head over heels. He groaned in pain and clamped the back of his neck that ached.

"I need to work on that landing," James thought as he staggered to his feet and dusted himself off. Heading for the garage door he knew would be unlocked; he let himself in and spotted his friend in a lightweight cardigan and chinos at his workstation, surrounded by machine parts.

"Hey, Allen," James called cheerfully.

"James?" Allen answered back as he pushed up his large framed gray plastic eyeglasses that threatened to fall off his nose.

"It's me." James leaned over Allen's shoulder, watching him tighten bolts on a chassis of a computer case. "What's that you're building?"

Allen set his screwdriver aside and turned over the project in his hands, admiring his work. "I'm working on creating my own microcomputer," he replied and set it back on the workstation. "Smaller faster computing machines are going to be the wave of the future!"

James laughed. "Yeah, right," he said and blew a raspberry. "With that logic, they'll have miniaturized laser disks and tiny cellular phones too!"

Allen snorted. "Don't tease," he retorted. "How'd you get here?" he asked instead. "I didn't hear your car!"

"Well," James responded, chuckling, "it's cos I *flew* here!"

"Right!" Allen scoffed. "Next, you'll tell me there are aliens too!"

"Err... that too!"

Allen glanced up at James over his glasses, raising an eyebrow. "What?"

James pulled out the pocket device and showed Allen. "Yeah, and I brought this just in case you didn't believe me!"

"Amazing!" Allen cried, reaching out for it. "May I?"

"I doubt you can break it, Al," James said, grinning.

Allen took it from him, going over the machine in awe. "I might have to if I'm going to reverse engineer it!"

"Not with the technology we have! I can tell that's too advanced with what parts we can get our hands on now."

"I still want to give it a try. This is an interesting device!" Allen glanced up as his face flushed from excitement and motioned James to follow. "Let's have coffee!"

Later, at the parlor table, James toyed with the machine, pecking at the keys in an effort to figure out its commands. He wondered why the strange portable reacted only with his left hand that had the brand, while it did nothing with his right hand. Allen sat across from him with a mug of coffee, sipping its contents.

"Of course I believe you, Jamie," Allen murmured, "at least about what you can do. I can't argue with solid evidence!"

"So you wanna test it out?" James inquired.

"Sure!" Allen smiled brightly. "It's important; maybe the most important thing in history!"

"History, huh?" James cracked.

"Seriously!" Allen paused and glanced out the parlor window. "Did you hear something?"

"Hear what?"

Allen shrugged his shoulders, returning to his coffee. "Never mind."

"Yeah, Al, I know," James murmured, "I keep wondering if I should *call* somebody, though."

"After you get more info first!" Allen snapped, bristling. He quickly slammed down his mug and the coffee splashed on the table. "You don't know for sure *who* might get too interested, *especially* the Government! You know how *they* are about these things!"

"It's weird," said James softly as he continued pecking at the keys, "I keep recalling some of the stuff the Space Guy said, like that it took courage to use 'the weapon'! How is this Signet thing a *weapon* anyways?"

Allen shrugged. "Is it like mind over matter?" he interjected. "If you have to 'think' it 'on' like you said, then it'd be hard to do if you're busy wetting your pants!"

"Ha," James replied wryly. "He said that he trusted me, because I had guts, that I always asked questions and I'm capable of reason!"

"Sounds like a put-on to me." Allen picked up his mug and sipped at his cooling coffee. "You're not a bad looker yourself, ya know…"

"I'm serious, Al!" James complained. "You wouldn't put the most deadly weapon in the hands of a cowboy, would you?"

"No; in fact, there are a lot of people I wouldn't *trust* with that thing..."

"Exactly! So maybe we *shouldn't* go public with it. Not yet, anyway."

Allen nodded. "If Big Brother finds out about this machine, you *know* they will want their mitts on it."

"With this thing being a weapon of some kind, I see your point. They could start a third world war if they want to!"

"People can't want what they don't know, I guess..."

"Right!" James nodded. "Even the Space Guy's last words to me were to 'guard it well'!"

Allen stiffened and pushed back his chair, dropping his coffee. The remaining drink splashed everywhere and the cup rolled off the table, shattering to the floor. "Did you hear that high-pitched whine?" he asked.

"You're being paranoid!" James retorted.

"No, Jamie--!"

A loud explosion burst through the sidewall of Allen's parlor, throwing over Allen and James as well as glass, wood and plaster. James cried out when debris fell over him and Allen wailed in fear, quickly diving under the table.

Storming through the wreckage in the wall stood a large robust tall humanoid figure who wore a dark helmet with a smoky reflective face and a uniform similar to what the mysterious young man wore. The star fighter was armed with a glowing orange high-powered weapon that resembled a heavy rifle strapped to its waist and in its hand it held a triple-barreled pistol that gleamed in golden light.

"Arrest or death!" the star fighter demanded.

"Allen, run!" James shouted and ducked for cover behind a ruined bookcase as the mysterious fighter fired at the semi-destroyed parlor table, engulfing it in flames.

Allen screamed when the force of the blast threw him back. Bowling over, James landed on his arm and quickly flipped over, crawling back as the alien stormed through the wreckage, making a sweep with a pocket device it held in its free hand.

"*That must be that Corpii the Space Guy warned me about!*" James thought. "*He must be after The Signet!*"

"You have what I seek!" bellowed the fighter before Allen who huddled on the floor, shuddering in fear.

"Jamie!" Allen screeched, "What the hell is going on?" The star fighter slipped the device back into its pocket, raising its triple-barreled pistol at Allen's head. "Oh no," Allen whimpered as the gun flashed in orange light. "Oh no, why me?"

James's eyes widened as the weapon made a high-pitched whine. "*He's going to blow his head off because of me!*" he thought in horror. "Stay down, Allen!" James declared and quickly made a mad dash out the hole in the wall, taking flight. Three spheres of plasma-like substance immediately hurled past him. "*I wonder what's that he's firing at me with,*" James mused as he quickly rolled out of another trio of shots. "*Whatever it is, he's a hack shot!*"

"Return what you have stolen, infidel!" the alien thundered.

James cringed when one of the shots singed his arm. "*Could it hurt me though?*" Checking behind him, James noticed the star fighter in flight behind him by several yards, surrounded by pale bronze light. "*He can fly too! If I can lead him away from here--!*" James grunted in pain when struck again, forcing his shoulder to bleed as he fell slightly. He then changed course, increasing his speed further from the Cedarwood area. "*I should take a chance and fight back... This guy isn't kidding around now!*" Looking down, James noticed cars racing below on a darkened street. "*I'm over Industrial Street! There should be a slag dump from the coal plant near here.*" Approaching an area near a railway and several cars, James slowed his speed. "*This is a good deserted place for a showdown, if the drag racers aren't watching...!*"

Slamming onto the ground behind a railcar, James groaned as he staggered to his feet and darted out of the way from several plasma blasts. The star fighter also touched down, sheathing the triple-barreled pistol and hauled out the plasma rifle that gave a high whine.

"You have taken Decamundi Federation property!" the alien sneered from behind its helmet as James backed away. "Return it or die!"

"What the hell?" James cried and the star fighter pointed the rifle in his direction. The alien fired, blowing away the nearby railcars and everything surrounding it.

The force threw James back, hurling him into the earth on his face. He groaned as his body reported with abundant signals of pain appearing in various forms: burning, prickly, searing, sickening, crushing, and throbbing in fierce agony.

Thudding stomps came nearby as the alien star fighter stormed over to him.

"*My body will pay for this later,*" James thought and let out a yelp when the alien grabbed him by the collar of his shirt with a heavy hand, yanking him up with force.

"Surrender the weapon!" the alien shouted, gripping James's neck firmly with one hand. "You do not understand what you put yourself in! If you keep this weapon, you will be part of a master plan that will bring nothing but desolation and waste to your planet and its inhabitants!"

"*What if he is telling the truth?*"

The alien pulled him up to eye level and James took in a weak ragged breath, realizing the alien was bigger than he was in weight and height. The color quickly drained from James's face and he fought to keep from passing out in shock.

"Keeping the weapon will only bring domination to your planet, as well as your universe," roared the star fighter. "So save yourself the trouble and give up the weapon!"

"I don't know if I can--!" James croaked.

"Do not force me to terminate you!" the alien shouted as it dropped James, only to swiftly grab him by the wrist that glowed brightly in orange flames.

"*Should I let it go?*" James pondered. "*But what if that Space Guy was right?*"

"You are too weak to protect the universe," the alien bellowed, shaking James forcefully. "I am the perfect one to possess such vast power!"

"*What if he's that Corpii that Space Guy was talking about? What if...*" James felt the faint coming on and his eyes closed as his body began to give up the fight, tapering the power that surrounded him.

"Yes, give it up and return it to me," hissed the alien, "I am the rightful owner!"

"*No!*" James snapped open his eyes. "*What the hell am I thinking? The Space Guy got <u>killed</u> over this thing! I gotta fight back, hold on and not lose it!*" James glared back at the alien and the fading energy abruptly flared around his body.

"You have a long walk home, puny human," the alien snarled, squeezing James by the throat. "Either die here in vain, or give up with your life spared!"

James struggled beneath the alien's titan-like grip, trying unsuccessfully to loosen himself free. "*This Corpii guy is trying to kill me, using some mind control to make me give up fighting! Why? Why me? Why did the Space Guy give it to me?*" The power that blazed around James intensified, turning from red to orange. "*I need to know... I can't know if I'm dead!*" Sudden silence filled their immediate environment and a burst of flame knocked back both the star fighter and James.

Skidding back several yards on the ground, James clenched his hands, feeling renewed strength as reddish-orange flames engulfed his body.

"Stand down or face retention!" the alien shouted, brandishing the triple barreled pistol that gave a high whine. At his feet lay the charred rifle.

"Not tonight, buster!" James declared. "For a minute there, you scared me!" He quickly dodged six high-powered plasma blasts. "I got it together now and I don't like being almost scared to death!"

Taking a leap, the alien fighter lunged forward, grabbing James by the face and slammed the muzzle of the gun to his forehead.

"You know nothing of this power!" the alien bellowed.

James fell back, dazed and quickly darted out of another swipe. *"Can't give up now!"* he thought and shook his head to clear his blurred vision. *"That was a helluva hit, but you're just as strong as he is! Get it together!"*

The alien charged the pistol for another shot and James gave a wild kick, knocking the pistol away. The alien grunted when a sickening crunch snapped his wrist. The alien grasped at James with its good hand and James kicked again, hitting the alien in the chest that hurled him backwards.

Somersaulting over the alien, James thrust himself in the air, suspending over the fighter who withdrew another pistol harnessed at his back, levitating beneath him. The alien appeared rattled as he steadied his good arm and focused his energies into his next shot.

"You want this power so bad?" James screeched and raised his hand that burned intensely in orange flame. "Then eat this!"

The blast of light that released from his body washed out everything in harsh white luminance before turning dark once again.

CHAPTER THREE

Sitting on a pile of steaming rubble once the dust cleared, James's body smoked slightly as the last thread of his clothing burned away. James felt nothing, not even the cool evening winds that blew around him, completely overloaded with numbness and shock as he finally took in what happened.

There were no traces left of the slag dump, the railway cars, and the annoying Corpii. In the distance, he heard footsteps crunching across the decimated metal and tensed.

Turning, James spotted a small figure carefully approaching the plumes. The figure became clearer as it neared, cutting through the cloud of smoke and dust and James sighed in relief once he saw his friend Allen wielding a baseball bat.

"Jamie," Allen called, "what happened?"

"I don't know," James replied, turning away. His face flushed in embarrassment. "I got so worked up, that I released all this energy like some atom bomb or supernova star or something."

"I'm not sure I follow. Where are your clothes?"

"Burned off I guess!" James hung his head, the flush spreading from across his cheeks to his ears. "But it's no big deal... When that alien grabbed for me, I kinda wet my pants!"

Allen nervously looked around and tightened his grip on his clubbing weapon. "Let's get you into something before somebody like the Feds show up!"

James smirked and glanced up. "Man, you're always worried about those Feds!"

"Jamie, this is serious stuff! Big Brother's always watching!"

James shook his head, cracking into a wide smile. "Alright, fine... So where are you parked?"

An hour and a half later, after gaining a change of clothing from Allen, James muttered his thanks once dropped off at their mutual friend's apartment in the low-class district of Briar. He dragged his sore body up the steps, feeling somewhat at ease that his friend lived on the first floor. James approached the door on the immediate right from the main entrance and knocked.

Through the thin walls, James heard the news reporter talking of current events. He took a glimpse at the nearby mail drop box, checking that he was at the right door and sighed in relief reading the label, 'L. Gibson'.

"... Explosion of the Industrial Street slag dump has the police baffled!" droned on the reporter. "Officials dismiss that the Federal Government is conducting secret nuclear tests near the Medium Security Prison, also known as The Workhouse Institution..."

"I need to be more careful," mused James as he knocked again. *"Allen said he saw a mushroom cloud come from where I was fighting. At least <u>he</u> got to me first and not the Feds he's always worried about!"*

"Who's at the door this late?" a voice from inside answered.

"Leila, it's me!" James called back and moaned in pain. Just talking hurt as that hard jab in the face bruised him badly. The door opened and a young woman with bright green eyes and spiky raven mullet wearing a gray tracksuit looked warily back at him.

"Jamie," she complained, "it's late!"

"Hey, Leila," James murmured. "Yeah, I know; some stuff came up." He leaned against the frame. "Can I crash here tonight?"

"Sure," Leila replied warmly and stepped away to let James entry. "So what's with the weird clothes? The last time I've seen threads like that, my dad was finishing college at Roberts University!"

"Ha, funny," James spat sourly and blew a raspberry. "I kinda lost my clothes for your information, including my keys and my wallet and--"

"At least Allen loaned you some of his old stuff!"

James shuffled for the couch and sank into it, groaning. He found breathing difficult, even after Allen taped his chest, fearing cracked ribs. James felt sure he broke something though Allen warned him it was too risky to go to the hospital appearing like he did. The doctors and nurses would definitely connect his injuries to what just happened at the slag dump.

Leila shut the door and went to her hall closet, withdrawing blankets. "That's terrible," she said as she took out an afghan. "You look like hell, James. Did you get jumped or something?"

"You can say that!" James replied.

"Here's a blanket." As she returned with the afghan, she saw James nodding off once his body accepted the softness of the lumpy couch and the relative warmth of the apartment. "Huh, gone off to dream world already...!"

The next morning, James sat at the kitchen table sipping coffee and munching on toast with cream cheese and apricot jam as Leila made phone calls for him. He had caught sight of himself in the mirror, surprised to see that he managed to heal perfectly during the night.

Relieved being able to breathe again, he noticed that even his face didn't appear busted and the bruises had disappeared. After Leila made her last phone call of the morning, she came to the kitchen doorway, tossing her keys in her hand.

"Let's boogie, Jamie," called Leila. "The locksmith is on his way and I gotta get to my job also if I wanna keep paying my rent!"

"Sure thing," James replied, downing the remainder of his coffee.

"I called P and P for ya already so don't worry about that!"

James nodded, following her out of the apartment and to her car. "Leila..."

"Here," Leila murmured, palming James a bill before he made his way to the passenger side. "Emilio says relax! You'll need it!"

James glanced down and blushed when he noticed it was a hundred-note. "Thanks Leila," he murmured gratefully and pocketed it. "You're too nice to me!"

Back at the Verde Court apartments, James exited the shower to change into a new set of clothing. *"Man, that Leila!"* he thought, stepping into a pair of worn jeans. *"Next payday, I gotta remember to give her back the bucks she loaned me and take her out to dinner or something!"*

James noticed the small red light flashing on his answering machine after pulling on his T-shirt. He pressed the playback button and as he searched for his sneakers, he heard the voice of a woman he currently dated on the tape.

"James, this is Roxanne," said the woman. "Don't forget you have a date with me later tonight! I know how you get so caught up on that Orichide stuff. I swear, it's not gonna get you anywhere. Pome doesn't stand a chance against WCM! Anyways, we have to talk. Seriously..."

"Damn, that reminds me," James grumbled after he quickly laced his shoes. He left the room, grabbing a leather driving coat draped on the nearby chair. "I have to get a new driver's license and credit card! Good thing I had a spare key at Leila's."

Leaving his apartment, James hurried over to his nearly thirty-year-old lime green coupe sedan parked on the lot. Even though one of Allen's friends, who owned an auto body shop, restored the car in exchange for a computer, James hated the coupe. The car had constant problems and James couldn't afford to get rid of it for a newer model. Also, he felt excessively attached after getting the vehicle from his parents.

"*Please don't be fussy today,*" James prayed, banging the door to get it pop open. The window rattled from the blow and he pulled against the handle, giving a firm yank. The handle broke off with a snap and the door finally yawned open.

"Damn it!" James growled and threw the wrecked handle on the dashboard as he got in. "Got to gauge my strength..."

James slammed the door shut with enough force that cracked the window. Putting the key in the starter, he blew a sigh of relief when the engine turned, roaring to life.

Later, pulling up behind the Parsons and Parker office park, James left his car on the deserted back road and returned to the crater. After taking a cautious look around, James took a small jump and hovered several feet from the ground.

He took flight and rushed through the heavily wooded park, satisfied there was no one around that early in the day.

"*Will P and P be miffed at me for taking the day off?*" James wondered as he flew for the rear of the park, checking out the scene around him. "*They probably won't mind, figuring I'm planning my suicide attempt... I hope they haven't found a replacement already!*"

He finally approached the burned-out area of the office park and touched down then stumbled forward. James smiled at his feat for landing without crashing and walked over to the area where the two bodies left behind lay in the earth.

James searched for evidence from a few days before. He spotted a dark scorched mark on the ground and the bodies previously left behind now gone.

"What the hell?" James murmured and ran forward, finding a hole in the earth instead. "The Space Guy and his killer are gone!" Dropping to his knees, James dug at the shallow impression in the dirt, finding a set of clothing buried there. He uncovered a reddish-brown jacket, similarly colored pants with a black stripe on the side, red and black gloves and black long boots, as well as a closed-face red helmet with black polarized visor. "There should've been *two* decaying bodies here, unless that *other* alien incinerated them!"

James pulled out the jacket and examined it, finding it like new, not even torn or burned. He saw it was similar to the jacket the mysterious young man wore and had the same sigil on the right breast matching the brand on James's hand.

"How odd," James murmured and headed back for his car. He threw the clothing and helmet into the passenger seat and sank into the driver's side. His vision blurred and he left his body, staring back at an alien that had his appearance. It drew his weapon and fired...

A knock at the car window brought James out of his fog and he screamed in surprise. He turned and saw a Parsons and Parker's security officer peering at him through the glass.

"Oh, goodie!" exclaimed the officer. "You're not dead yet!" He stepped away and spoke into his small two-way radio. "It's cool guys," he said, "Employee JR-703 in Department 387 is still kicking."

"What is it?" James grumbled.

"We got a call earlier that you wasn't coming in today," explained the officer after he hooked his radio back to his belt.

"Then someone spotted a strange car out here, so I ran the plates to find it belonged to you and, well... you know the rest."

"I hadn't taken anything," James retorted, "if that's what you're wondering about."

"Thinking about the usual?"

James shook his head. "Not yet."

"That's excellent!"

James slammed the door and turned the key in the ignition. The starter clicked and the engine sputtered in response. Grimacing, James threw the gear in neutral and tried again.

Moments later, a squelch came over the radio, followed by a gruff voice. "Yo, Carrington," said another guard, "should we cancel the order of Dummy Round?"

The officer pressed the radio's button he had holstered to his hip. "Yeah, yeah," he answered. "He's still kicking."

"Ya sure?"

"Not yet, not yet!"

The engine continued to whine when James pumped the accelerator and kept turning the key. The security officer then knocked on the glass. Growing exasperated, James leaned back in his seat and rolled down the window. "What?" he spat.

"So how long do you need time off?" asked the officer.

"I'll be in tomorrow, promise," James replied halfheartedly.

"If you don't show up, we'll get somebody else!"

"I doubt it!"

James grunted when the officer guffawed in response and tried the ignition again. Relieved when the car finally came to life, James immediately switched the gear in drive and drove away. He glanced in his rearview mirror and saw the officer waving him off.

CHAPTER FOUR

Driving up to Roxanne Citovecca's large ranch home in the quiet suburb of Pomaderris, James pulled into the empty driveway and sighed heavily as he cut the ignition. He drummed his fingers across the steering wheel in trepidation, lost in the sea of myriad worrisome thoughts that floated about in his head.

"*It took me all day to get this stuff together,*" James thought in disgust. "*I'm so fake, sitting in this rented car and wearing this wash and wear suit...Polyester is so out of style!*" He glanced at the blazer that matched his slacks lying draped over the passenger seat. "*If I show up like this, she'll just <u>know</u> I have no money, hustling a dead end job and she'll drop me like a fake handbag!*" James turned his attention to the dashboard clock and groaned when he saw the time. "*Almost a quarter to seven. I'd better boogie!*"

James grabbed his blazer and stepped out the car with much effort. Shutting the door, he leaned against the car and took in a deep breath then exhaled slowly, dispelling his paralyzing fear. James forced himself up the steps and rang the doorbell. He readjusted the sky-blue silk tie he wore and draped his blazer over his shoulder.

"In a minute," a sweet voice called from inside.

James put his free hand in his pocket and leaned casually against the frame. *"Why did I even bother coming here? I don't have any cash to go out other than what Leila loaned me and all I can afford is Japanese – the cheapest thing that's fancy enough for this woman's taste!"*

He forced a smile when the door opened, revealing a beautiful young woman with long red hair and striking violet eyes who wore a smart red pantsuit with a pearl necklace around her neck. She held one diamond earring in hand while the other dangled in her ear.

"James," she said happily, "you're early!"

"Heya, Roxanne, I decided to surprise you!" James replied in false cheer. Roxanne stepped back, letting him indoors. "So we're catching the happy hour special at my favorite Japanese restaurant."

"The kids--" Roxanne started.

"They won't be a bother," James said quickly. "I'm sure the babysitter will come for them soon."

"That's what I wanted to talk to you about." Roxanne walked past James for the parlor where a young boy and girl were sitting on the couch, watching television. "It's late you two!" she reprimanded. "Dinner's long over and you've got school tomorrow!"

"But, Momma," the girl complained, "*Cosmocats* isn't over yet!"

"Darlene, not tonight! It's time for you and Mikey to go on upstairs for bed!"

"Goodnight kiddos," James said sheepishly, waving slightly. "I promise me and your mom won't make too much noise." The children giggled as Roxanne slapped James on the shoulder. The kids left the couch, scurrying for the rear rooms.

"Don't forget to brush your teeth and floss!" Roxanne called after them.

James headed for the couch and draped his blazer over the arm. He heard a snigger and glanced up, spotting Darlene in the hallway who peeked around the corner. "Hey," James started, "didn't your mom...?"

"Go get 'im, James!" Darlene cheered and James chuckled, blushing. Roxanne shook her fist at the girl and Darlene ran off.

"Too cute," James murmured and leaned against the couch, folding his arms across his chest.

"Good night," Mikey called.

"Damn kids," Roxanne grumbled and the bedroom door slammed shut. She turned to James, touching his arm. "Alone at last!" she purred.

"So, are you going to tell me what's on your mind?" James asked once Roxanne let go and headed for the mini bar across the room. She turned off the television along the way and James wandered into the kitchen, spotting the remains of dinner on the counter: a pot roast with potatoes, green beans, corn, peas and carrots in the gravy.

"I wrote a poem for you today," Roxanne said gaily as she returned to the kitchen with two glasses in one hand and a bottle of wine that had a loosened cork in the other.

"Sock it to me," responded James.

"Roses are red, telephones are plastic; Disco is dead, but you are fantastic!"

"*My god,*" James thought as he faked a laugh. "*What am I getting myself into?*" He took a glass from Roxanne and held it ready as she opened the bottle and filled the goblet. "You're such a romantic," James murmured and threw back the drink with a gulp.

"Do you want dinner?"

"Sure!" James quickly bit his hand and his face immediately grew warm. "*I said that a little too quickly,*" he mused. "*Man, I'm so cheap!*"

Taking a seat at the dining room table, James set his glass on the placemat and moved aside the cloth napkin that held a clean spoon, fork and steak knife wrapped inside. Roxanne approached, pouring him another serving.

"You know," Roxanne said softly as James sipped his drink, watching her with a careful eye as she returned to the kitchen, bottle in hand. "I have this great dinner and this great home and two great kids..." James clenched harder to his glass and cleared his throat when the realization hit him hard and fast at once amid the rattling of silverware and plates.

"*Please, please, don't ask me what you're planning to ask me!*" James prayed as he finished his second serving of wine. "*I'm not this rich guy you think I am! I'm just some two-bit player that's not rich <u>yet</u>.*"

"I know you'll be a shoo-in at WCM, James," Roxanne cooed once she returned with a large plate of the former dinner. "You're so smart and sexy to boot..."

"More wine please?" James asked, holding up his empty glass. "*You just don't know it yet,*" he contemplated as Roxanne set the plate before James and took his glass away. James unfolded the napkin and took the fork in a tight grip, breaking out in cold sweat. "*Wait until my friend Allen and I invent this awesome new computer and we'll blow Shellacker Corporation, Micron Industries, and Pome away!*"

"We can have the perfect everything and it'll be beautiful if you're in it!" Roxanne went on and arrived with the refilled glass and the wine bottle. She set the glass next to James and put the bottle at the center of the table. James glanced up as she sat on the edge of the table, holding her half-filled glass. "So, I'm all yours, James!"

James suddenly dropped his fork. "Is that what you're worried about?" he asked in a strained voice. "Are you asking that we should get married?"

"Oh, James, it would be so wonderful!" Roxanne squealed and James quickly leaned back as Roxanne put her arms around him.

"Roxanne, baby... I..." Roxanne's eyes widened in fear as she loosened her grip and withdrew. "I, um, don't think--!"

"Oh, I'm so sorry!" Roxanne wailed and quickly gulped down her drink. "Forget I ever mentioned it; it never came up! Poof - gone, just like that!" James turned away and clutched hard to the stem of the wineglass, concentrating on keeping his hand steady. "The last thing I want to get into tonight is some heavy discussion about our future!"

"*You gold digger!*" James thought in abhorrence and blew a weak sigh.

"Now, where were we…?" Roxanne pulled at James's tie and he let out a yelp when forced to his feet. She led him to the couch and pushed him down onto the cushions, straddling him. James gave no resistance when Roxanne kissed him softly on the side of the neck. With her free hand, she took the glass out of his hand and set it aside on the nearby end table. "We were on the verge of some goofing around like ferrets!"

"Hey!" James cried and immediately fell under her spell, becoming more interested. He returned her kisses and loosened his tie as she undid the buttons of his shirt. A soft thump startled James and he quickly stiffened as she yanked out his shirttails.

"What's wrong?" Roxanne muttered.

James gently pushed her aside. "Did you hear something outside?" he asked nervously.

"Somebody coming in from work, most likely," Roxanne murmured. "Now come on, before I cool down!"

Hearing a chirp, James pulled away, growing alarmed. "*That sound is unmistakable!*" he thought as he stood. "*That's from that GEARS thing the Space Guy had!*"

"James," Roxanne complained, "what's going on?"

"Didn't you hear *that*," James demanded, gesturing toward the large bay window covered by the dark curtains, "that beeping sound?"

"Relax, James…"

"I need to check it out!"

"Honestly, James!"

James hustled for the front door, threw it open wide and stormed out onto the lawn. He spotted a flash near the rear of the house and hurried for the backyard.

James paused dead in his tracks when Darlene, with blank white eyes and wearing blue pajamas, pointed a golden pulsing pistol in his direction. He clenched his teeth to keep them from chattering when the cold evening winds picked up, blowing around them.

"The cold isn't even bothering her!" James thought in horror and stiffened when she stepped forward toward him. "Darlene!" he barked as she stepped closer. The pistol she held gave a high whine and James backed away, clutching his left hand that flared slightly in golden light.

"James!" Roxanne cried. The pistol discharged and James quickly turned out, its shot nearly striking him. He dove for the gun, snatching it out of the girl's hand. "James, what the hell are you doing?" Roxanne shrieked once she approached the scene. James fell onto his back, pointing the glowing gun at the possessed Darlene.

"That's not the little girl you know, Roxanne!" James shouted. "That's some alien posing as her!"

"James!"

"Look, Roxy, she should be freezing to death out here, but--!"

The spell broke and Darlene wavered as she blinked slowly and her eyes came back to normal. "Momma," she moaned.

James lowered the gun and slowly rose to his feet as the blazing light died.

"Don't scare Darlene like that!" Roxanne fussed, grabbing for her daughter. "She was probably playing with Mikey or--!"

"You never buy Mikey toy guns!" James snapped, slipping the pistol into his rear waistband.

"He probably borrowed it from a neighbor or a friend from school!" Roxanne ushered Darlene back for the house with James following in step, fuming in silence. "Besides, why does that matter?"

"It matters because these Corpii mean serious business!" James thought, grinding his teeth as he approached the couch. *"Who knows what these things are capable of?"*

"Momma," Darlene whined, "my head feels funny."

"Now go on to bed and we'll check it out in the morning," Roxanne said softly. "You're probably worried about that test tomorrow huh?"

James grabbed for his blazer. "I gotta get going," he called over his shoulder and stalked outdoors.

"Why?" Roxanne wailed after him and rushed outside. James approached the car, keys in hand. "So she was sleepwalking," Roxanne called after him, "It's no big deal!" She ran up to James and grabbed him by the sleeve, turning him around.

"I can't have you involved!" James spat back and pulled out of her grip.

"Involved in what?"

James cupped Roxanne's face with his free hand. "Don't worry." He gave her a quick peck and ran a hand through her hair.

Roxanne frowned as worry masked her face. "Oh my god," she cried, "Don't tell me you're involved with the Syndicate, are you, James?"

"Syndicate?" James laughed. "Don't be silly!"

Roxanne's expression turned from worried to frightened and she stepped away. "It's about my half-brother Nicoterra, is that it?"

"What the --?"

"Please, don't agree to anything he asks," Roxanne begged. "Just stay out of the way!"

"Roxanne!" Reaching out, Roxanne pulled away and ran tearfully indoors. "Man, this is new!" James took a quick check around on the darkened streets and finding no one around, he took a leap upwards, taking off in flight.

CHAPTER FIVE

After several hours of aimless flying, James returned to his apartment, shucking his blazer and necktie aside on the chair in the parlor and pulled out the golden pistol that blazed brightly in his left hand.

"What is this," he wondered, *"some kind of warning?"*

Stomping into his bedroom, James approached his phone and picked up the receiver, glowering at the radiant weapon as he dialed with a free finger. James held the receiver to his ear, waiting for the rings to end.

"What youse want?" a weary voice grumbled from the other end of the line. "It's four in the flippin' mornin'!"

James slammed down the receiver, stunned. *"Did I dial that right?"* The phone rang moments later and James picked it up, growing even more uneasy. "Um, hello?" he answered.

"James!" Allen's voice called from afar amid static.

"Yeah, I just got in."

"Jamie, don't call my house!"

"I was about to ask you about that--"

"I've been trying to call you all day," Allen went on, ignoring the previous comment. "You know that thing that attacked us last night; I thought I saw it near your girlfriend's house when she had me come over, asking about our latest project."

"How can that be?" James wailed. "He's supposed to be dead!"

"Well, he's not, huh?"

"Now I'm worried," James said and moaned. "Whatever that thing is, it took over Roxanne's little girl somehow. I can't trust anyone else to be near me right now!"

"You think you've got a problem, and I'd hate to worry you more, but I figured I'd better tell you this--"

"Tell me what?"

"The Feds that I'm not too fond of are crawling around, asking folks in my neighborhood questions about me!"

"I don't want anyone to get hurt in this mixed-up mess!"

"How can I explain the blasted out window and the other damage, James?" Allen squawked. "What about reports of a flying man?"

"Did you tell them anything?" James demanded.

"Of course not, Jamie; I didn't tell them squat!" Allen scoffed. "I'm even calling from a pay phone in the case my line is tapped!"

"*Too late*," James thought, sighing heavily. "Hey, Al, man, I can't go to sleep with this going on now," he complained. "All I wanted was an early lunch break..."

"Now don't freak out," Allen said confidently. "I've been thinking about this, about the whole deal with the alien thing, about your safety and about the effect this business could have on the whole world!"

"What have you thought of...?"

"You have five minutes left," interjected the operator's voice.

"I'm getting real concerned, Jamie," Allen said quickly, "We'll talk more about it once the heat dies down. Now remember, until then, don't talk to anybody, and not even your other friends or your girlfriend!"

The line disconnected before James could say more. Hearing the front door open, he dropped the receiver and raced to the doorframe, holding the pistol at ready.

"Who's there?" James barked.

"Jamie, it's me," Leila called.

"*Why is she here so early?*" he wondered and set the pistol aside in the chair near the door. James walked in the main area of the apartment, finding Leila sitting on the edge of his couch, biting her fist in worry. He gave a critical once-over, admiring the brown baseball jacket she wore with bright yellow jogging pants, scrunched purple leg-warmers and gold moon boots. She ran a hand through her raven mullet, making the yellow plastic bangle bracelets clunk against her wrist. "*She makes a workout outfit look cute...*" James cleared his throat and Leila looked up, smiling faintly. "What's wrong?" he asked in concern.

"I had a call from P and P's Resource Department and they told me your boss, Mister Parker, had a fit like a Georgia thunderstorm about you not coming in for the past two days."

"What?" James looked at her warily. "This doesn't sound right at all," he grumbled under his breath.

"What?"

James shook his head. "It's nothing -- go on..."

"They even left me a message saying that if you don't come in by tomorrow you shouldn't come in ever again!"

"I talked to the security officer not long ago!" James protested. "They knew I needed some time off to clear my head..."

"So, what's going on?" Leila asked, raising an eyebrow. "If you're not taking the mandatory three days off to consider killing yourself, then why would Parker have a bitch fit?"

"Parker's not even my boss!" James thought, turning away. *"Something's not right here... Why is she being weird on me?"*

Leila rose upright and touched James on the arm to gain his attention. "Hey," she murmured, "you're not having problems with Body-Rockin' Roxanne, are you?"

"No," he answered, "but I'm probably gonna screw that up too with her brother Nicoterra and all..."

"She's got a brother?"

"Forget I said anything," James mumbled, pulling away.

"Look, you'll always have me, right?" He said nothing as Leila headed for the front door. "Well, I'll catch you later."

"Later," James muttered.

Returning to the bedroom, he stiffened when he heard a high whine. James quickly snatched up the plasma pistol from the chair and turned about-face, pointing it ahead at Leila who stood frozen at the door in stark fear.

"What are you trying to do, Jamie?" she cried, cringing. "I was only coming back to ask you something..."

"My god, I'm sorry!" James yelped and tossed the pistol aside on the floor. "What's gotten into me?"

Leila approached James and touched his cheek. He turned away "You sure you're alright?" she asked. James nodded. "Where'd you get that thing from anyway?"

"I'll be all right," he said softly. "So, what were you going to ask me?"

Leila glanced behind him and gave a tight smile. "I'll ask you later; besides, I gotta get going anyway... It's pretty late."

"But...!" Leila left his side and headed for the door. "I'm sorry if I scared you, okay?" James said after her. "Trust me, everything will be fine later."

"Good night!" Leila left the room and James heard the front door close with a firm click.

James let out a hard sigh and drifted into the kitchen, pulling out an orange soda. He returned to the couch, levitating over it as he popped the tab and sipped the contents of the frigid drink.

"Yeah, everything will be fine," he thought incredulously.

Two days later, James returned to Parsons and Parker's office in downtown Petoria, close to the riverfront. He had taken the day off, sleeping the afternoon away and tried to figure how to make the plasma pistol work.

James tried not to think much about the Signet as he threw himself into work. He gave no mention of it when he noticed his coworkers giving him odd looks and they said nothing in return.

After a long day of data entry and filing that became backed up due to his absence, James heard a knock and spotted the coworker who had a crush on him standing at the entranceway of his cubicle. The coworker pulled out the tie holding back his frizzy strawberry blond hair and ran a hand through it, loosening the strands.

"It's quittin' time, Russell!" he chirped. Sifting through his chinos pockets, he withdrew a black eyeglass case and took out rose-colored glasses. "Guy, you totally busted butt putting away all those papers today!"

James turned away from his file cabinet and reclined in his chair, sighing. "With all the forms I generated," he replied, "you'd think I let that mess sit for three months, not three days!"

The coworker chuckled and put on the tinted lenses. "You must like this job, huh?" he cracked.

"Nah, Adnan, I just like being around you," James quipped.

Adnan blushed in response. "Yeah?"

"Nope, you're not my type." James gave a sardonic grin. "Grow a shelf and a trunk and *maybe* I'll consider..."

The flush darkened on the Adnan's face and he cleared his throat, loosening his tie. "Um, well--" Adnan turned away, suddenly growing tense. "How about getting your scrawny behind downstairs to Mainframes and haul up some beige boxes to Department 3126?" he said in a controlled tone. "I'd do it, but I've got a date tonight."

"You suck," James muttered, standing to his feet.

"Oh, really?"

James pushed past Adnan, heading to the elevator out in the corridor and pressed the button, waiting for the cable car to come up. Glancing back behind him, James noticed Adnan walking in the opposite direction. Before the elevator came up, James went for the staircase, pulled out of his blazer and hung it on the guardrail.

"Any other time I'd be wishing to shove those microchips where the sun doesn't shine!" James thought as he took a jump down to the stairwell. *"But maybe having this Signet isn't too bad!"*

After carrying several computers marked for transfer all at once to the intended department, James returned to the stairwell, grabbed his suit jacket and slung it over his shoulder. He confidently walked past Adnan who stood near the smoking shelter, lighting a cigarette.

"See ya tomorrow," James called over his shoulder.

Adnan dropped his cigarette and looked at James with wide eyes, taken aback. "Hey, wait a minute!" he called after James. "You can't be done that fast!" Adnan rushed indoors and James grinned, strolling toward the bus stop.

Later, at the Verde Court apartments, James came out of his clothing piece by piece until he stood in his underwear. Entering his bedroom, he approached his answering machine and pressed the playback button.

"You have what we want," a low mechanical voice warbled. "Give back the GEARS unit or people die!" A beep followed and the machine whirred as the tape rewound.

"No other message, huh?" James muttered and approached his closet. Opening the door, he gasped when he found the outfit he salvaged from the crater hanging inside, neatly pressed and the gloves hanging inside the boots. "What the--? I never took this out the car; it's like he's *expecting* a fight!" James took the jacket and pants off the hanger and pulled into them, finding they were slightly loose. "Huh, I'm thinner than the original owner... Oh well, my only worry is if this junk is durable enough to stand up to a pummel I *know* I'm getting."

Taking the gloves from the boots, he slipped them on his hands and they hung loosely from his wrists. James then stepped into the boots that were two sizes too large and the faint power suddenly flashed around his body. The suit and gloves he wore shrunk down, fitting his body with better form and the loose boots molded to his feet. A mechanical chirp sounded behind him.

"Jim, what sort of mess are you getting your fool self into?" he mused as he picked up the gun that continued to beep. The gun glowed brightly, transforming into the small pocket device with the screen on top and the keypad on the bottom. On the screen's face displayed a single acronym followed by other information.

GENETICALLY ENHANCED ARMAMENT RESTRUCTURING
SYSTEM
GEARS: ACTIVE
SIGNET: LUMINIS (IN USE)
MOLECULAR STRUCTURE: HUMAN
DEFAULT MELEE WEAPON: UNKNOWN
DEFAULT PROJECTILE WEAPON: UNKNOWN
DEFAULT AUXILIARY WEAPON: UNKNOWN
TEK DEK: NOT AVAILABLE

"What's all this mean?" James wondered. *"Well, no time to dwell on it now!"* He folded the machine, pocketed it, and

hurried outdoors. *"It's time to kick booty or get it handed back to me!"*

James took off for the sky without taking a leading jump first, leaving the parking lot with a multitude of cracks on its surface from a transonic wave. The apartments shuddered, the windows rattled and the trees swayed from the force.

Coming near the Parsons and Parker's office park, James gasped when he noticed a white-gold levitating machine in the forested region where the back roads ended.

"Is that a space ship?" he murmured and touched down lightly on his feet. James raced ahead for his intended destination, blowing back trees and rustling leaves in his wake. His energy increased as he neared and took a leap, hovering in the sky overhead.

James spotted a large helmeted fighter emerging from the rear of the craft, wielding a powerful rifle that had four barrels with a large pack of dark matter coursing inside its chambers. The fighter held a small pocket device similar to the one James had and typed data into it as three more star fighters appeared nearby with a flash of light.

"There he is!" one shouted, pointing at James who swooped down from behind.

James gritted his teeth, noticing that the assembled alien fighters also wore suits similar to the one he had on.

"I've been flying around trying to find you," he snapped, backing away when the three others with plasma pistols stepped closer while the one with the rifle steadied his shot. "I bet you were hoping I'd finally get my stuff together and look you up, huh?" James clenched his hands that glowed in faint red as the alien fighter hoisted the rifle over its shoulder. The rifle gave a high whine and a large sphere generated from the four barrels. "What's this fascination with P and P anyways? You've got a contract with them, or you've secretly got a base going on and getting parts from them?" The high-powered beam blasted into James, knocking him back as well as the alien fighter. Bowling over, James struck a tree and moaned when his world tilted from dizziness. The other three aliens approached, pointing their pistols down at him. "I take that as a yes," he groaned. "Who are you whack jobs...?"

"We are Corpii," hissed one alien to James's right from behind its helmet. "We are elite assassins and we have been ordered to take out one irritant that threatens to destroy the universe!"

"If you think I have enough power to destroy the universe, then maybe I won't play nice!" James thrust forward his left hand and released a flaming sphere, burning the alien closest to him. The two remaining star fighters slowly stepped back as the one with the rifle readjusted settings. "What's it going to be, guys? We can tussle all night!"

"Take him down," the alien with the rifle ordered, "and neutralize his power!"

"No dice!" James thrust forward his hand once more, taking out one alien with a blast of flame and jumped back, hovering in the air. He released another fireball, incinerating the last pistol-toting fighter into dust, leaving only a charred suit behind. "I might not understand right now what's going on, but I'll be onto you if you keep coming after me!"

"You do not need what you have no understanding of!" the last alien barked. A high whine emitted from the rifle as a bright black light with cackling white and violet electricity around it formed.

James clenched both hands, releasing dark red and orange flames around his body. "More guns won't help you, sucker!" he shouted. The alien released the sphere from the rifle, blasting directly into James. He took the brunt of the hit, shoving back his body from the force. James shook off the initial stun and lowered to the ground with ease once the threads of antimatter faded. "I got it together, this time for good!" he declared and stormed forward toward the alien. James snatched the rifle away and crushed it into pieces with his charged hand.

"There will not be just one," the fighter shouted and bright green energy blazed around its gloved hands. Gold light cackled around them as it clutched its hands into fists. The alien backed away, cringing slightly when the red-orange energy that engulfed James turned yellow-orange. "There will be more!"

"You see, you got me angry now cos I'm starting to get sick to death of being hounded and harassed!" James shouted and grabbed the alien by the collar. The space fighter threw a punch and James leaned back then hurled the alien forward onto the ground. The alien bowled over and James levitated in the air. "I've had it with you!" James screamed and his hands burst into red and white flame. The space fighter jumped to its feet and rushed forward for James. James threw a charged punch, delivering a powerful blow into the alien's face, cracking the helmet. The alien stumbled unsteadily off its feet and James grabbed it by the throat. "You leave me alone with this Signet mess and get the hell off my planet!" He hurled the alien aside, crashing it to the side of its spacecraft, denting the metal.

The alien peeled off and hurried inside the ship. The craft's door whirred closed and the vehicle whined, gaining power from an unknown source. James watched in subdued awe as several bright spotlights turned on and the ship hovered from the ground as a propulsive force caused a loud rumble, blowing back trees, grass and shrubbery.

"We have our answer now," boomed the alien's voice through speakers on the craft. "You have brought war to your planet!"

"Bring it!" James shouted and shook his flaming fist at the ship. It took off with a sonic boom, destroying trees nearby when it shot for the sky. The force threw James back on his rear and he looked skyward, watching the white-gold starcraft ascend into the evening sky, joining the stars.

"*Whether that Space Guy meant it or not, he picked the right guy; I've got the power and I'm going to keep it, no matter what!*" James considered as he took a jumping leap, flying off in the opposite direction. "*That means I gotta get it together and turn this up into high gear; even if it means kicking every butt in the universe -- I need to handle anything that'll come after my scrawny behind!*" James glanced up at the darkening dusk sky, noticing the stars. "*Those alien assassins are just the beginning...*"

PART TWO

TAKING CHARGE

CHAPTER SIX

James let out a whoop in joy, bounding skyward over the Verde Court apartments.

"This is friggin' unbelievable!" he cried, piercing the clouds as the winds whistled in his ears. "How much higher can I go?"

James willed himself faster, bulleting toward the heavens. The temperate air turned frigid around him and ice formed on his clothing and skin from the force of the thinning air. He immediately fell back with a crack and let himself free fall back to earth. As the world blurred before him, his fears shot to the surface.

"Don't panic, Jim," James thought. *"Calm down; don't let it fade out on you or becoming road pizza will be the least of your problems..."* His body warmed quickly as his speed increased once he hurtled back for the ground. *"Well, I can't get to mesospheric without freezing <u>and</u> choking to death!"* Flipping over before he struck pavement, James bulleted ahead, seeking out places to fly around. *"I'll probably make stratospheric when I get better at this, or perhaps get some of that fancy equipment I keep finding on those aliens..."*

After twenty minutes of trying to figure his bearings, James touched down along the riverfront in Carolus County and let out a cry when he slammed onto the ground, throwing stones along the riverbed. He bowled to a stop and held his hand to the back of his neck, groaning.

"Take off is great," James moaned, "but my landings...!"

He rose to his feet and dusted himself off, then walked along the riverfront, kicking up stones. He grabbed a few and skipped them across the water, watching them sink. After several minutes, he heard a rumbling engine and looked up, noticing a driver in a pickup truck along the roadside. The driver parked and cut the engine, then got out, pulling out a tackle box and fishing pole. James noticed the driver wearing red and white, giving him an idea.

"*I wonder if anyone would notice me near Breyer Stadium,*" James mused and ran along the muddy river's edge. "*Would those nine-to-fiver's freak out downtown? Maybe the ballgame-goers would think they had one too many...*" James took off with a leap and zipped toward downtown Petoria, admiring an evening game underway. "*I know I'm a cheap bastard and could probably sneak in, but I wouldn't want The Awesomeness and company to get gypped out of their paychecks!*" Passing the front sign, he sighed when he noticed the teams playing. "*So the Redbirds are up against the Kickers today! Too bad I didn't record it...*" Flying away, James wistfully thought of the game currently in play. "*Maybe Coach Larson's crew can cream Majestic McGowan before he scores another run for Oakdale if they're not wimpy enough to let him walk...*"

Passing the Old Courthouse, James spotted the Porta Archway in the distance and flew to the top, hovering near the keystone.

"I'm king of the world!" he whooped and pumped his fists above his head. James then looked up at the evening skyline, admiring the stars.

"*What's going to space like?*" he wondered. "*I could try, but flying around town is more awesome!*"

Looking down at the people below, he made a backward leap off, flying toward the Riverfrontenac Amphitheater, where he found a lively heavy metal concert in progress. Coming down amidst the trees scattered offside, James peered behind one large oak and huffed when he couldn't tell which band performed on the stage.

"Ooh, I hope that's *Incus*," James muttered to himself. "I guess it's not too cold for them with them being Canadian and all..." He sighed as he reminisced. "I missed their *Super Rockin' Japan* concert three years ago since it was the same day I started at Parsons and Parker..."

Lowering to the ground, James stumbled forward and caught himself before he fell on his face. Walking away, he grinned, recalling when he met Roxanne.

"*I left that evening depressed and hit up the <u>Barcelona</u>, where I found her doing that break-dancing stuff, which reminds me...*" He left the grounds of Riverfrontenac and sped to Roxanne's house.

Upon approach, James hovered outside her bedroom window, watching her readying for bed and his face burned in response. He turned away, flying for home. "*You gotta quit this stuff, Jim,*" he chastised to himself. "*Turning into a tacky perv is so not cool!*"

Arriving back at his apartment, James grunted when he slammed onto his porch and banged against the door. He crawled up to the door and unlocked it, then staggered to his feet.

"Ouch..." James grumbled and entered. He pushed the door shut and walked over to his black and white television set on a cart in the parlor, flipping the switch. James then headed into the bedroom and checked his answering machine for messages.

"... Coming up at eleven," squawked the reporter, "the latest on the pirate hijacking of the German cargo ship, the *Maserk!*"

"*Pirates, huh?*" James mused when he noticed there was no flashing light. "*It would be too easy to become a jerky slime ball with these powers... so what <u>should</u> I do with it?*" Leaving the room, he went into the kitchen and a knock startled him out of his thoughts.

"It's open," James called and the door opened moments later.

"James," Leila called back, "I'm glad you're here."

"What are you doing here?" James asked as he opened the refrigerator and searched for something worth eating. He pulled out two cans of soda and tossed one to his friend who stood at the archway. She caught it, popped the tab then raised the can to toast.

"Well, Allen's been trying all day to call you and I came by to leave an important message..."

"All day, huh?" James muttered and shut the refrigerator door with his hip. *"I checked the machine when I came in from work,"* he considered, *"and when I got back not too long ago... She's lying to me, but why?"* James headed for the parlor and reclined on the floor.

"So, you want the message or not?" Leila asked.

James looked up from his place on the floor at Leila standing above him in jeans, black blazer, boat-neck navy and white striped T-shirt and gray sneakers. "Do a jig for me," he said, giving a wolfish grin. "I wanna see those perky boobies bounce!"

"Jamie!" Leila huffed, nudging his head with her foot. "Seriously!"

"So, are you staying tonight?"

"Sure, why not?"

"Let's see what's on *Nightly News*, huh?" James sat up on his elbows and Leila sat next to him, sipping her soda.

"What happened to your clothes?" she asked. "They have little tears in them."

"Erm, running through the woods?" James answered and Leila chuckled. *"That means no more extended flying with my regular clothes on,"* he thought.

"Allen wants you to meet him at the workshop at three tomorrow," Leila said.

"Yeah, remind me if I forget," James answered nonchalantly.

"You've been out of it lately," Leila murmured. "Are you sure you're okay?"

"Sure, I'm just under a little stress..."

"Is there anything I can do to help?"

James stiffened, growing slightly uncomfortable when Leila touched his thigh. "*We're close, but not this close...*" he thought and shut his eyes when he felt himself stir slightly. "*But if she doesn't hold it against me, I'm not going to mention it!*"

Later that evening, James lay in bed with Leila sleeping next to him, her arm and leg draped over his body. He put his arms behind his head and stared up at the ceiling, listening to Leila snore softly.

"*I need to figure some stuff out,*" James thought. "*I need to know what to do with this power; what I should be doing!*" He glanced at Leila who had her head against his chest, withdrew a hand, and stroked her hair.

"Why can't I just quit wasting your life and let you go?" James muttered, "You deserve more than me always jerking you around..."

"I like being jerked around," Leila murmured.

James stiffened. "That's not what I meant!" he cried.

"Rise and shine..." James gasped when Leila reached beneath the sheets to make a grab. "I see someone's up and moving!" He sat up on his elbows as Leila shifted her weight and became lost underneath the covers.

The next afternoon, James woke up with a start and glanced at his clock. He groaned when he noted the time. "Man, what's wrong with me?" James moaned, sitting up as he ran a hand through his hair.

"Let's get going," Leila called from the next room. "You've been out all morning! I called the folks at P and P for ya, told them you had Mono!"

"Why?" James cried. "What the hell was with that excuse, *Mononucleosis* of all things?"

"Oh yeah, Body-Rockin' Roxanne called you and she sounded straight pissed!"

"I was supposed to call her, right?" James threw back the covers and stumbled out of bed and stopped dead in his tracks when he saw the GEARS unit nearby on the night stand. James clenched his teeth.

"I didn't leave that there," he thought. *"I left it in the closet with the other space stuff!"* James picked it up, frowning and looked out his bedroom door. *"Just <u>what</u> is going on?"* He quickly hid it behind his back as Leila came to the door, fully dressed in the clothing she wore the night before.

"So, are you comin' or what?" she complained. "I walked here, so you'll have to drive!"

"Did your car break down?" James asked, raising an eyebrow.

Leila shrugged. "Erm, sure."

"Banging on machines can't be too far out of your league. You know I'm a klutzy ditz when it comes to cars."

"Between fixing teevees and radios and computers on my downtime, I guess I forgot to get around to it." Leila waved at James. "Come on, hurry it up!"

"Yeah, give me a minute," James said quickly and Leila left the doorway. He gripped hard to the GEARS unit. *"There's <u>no</u> <u>way</u> she could've walked here!"* he realized. *"She lives all the* *way on the <u>other side</u> of friggin' Briar and it's a forty-five minute <u>drive</u> from her house to mine and even <u>longer</u> to walk!*" James tossed the GEARS unit on the bed and hastily threw on his clothing as well as a lined windbreaker. "*I don't like this at all... not one bit!*"

Scooping up his keys that lay on top of his chest of drawers on the other side of the room, James motioned Leila to follow him.

Pulling off the exit ramp, James noticed the needle on the fuel tank monitor hovered near empty and drove the short distance to a gas station nearby.

"You refill and I'll make a phone call," he ordered, idling near a pump. James exited the car and walked briskly to a nearby pay phone and dug in his pocket for change. He dropped several coins into the slot and dialed Roxanne's home number. After two rings, the line picked up.

"Roxanne Citovecca speaking," Roxanne answered.

"Roxy, hey," James said brightly. "I know you wanted me to call last night, but I can't make it tonight."

"What?" Roxanne fussed.

"Well, something came up," James rambled, cutting her off, "and Allen left me this urgent message, something I don't know about yet..."

"James, why didn't you call me last night?" Roxanne demanded.

"I know, but right now, my life is getting too weird, with the Feds and all..."

"Feds? James, what's going on?" She immediately lowered her voice. "It's not about Nicoterra, is it?"

"Huh, what?" James glanced back at Leila leaving the refuel station with change, heading for the pumps. "No, look, it's nothing major, really!"

"I love you, James," Roxanne said sadly. "Please, don't get hurt!"

"I feel the same about you too."

"Please tell me," Roxanne cried. "You act like you're afraid to say it!"

"Look, I'm not afraid to say it, okay?" James snapped, bristling. "I love you. There, I said it."

"It's not that difficult, James!"

James watched Leila enter the car after finishing filling the tank with gasoline. "I'll have to finish this later," he said quickly. "I'll talk with you soon, alright? Bye now." James hung up the line and hurried for the car. With a firm kick, he forced open the door with a pop and got in.

Leila rolled her eyes. "Can't you just get the door hammered out instead of causing more damage?' she asked wryly.

James slammed the door. "It'll cost too much!" he protested and turned the ignition.

"How can replacing the handle cost so much? It's cheap at the junkyard, right?"

"The lock's broken and all the dents need to be pulled. With this steel body, it'll be damn near impossible!"

"So stop banging it up!"

"Oh, would you rather I bang *you* up?" James's face flushed scarlet and Leila giggled in response. "*With this enhanced strength,*" he thought, adjusting his mirrors. "*I could probably give it a few whacks with my fists no problem!*" He pulled out the lot and returned to the road.

Leila touched him gently on the arm. "Did you have a nice conversation with Roxanne?" she asked gently.

"It's cool," James answered.

"I hope I didn't ruin anything between you two..."

"Nah, you can't break anything that's already falling apart!"

"I want you to be happy, James," Leila murmured.

"Whatever Allen wants better be important!" James replied, changing the course of the conversation. He stiffened and clenched his teeth when Leila leaned against him, resting a hand to his chest. "*C'mon Jim, keep your head on,*" James told himself. "*Now's not a good time to let your nasty brain wander!*"

CHAPTER SEVEN

Finding most of the lot behind Allen's workshop occupied by people refurbishing cars in various states of disrepair, James parked on the lot's edge. He cut off the engine and leaned against the wheel, watching the work.

"Are you okay?" Leila asked.

"I'll be fine," James murmured.

"Get your head out the gutter and let's go."

"I'll follow in a minute."

Leila laughed and pulled against his sleeve. "Come on, Jamie. You act like I felt you up or something!"

James blew a hard sigh. "You know how I get, so please, don't do that again! Next time, I might not concentrate as hard!"

Leila laughed harder and punched him playfully on the shoulder. "Am I that hot?" she teased. "I thought you only had eyes for Body-Rockin' Roxanne!"

"I might just change my mind..."

"Too cute!" Leila stepped out and shut the door. "Want me to give you some space?" she called. When James didn't answer, she walked ahead for the building across the lot.

"Wait up!" James cried and clamored out. He slammed the door with a bang that rattled the windows and hurried after her.

"Jamie! Leila!" Allen called brightly as he came across the lot, waving. James stifled a laugh when Allen approached, as Allen wore leather sandals, Bermuda shorts and an open Aloha shirt, displaying his pale narrow chest. A pair of gray-tinted sunglasses rest perched atop his head.

"Did you forget you already have a pair of glasses on your head?" Leila asked and James chuckled.

"Oh!" Allen said and reached up, feeling for the frames. "I forgot I put them there. If I lost these, it's another three hundred for a new prescription!"

"That's harsh," James said.

Allen shrugged his shoulders. "I've got to be more careful then, hm?"

"Yeah, without them you've got to guess what you're looking at!" James laughed harder and Allen blew an annoyed sigh.

"I was born with poor eyesight, okay?" Allen grumbled.

"Aren't you cold?" James inquired instead.

"It's unusually warm today," Allen answered, "so we decided to take the advantage!"

"Who's 'we'?" Leila asked guardedly.

"Follow me," Allen said, beckoning them over, "I want to show you something!"

"Show us what?" James drawled, smirking.

"Come on, this way..."

James and Leila followed Allen to the tinkering mechanics and their older cars.

"So, what's with the junk?" James asked.

"This will be the future, James; I can *feel* it!" Allen gestured toward one old rusted chassis of a former sedan.

"Okay, so you got rusty scrap metal, and...?"

"This old beauty will run on electricity. Electric cars *will* make a comeback when the next oil crisis comes and I wanted to test out a few theories..."

"That crazy old Allen," Leila drawled. "We've got ourselves our personal own conspiracy theorist and part-time machinist, huh?" She nudged James in the chest with her elbow and he chortled.

"I mean it guys," Allen complained. "This feeling I've got is never wrong!"

"I hope you didn't call me here to help you fix this 'old beauty', right?" James said dryly.

"Well, I don't know all you can do..."

"So you want me to test it out."

"You promised, remember?"

"Right," James moaned, wincing. "The most important thing in history..."

"So who are your friends?" Leila asked, gesturing to the other people who chatted and worked on parts.

"We call ourselves 'Makers'," piped one young man in ripped jeans and sleeveless shirt. "We like to make things out of old stuff and give it new life so that we won't be dependent on a consumerist society!"

"True that," said a young woman near him in overalls and tank shirt. "Planned obsolescence is bad for the environment. We have landfills high with junk and no where else to put it!"

"So, everyone," Allen called, clapping his hands. "Let's take a break of lemonade and cookies. I also have some questions and I'm sure my friends do too!"

Everyone left their project cars, filing into a large building with many windows and skylights. James and Leila followed them and James stood near the wall closest to the door, watching the others while Leila mingled.

"Hey, Jamie," Leila called, waving to him, "some of your friends from college are here."

"I'm sure I know most of the people here," James muttered, recognizing many of the faces in the crowd. "Allen and I met most of these mecha nuts at Central!"

"Hey, everyone," Allen called, waving his hands. "This is James Russell and his friend Leila Gibson. Meet, greet, and have fun, okay?" Allen left the room and James blew a sigh as several people came up to him to talk and catch up on events.

After answering their questions halfheartedly, James turned to leave and bumped into a young woman with hazel eyes and bobbed sandy hair, wearing a green blazer over a yellow tank, white high-cut shorts and low-top sneakers.

"James, is that you?" she asked, startled. "It's been a long while...!"

"Um, er, hey Nadine," James said, surprised. "So, how's the kid?"

"Tony's fine... He misses you though."

"Really?"

"You were like a surrogate father to him when we were together. You ought to call once in a while."

"I didn't realize I made that much of an impact," James murmured, flushing darkly. "You know how hectic college was... Especially with the *Funky Fresh Fellas*..."

"Oh, those nuts." Nadine blew a sigh and shuddered. "I'm not too fond of the reunion coming up."

"When is it?" James jammed his hands into his jeans pockets.

"Sometime next year." Nadine ran a hand through her hair. "When the date gets finalized, I'll let you know."

James grinned. "Maybe we ought to get together sometime?"

Nadine narrowed her eyes. "Oh, I see you've been busy lately."

"Huh?" James stiffened when Leila approached, taking his arm.

"This one is very pretty, James," Nadine said flatly. "Congrats are in order."

"Now, hold on," James protested. "She's just a friend!"

Nadine scoffed. "And we were too, right?"

"I need some air!" James pulled out of Leila's grip and stormed for the door.

"Jamie!" Allen cried when James bumped into him. He held fast to James's arm to keep him from walking out. "Where are you going? I was about to start..."

"Al, I don't need this," James retorted, "and it's just too weird!"

"I need your help!"

"I don't need the help of your weird anti-establishment friends!"

"You're bright and perceptive," Allen whined. "You can take their so-called weird ideas and turn them into something useful!" James shook out of Allen's grip. "Now come on, please, just this once?"

"One weird thing and I'm gone!" James snapped.

"That's fine, now come with!"

James blew a hard short sigh and returned with the others assembled on the floor. He took a seat next to Leila who sat next to Nadine, who sat next to Allen, seething.

"*Please, Nadine,*" James prayed, rolling his eyes to the ceiling, "*don't jump Leila!*"

"So, before we get back to tinkering on our world-changing products," Allen started, "I wanted to discuss something."

"Let's hear it!" one member of the group called.

"What would you do if you suddenly acquired the power to control or even destroy the universe?"

"*What is he doing to me?*" James thought, horrified.

"Well," Nadine answered, "I'd probably destroy those pesky meters downtown off Market District." Several members of the group laughed.

"I'm out of here!" James spat and quickly rose to his feet.

"James, wait!" Leila cried, hurrying after him as he stormed out.

"Where are you going?" Allen yelped and rushed to the door after him.

James whirled around, grabbing Allen by the collar with his flaring hand. Allen paled when James's hand burned through the fabric.

"You get your manipulative butt off my case, Allen!" James sneered.

"I thought this might help you," Allen complained. "You know, figure things out... Besides, I saw you flying around downtown earlier!" James bared his teeth and pushed him back. "You have to be careful! The Feds..."

"I'll figure out things myself!" James growled. "I don't need your paranoid help and if the Feds want me, they already know where to look!"

"Sorry," Leila murmured to Allen as James stomped off back to his car. "Jamie, what's your deal?" she called at his back and ran after him.

James grunted, too steamed to answer and kicked open the door. Getting in, he slammed it shut and the force rattled the windows. Leila went around, getting in with him and he started the engine with a roar.

"Leila, it's like this," James replied, "What if you trusted somebody with a secret and the one who knew put you in this large group of nobodies who can't keep their mouth shut and wanted to expose you?"

"You're getting paranoid," said Leila, shaking her head. "I think Allen's infectious!"

James snorted in response. Shifting gears, he peeled out the lot and sped away. "I'm serious, Leila!" he fussed. "You'd be uncomfortable too if you were up against the wall and the people around you already assume you're nuts!"

"What are you getting at exactly?"

"I'm telling you that I trust you enough to show you *exactly* what I'm talking about!"

James pulled off on the side of the road and came out the car, motioning Leila to follow.

"This is something I definitely have to see!" Leila said with a grin as she stepped out.

James stood staring at his car, holding his chin in thought. "How heavy is a car this old?" he murmured.

"With a steel body like that, probably close to a ton at most..." Leila stepped back, apprehensive. "What are you getting at?"

"I'm going to pick it up!"

"You're going to rupture something!"

"Just watch!" James crawled under the car as his body flared in golden light. "Let's see if I can do this," he said and pressed his hands against the car, struggling to lift it. James grunted and Leila laughed when the car rocked but made no effort to move. "I thought I was insanely strong," James muttered, miffed as he crawled back out.

"Okay, I *know* you're insane now," Leila cracked and laughed even harder.

"Hey, I *am* strong, okay?" James snapped. "I can show you!" He withdrew the keys from the ignition and walked around to the trunk, opening it. James pulled out his bag of tools, digging around for an object he wanted to show, then withdrew a wrench. "Now watch," he said seriously and tossed Leila the keys.

"What are you going to do with *that*, Super Spud?" Leila teased as she caught the keys.

"I'm turning this monkey wrench to sculpture!" James declared.

Leila's eyes widened as he twisted the metal into a ball. "Okay," she yelped, dropping the keys, "I believe you!"

"I think the better I get at this, the stronger I can be," James said and he tossed the twisted metal to Leila who had shock written on her face. She let the crumpled wrench fall to the ground at her feet, too astonished to catch it. "It takes practice you know? I can't topple cars overnight!"

"I... I don't know what to say!"

"Then don't mention it to anyone!"

"What else can you do?" Leila returned to the passenger side, dumbfounded while James slammed down the trunk and scooped up the dropped keys.

James returned to the driver's side. "I can fly," he said, "and I can light up like a star too..."

"Yeah, right!" Leila scoffed.

"I'd show you, but then half of Petoria would be blown away!"

"No way!"

"Really!"

"So... how did you get that way?"

James returned to the road, heading for home. "That's a long story... one I don't even get all the way myself."

"I promise; my lips are sealed!"

"So what do you think I should do with this power?"

"If you put on a mask and a cape and a spandex suit, I'll be sure to commit you to Metro Psychiatric myself!"

James grinned, adjusting the rear view mirror. "Point taken!"

CHAPTER EIGHT

The next day, James welcomed the weekend, spending his morning sitting on the floor in front of his small black and white television set on a wheeled cart. He sipped coffee and watched the early newscast in his A-shirt and boxers, completely engrossed. Behind him in the nearby kitchen, Leila worked the stove frying vegetables and rice in a skillet while wearing his bathrobe.

"... The hijacked German cargo ship, *Maserk*, is still sailing across the Atlantic," rambled the reporter on the screen. "No one knows for sure who these pirates are, but they have successfully deterred any attack made by officials and have not made any demands yet..."

"Maybe you could save that ship out at sea," Leila suggested as she scraped the pan. "That'll be a job for Super Spud!"

"Nah," James demurred. "I failed Geography in high school; I wouldn't know my Atlantic from my Pacific!"

"Well, try the superhero thing closer to home, huh?"

James leaned in closer to the screen as images of downtown Petoria appeared. "Wait," he said excitedly, "there's some breaking news!"

"Meanwhile, another tense drama is unfolding in uptown Petoria," droned the reporter. "Around nine this morning, in the 4300 block of Dandycuss..."

"Turn that up," Leila called as she turned on the water in the tap.

"... Terrorists have attacked the Federal Center and have completely taken over the nearby bullet plant! A rescue team is trying desperately to drive the terrorists back out of the AMASTCOMS offices to spare the sensitive documentation kept there..."

"Do you think you can handle terrorists?" Leila asked.

"... and there are rumors that a bomb has been placed among the National Reserve which is housed on-site..." continued the broadcast.

James grinned deviously as the orange light flared faintly around his hand. "Maybe I can!" he said with confidence.

Later, after changing into his uniform, James quickly bounded out the door and took a hesitant leap before pausing, levitating above the ground by several feet.

"*If I fly there,*" he thought, "*then everyone in the world would know I have this ability...*" He touched down with ease and pulled out the folded electronic device from his rear pocket then glanced at the screen. "*It says that I have double my base speed... what does that mean?*" He punched several buttons with his non-glowing hand, scrolling through statistics. "*According to this, with this power I can run at best 60 miles per hour, a little slower than a cheetah... Well, that's all I need to know!*" Pocketing the device, James took off in a sprint.

After an hour, between checking his orientation and making sure he ran in the right direction, also following traffic laws, James approached the scene where numerous flashing lights and cars blocked the way from several directions.

"*No wonder traffic is backed up on the nearby highway,*" he mused, "*since the interstate is right behind the bullet plant!*" James pushed his way through the crowd of people clustered nearby.

"Um, excuse me," he said to a woman who peered over the interested. "What's going on? I just got here..."

"The police just sent in some ABLE Team guys to rout them out," she replied. "So far, three national guardsmen were let go because they were badly hurt from trying to fight them off..."

"Who are these terrorists exactly?"

"Nobody knows for sure..."

"Thanks." James walked around, observing the scene. "*What should I do?*" he thought. "*Just kick in the door and go in fists a-blazing? I could return a hero and have instant stardom...*" James blew a heavy sigh. "*Can I deal with that right now? How would I explain and not sound crazy? How can I deal with all the new changes in my life?*" He turned away and headed down another part of the street on the opposite end of the blockade near the bullet plant. "*It might be worth it if I could save the other National Guardsmen, but it's clear they're outnumbered. What if those terrorists won't be nice and blow them all straight to Hell? What if those three were just icing to calm the police down before the big number?*" James glanced around and made a quick dash to the rear of the bullet plant. He took a leap over the barbed wire fence and hid behind a large refuse bin. *"This is more complicated than I thought!"* Hearing shouts, he looked up and gasped upon sight of an armored flying machine heading directly for the National Guard building. *"What the--? Is that some kind of robot?"*

"What is that thing?" a voice cried.

"Is it some kind of Air Corps project...?" called another.

"It's going inside!" yelled a third as the nearly eight-foot-tall robot touched down and marched directly inside. "Get ready!"

James clenched his teeth as gunfire resonated from within. Moments later, the many guardsmen exited the building, followed by the machine and the police forces infiltrated the bullet plant.

"My work here is done," a mechanical voice boomed through the machine and took off, flying away.

James took off after it as the fight at the bullet plant went under way. *"I've got to check that thing out,"* he considered as he kept close behind the machine. *"As long as I stay out of its sights, I should be okay..."* Growing concerned when he noticed the robot flying toward the small, disenfranchised county of Keyes Inlet, James increased his speed. *"Why would it come from here? I know the Landers Field airport's started their project of tearing down housing to expand their field space, so why would there still be any holdouts if they were all bought out by now?"*

James landed behind a half-demolished house several yards away of the robot that landed near an abandoned home.

Peering out, he saw several cars parked at the rear and a young woman emerged from the head of the robot. Several young men that surrounded the machine cheered in response.

"We heard it on the radio," one said brightly. "Nice work, Arice!"

"*A girl in that robot, huh?*" James thought from his position. "*She's got red hair and a nice body to boot...*" He felt himself flushing. "*No sense tipping my hand yet...*" Walking away, James clenched his hands, feeling the power that surrounded him fading. "*This is too weird. I just can't walk over there and say, 'Hi fellas, how's the superhero thing going?' or something stupid like that!*"

"Ay," a voice snapped from nearby. James whirled around, spotting a young man with a shock of blond-tipped fiery red hair, wearing a sleeveless shirt with sweatpants, red suspenders that hung around his waist, and running shoes. On his face, he wore darkly tinted wraparound sunglasses.

"What is it?" James demanded.

"You ain't from around here," the young man demanded, "is ya?"

"So?"

"So, from the way you sound, you ain't from Keyes Inlet."

"If monosyllable helps," James drawled, putting up his hands, "then hey, you got me."

"What's it to ya; you comin' to inspect the damage already done?"

"What are you talking about?" James stepped away, feeling his left hand burn in response. "I'm not with Landers, okay? I'm not part of the demolition team!"

"You sure look like some kinda pilot though…"

"Well, I'm not!"

"Put them up, yo!" The young man snapped his fingers, unleashing a glowing switchblade.

"That'd better be some fancy theatrics!" James thought as the young man advanced. James quickly dodged a cut and shoved the young man away with a flaring hand, stunning him as he bowled over. The young man fell head over heels and the weapon he held vanished.

"Man!" the young man yowled in pain. "What the hell?"

"Am I stronger than I thought?" James stared down at his hand in awe. The GEARS unit in his pocket beeped frantically and James took off before the young man could get up, leaving him behind in a cloud of dust. *"I'll figure this out later…"*

Finding a note on his apartment door, James ripped it off and quickly scanned it.

"Sundays are my day off," it read in heavy angular strokes. *"We'll fool around later."*

James entered his apartment and made a direct line to his bathroom, shucking his clothing along the way to his shower stall. *"What's wrong with me?"* he thought once he started the tap and pressed his head against the stall wall as hot water ran down his back. *"Why couldn't I just barge in like that cute girl in the robot suit and kick terrorist butt?"* James groaned when the phone rang moments later, scattering his thoughts. *"So why am I upset that somebody else saved those guardsmen guys? Is it because I wanted to feel important?"* He turned off the water, grabbed a nearby towel on the rack and wrapped it around his waist. *"I can't believe that I'm jealous. <u>Jealous!</u> Maybe I shouldn't have left Allen's little hippie group so quickly and heard what they had to say..."*

James padded out the bathroom and entered his bedroom, approaching his phone that rang again. He picked up the receiver.

"Hey," he greeted.

"Hello, James?" said a nervous voice over the line.

"Nadine?" he answered in surprise at once finding recognition in the sound. "Well, hello! I was about to call you..."

"I'm sorry about being so catty the other day," Nadine murmured. "You know, some old habits die hard."

"Well...!"

"Hi, James!" a voice called from the background. Nadine giggled in response.

"Tell Tony I said 'hi'," James drawled, blushing slightly. "So how did the discussion go with Allen?"

"Well, people said what you'd expect, like 'end apartheid', 'lower taxes', and liberate whatever countries being repressed..."

"Of course," James muttered, "but what about you?"

"What about me?" Nadine scoffed. "Really, James, you don't want to hear it."

"Come on, Nadine!" James leaned against the dresser, running a hand through his wet hair. "I know what you said about destroying the parking meters on Market District's a joke. Now let's be serious."

"Well, seriously..." Nadine sighed. "If I had a power that could destroy the universe, I'd enlighten everyone in the world to be like me, so as to not destroy it."

"Isn't that what the States did with their nuke program?" James retorted, chuckling.

"Hey, I'm being serious!" Nadine spat. "I'd never use my power, only to threaten those that want to harm the Earth and get them to straighten up! We've only got *one* planet, James!"

"Yeah, that's something to think about..." James sat on the edge of his bed, sighing heavily.

"You know, we *already* have the power to make a difference in this world," Nadine said softly. "Magic powers or not, we *can*, but only if we *want* to. Besides, don't we have the right to our *own* lives? Don't we have the *right* to live and die as we choose?"

"That's a good point..." James lay back onto the mattress, staring up at the ceiling. "Say, Nadine, what if there's a little kid's life at stake? If you could, would you save the kid? Is there any harm in that?"

"Well, James, that all depends. What if that kid is an evil demonic monster? What if saving him meant that he would kill his family who were nice people and me next; or, on the flip side, what if saving him meant putting him at the mercy of his depraved parents who had some diabolical plan to use him for body parts on another child they valued?" James snickered. "Really, James, it all comes down to one sure thing: why? Why bother? Why do it in the first place? All these questions..."

"You're right, Nadine. Why would anyone do anything?"

"People are so sure about what's right and what's wrong these days. I mean, take a look at the news. You know that German ship *Maserk* that's been hijacked by pirates?"

"Yeah, they've been talking about it nonstop for a few days now."

"Well, the Navy's on their butt willing to blow it up because the captain let mostly everyone else go and only he and his few mates that know how to run the thing are held hostage!"

"What is it; destroy the many to save the few?"

Nadine chuckled. "You see, we have a lot of choices, James."

"Thanks for calling Nadine."

"Yeah, no problem."

"Will you call later some time?"

"Sure, why not?"

"Maybe you can come over for a play date..."

"James!" Nadine squealed, "You are so bad!"

James grinned as Nadine's end of the line disconnected. *"A matter of choice,"* he mused as he hung up the receiver. *"Let's see what's on the television now..."*

Turning on the television that rest on the cart in the parlor, James curled up on the couch with a mug of coffee, watching the special report titled 'terror on the high seas'.

"... while officials neither confirm nor deny the speculation that the *Maserk* is used for handling and transport of test-grade devices," squawked the reporter, "and the presence of a secret test-quality nuclear weapon is aboard the ship, the United States has threatened to sink the vessel if it comes within two hundred miles of American coastline, despite the presence of twelve German officers held as hostages!"

James choked on his coffee, stunned. "What the hell?" he yelped. "This is serious!" He leaned in closer as the reporter rambled on.

"No demands have yet been made by the terrorists, and no specific group has made their presence known. We have been told by Government officials not to assume it is the work of Moslem extremists... Is this daring blackmail scheme by a new unknown group as an act of ultimate terrorism? The world watches fearfully..."

"I've got to check this out!" James set aside his coffee and turned up the volume of the set, then hurried into his bedroom, swiftly changing into his specialized clothing.

"Unless the *Maserk* changes course," the television blared from the next room, "it will cross the two-hundred mile limit around eleven this evening. The question is..."

"*The question is*," thought James as he picked up the GEARS device, "*can I keep sitting on my butt doing nothing, knowing that I could've actually <u>done</u> something?*" The machine beeped and James glanced down at it, noticing that it displayed the current time and the time he had remaining. "*This thing is smart...*"

Pocketing the machine, he went outdoors and grabbed for the national auto association-issued road map within the glove compartment in his car. After checking his route, he folded it into his rear pocket and took off skyward.

CHAPTER NINE

Approaching the scene, James noticed one spy plane flying ahead and flew close enough to stay underneath it, secretly hoping it would take him to his needed destination.

After the plane began to circle, James shot off in the general area, finding the ship within several yards on the ocean. He flew by, searching for signs of other smaller ships that could have aided pirates. Finding none, James landed on-deck and quickly ducked behind a post as a helmeted guard walked past, wielding a large laser rifle. James clenched his teeth in stark horror, trying to keep in a tight breath.

"Those aren't terrorists -- They're Corpii!" James studied the guard pacing on the edge of the deck, almost out of his line of sight. *"If they're here, then someone aboard this ship must have a Signet like I do!"* The GEARS unit in his pocket chirped and he pulled it out, grinding his teeth in frustration. *"I need to hurry... It's already ten-fifty and the Navy will torpedo this tub for real if we get too near that two-hundred mile limit!"*

"Was ist das?" a muffled voice cried.

Another voice in an unintelligible language suddenly shouted out to James and he looked up, startled. Quickly dropping all he held, he rushed forward and rammed his elbow into the alien guard that returned and smashed it against the side of the ship before it could ready its rifle.

"Son of a--!" James yelped as it cried out in pain, crumpling forward. "*He spooked me and I hit him too hard,*" he realized as dark green liquid began to seep beneath the fighter. "*I damn near forgot how strong I was!*" James stood over him, heaving for breath as the pool became larger. "*Don't chuck now, Jim; keep it together!*"

James picked up the rifle as the downed guard at his feet moaned in pain and James pointed the rifle at the fighter's face. "Stop making noise!" he hissed. James swallowed hard to keep the acrid burning down and winced when his shaking hands flared in response.

"*I need to tie him down, knock him out, gag him, something!*" he thought frantically. "*His moaning is going to alert the others!*" Shutting his eyes, James gave a quick whack across the guard's face, only to jump when the guard screamed from impact. "*Damn it, this always worked in the movies!*"

"*Wer ist da?*" another voice shouted.

James whirled around, dropping the rifle across the now still guard who had a busted helmet and crushed skull. He quickly took off in the opposite direction, finding security on the other side. Levitating near the edge, James caught sight of another fighter standing near the railing.

"*There's another one!*" James sucked in a shallow breath. "*Just hover over real easy, Jim. Right behind him, like his shadow...*" Inching closer, James tackled the guard from behind, bringing him down with a crash. Giving a fierce charged punch into his enemy's helmet, it cracked and the warrior made a muffled noise before becoming still altogether. *"Two down!"* He let go and floated above the still body, trying to resist the urge to vomit. *"Jim, you need to improve on your rate here without killing these guys or breaking their bones!"*

Descending onto the lower levels, James slammed into a guard and let out a surprised yelp, quickly throwing up a hand to shield himself from a return blow with the butt of the rifle. He released a sphere of flame and the guard let out a horrified cry as it quickly incinerated. James stumbled back, appalled.

"We have an intruder!" a voice squawked from within a nearby room. "Man the stations and kill the officers!"

"Hilfe!" other voices cried out. *"Helfen uns!"*

"That must be the German officers held hostage!" James considered as he quickly ran toward the sound. *"I need to get them out of there!"*

Finding a steel door, James grabbed the handle with a glowing hand and pulled against it, ripping it out in response. He kicked at the door, barely making a dent in the metal.

"Ready the device!" the head alien ordered as the others rushed about the deck of the ship. "Make sure no one lives!"

"Who am I kidding?" James thought in despair as his body flared in light. *"I'm running out of time! How can I stop them?"* The door crunched under pressure, slowly giving way to his glowing foot. *"Think, Jim; you gotta do something!"*

He let out a yowl as intense pressure slammed into his back, throwing him forward against the wall. Turning out, James found himself face-to-face against a large alien fighter in a similar suit with helmet, wielding a quadruple-barrel plasma gun.

"Die, intruder!" it growled.

"I'll blow myself up and take you all with me!" James screamed, thrusting forward a fiercely inflamed hand. The alien tensed and cautiously backed away.

"Can I control myself enough to fry these aliens and spare those officers?" James wondered. *"Can I just let the power rise enough, light up like a star and vaporize those guys?"* James clenched his teeth as the light flared brightly around his body. *"I doubt I can do it, not from this end-- they'd be incinerated from the flash!"* He let out a scream as a high-powered blast tore into his shoulder, throwing him forward from his inaction. *"Damn, what the hell I get myself into?"*

"Get him while he's unstable!" a voice barked as the air around him became charged.

"No!" James wailed, turning around. He kicked at the alien before him, throwing him against the wall and shook off another that pounced on him from behind. Shoving backward into another alien fighter from his rear, the alien let out a surprised yelp as its spine snapped against the metal railing and flipped over, crashing into the ocean.

James slipped forward once cracked on the head from the rear and let out a restrained cry as a heavy gloved hand grabbed his hair. His head yanked back, James stared up into a gleaming barrel of a triple-barreled revolving shotgun.

"Who are you?" demanded a gruff voice above him. "Who sent you?"

"I'm not telling!" retorted James. "Besides, the Navy's going to blow all your butts to Hell if you don't turn this thing around!"

"Tell us, or else!"

Another helmeted fighter rushed up to James, wielding his electronic device.

"The intruder's GEARS state we only have forty-six Terran seconds left!" said the second alien.

"Left for what?" the alien above James thundered.

"Before the Navy fires torpedoes into this thing!" James screeched. The unit chirped wildly.

"He's telling the truth!" declared the other alien.

"Get out of here!"

The alien let James go and James scrambled forward onto his feet, scooping up the dropped device as the aliens took off, flying away. Jamming the GEARS unit in his pocket, he flew for the door and rammed into it with all his might.

"I don't have enough time!" James thought as the door crunched from all his beating into the steel. *"They'll swamp this thing with so many Maverick rockets that it'd blow hotter than the Fourth of July!"*

The door caved in and James gave it another ram to blow it apart, revealing stunned German officers tied within.

"You've got thirty seconds to turn this thing around!" he cried as he hurried in and ripped off their binds. "Either do it or jump ship!"

The officers scurried out except for one with a hefty frame, wearing a different uniform than the others. He stood tall and adamant as faint dark blue light surrounded his body.

"*Als Kapitän, ich gehe mit diesem Schiff,*" the remaining officer declared.

"*He must be the captain,*" James thought as he grabbed for the man's arm. He let out a yelp as a sudden spark charged between them and the captain pulled back. "*He's got a Signet too! But we have fifteen seconds... can he run that fast?*"

James grabbed for him again and held him down as a blast rocked the ship. Getting up, he hustled the captain for the door as another concussive force hurled the ship and threw both of them out, flipping them end over end before crashing into the frigid depths below. James let go, sinking down into the murky deep while the captain swam for air above him.

"*That hurt!*" James fell slack and his body began to float upwards. "*Everything hurts... I need to go home, take a shower, and sleep the day off.*" Cresting, James gasped for breath, watching from a distance a Coast Guard boat several yards away, teeming with rescuers grabbing for the officers in the water. "*I wonder if that cute redhead and the robot even thought about coming out here...*"

Hearing a helicopter whir nearby, James made a straight shot out of the water, returning for home.

Making a stop in Keyes Inlet, after kicking up dirt from a hard landing, James walked up to the abandoned house that had spotlights hooked up in the front of the residence and surrounded by three large trailers.

The redheaded young woman pushed against the clunky robot set on a board with casters, trying to move it inside the garage. Several men aided her, shouting which directions to turn the machine.

"Are you sure the Galvanis suit is glitch-free?" the young woman demanded.

"Yeah, Arice," one young man complained, "it's as ready as it's gonna get!"

"I can't believe she thinks she can take a stab at that *Maserk* drama with *that*," complained another. "Doesn't she realize it's *weak* against water?"

"Ay," snapped the young man with frosted-tipped carmine hair who pushed at the foot of the machine, "my sister Arice knows what she's doin'! Now quit runnin' yer mouths and move yer arms!"

"No need to worry about the ship," James said as he approached the scene. "It was rescued by some commando group."

"Really, huh?" drawled one young man.

"Prolly Delta Force," said another, "or Navy Seals I think...

"So, who the hell are you, pal?" snapped a third.

"I've seen him snoopin' 'round here before," sneered Arice's brother. "He's up to something funny..."

"Hey, I'm just somebody who knows a lot about you and that robot suit thingy," answered James. "So no games, okay? Let's talk, got it?"

"Come around," Arice called, motioning James to follow.

James approached a trailer that contained numerous electronic parts and equipment. The GEARS unit in his pocket chirped and he quickly pulled it out with his right hand, folding it closed.

"So, first tell me," he said as the other young men filtered in moments later, surrounding him, "what's with that robot?" James clenched his teeth, noticing that they sealed off any possible exit. "*Smart move, Jim,*" he thought in disgust. "*Don't get lazy with the powers on, making stupid choices!*"

"This robot is a Gantry Engine Alternate Reactionary System," Arice answered. "It's a mobile armored robotic shell like a large exoskeleton, useful for various things... but that's the least you need to know about it!"

"*I wonder if it's similar to this GEARS thing I'm hauling around,*" James wondered. "So," he said instead, "what's with all this fancy equipment? Looking for something?"

"Specifically, this equipment gives a reading of any unusual radioactive activity, among other things..."

James clenched his hand as he took a step back in stunned silence. "*They were secretly trying to get a read on me!*" he thought. "What's your deal anyway?" demanded James. "Why were you out on Dandycuss earlier?"

"Let's just say it doesn't concern you and we can forget the matter."

"It *does* concern me," James spat. "Your well-intentioned interfering could've caused some people to die out there. I just had a hard lesson on that score -- a *very* close call!"

"We don't need your help, Super Jerk," Arice's brother grumbled from offside. James glared at him, sneering.

"Siegfried, cool it," Arice snapped. "I can handle this!" She stepped forward, poking James hard in the chest with a firm finger. "Look, bucko, we don't take demands from some nobody!"

"If you're going to take charge of some situation, just be aware of all the options," James said, putting up his hands. "Also be aware of everything, if any, that could go wrong too, including the potential consequences and who's got to put up with it."

"You act like you've been doing this for years!" scoffed Arice.

"I'm trying to do you a favor." James turned away. "Just think about it."

"Where the hell you think you're going?" spat Siegfried. "We ain't done with ya yet!"

"Now's *our* turn for questions," Arice said, grabbing James by the arm. A sudden spark flashed between them and he winced as she gasped, quickly pulling away.

"There's something on her hand!" James thought, watching her clutch tightly at her right hand that seemed injured. *"Does she have a Signet too?"*

"Hey, what's with you?" one of the young men growled.

"Look, I'm tired," complained James. "I want to go home."

"Get through us first, pally!"

Five other men from the group flanked James and he swallowed hard, noting their intent to cause serious harm to his bones. He glanced around and spotted a set of tools in a box nearby, immediately forming an idea.

"Hey, ever use this tire iron much?" James asked, grabbing for it.

"What the--?"

James quickly tied it into knots and threw it on the ground, forcing the young men who surrounded him to back away in stark fear.

"Happy birthday to anyone that wants it," James said and stalked away.

"*Oi vey*," moaned one of the men. "He's more trouble than we need…"

"See you around," James chirped and flew off.

Returning to his house, James pulled out of the uniform jacket and gloves, making a direct line to the television and turned it on.

"… Daring rescue of the cargo ship *Maserk* by a Navy Seal antiterrorist sniper squadron," droned the reporter on the screen. "A Pentagon spokesman said no nuclear device was found on board, clearing Germany of violating any peace agreements. However, the crew of the *Maserk* reported hearing an explosion after diving into the ocean once freed. The official statement that it were possibly grenades thrown by pirates during the scuffle with Special Forces…" James dumped his discarded clothing on the couch and slumped onto the edge, grinning brightly.

"*Yeah, I totally rocked my first good deed as a wannabe do-gooder,*" he said to himself and kicked off the boots. "*I barely get a mention in the news!*"

"Now, for this week in Weather," interrupted the reporter. James groaned when he realized the date.

"Tomorrow's Monday!" he moaned. "How will I even catch any sleep at this rate?" James peeled away from the couch, turned off the television and dragged his sore body to bed.

PART THREE
CLOSE ENCOUNTER

James moaned when his clock rang loudly and reached out blindly, groping with his hand to turn it off.

"Man," he groaned once he struck the button, killing the buzzing sound. "Everything hurts..." James sat up and rubbed at his face, then gave pause when he noticed the mark on the palm of his hand. Leaving his bedroom, James entered the parlor and spotted a small device near the end table next to the couch. He picked it up and unfolded it from its half-compact state, forcing the machine chirping to life, with data scrolling across the screen in cyan letters against a lime green background. "So it *wasn't* a dream!" Taking the machine back to the bedroom, he put it in his sock drawer and readied for the morning.

Getting off the bus, James entered the offices of Parsons and Parker, committing himself to his duties of typing, filing and answering telephone requests. After a round of filing, James grew irritated when his coworkers talked about him within easy earshot.

"Hey, Russell," a coworker called from the next cubicle. "How come you're so weird these days?" Before James could answer, another coworker piped up.

"Tell you what Xavier: word on the street is that Russell there is doing that crack mess. You know, party all night and come in zonked and half awake in the morning."

"Stop it, you guys," James complained. "I'm not zonked!"

"Hey, Reinhold, that can't be the only reason why!" called Adnan from close by. "I personally think he's on the straight shot for the gutter - he's got to since he got that tattoo and all!"

"Adnan, stop it," James fussed.

"So why *did* you get that thing on your hand in the first place?"

James stiffened, feeling as if his blood froze in his veins. *"How does he know about the Signet on my hand?"* he thought. *"Maybe I'm worrying about nothing; it's not like I'm exactly hiding it anyway..."* James cleared his throat. "Just because," he answered dully and the others hooted at him in return.

"You're partying all the time, dude," Reinhold drawled. "That only explains why you've been missing work! First the tattoo, then you become a hard-core wino..."

"What a shame," Adnan said and snorted. "Russell could actually *go* somewhere. He's smart, unlike Xavier over there!" The other coworkers chuckled.

"Yeah," spat back Xavier, "like Reinhold's ever going to catch up to me!"

"Hey, I don't have a girlfriend to blow money on at the disco," Reinhold retorted.

"That's because you stay at home with your momma!"

Everyone roared in laughter.

"Good burn!" Adnan jeered.

"Look, don't preach at me," James grumbled. "So I've got a nightlife…"

"And you like to boogie!" interjected Reinhold, causing the others to laugh even harder.

"Let me tell you," James said evenly over the laughs, "it's *not* as easy as it looks!" Blowing a hard sigh, James grumbled curses under his breath as he readied another stack of forms to be typed.

Adnan, with his frizzy strawberry blond hair pulled back into a loose queue, wearing a tailored dark brown suit with a yellow carnation pinned to the lapel, came around the cubicle's entrance. He approached the desk and clutched the sides, leaning in.

"How old are you, Russell?" Adnan demanded, staring intently with narrowed brown eyes.

"Twenty-five," James answered coolly, glaring back from behind his desk. "Why, you wanna buy me a present or something?"

"You've got your whole life ahead of you. You can party later!"

"But I'm *not* partying! I'm in *here*, wasting my life, grinding away at some electric typewriter!"

"You'll never break into Pome with those skills!"

James bristled and quickly pushed his chair back. "How did you know?" he snarled.

"You left some computer code lying around that you typed up." Adnan lowered his voice. "I checked it out... it's from the Orichide Programmer's Workshop." James paled as Adnan grinned darkly. "Now, how did *you*, a virtual nobody, obtain a software developer's tool when you're not even *hired* by them yet?"

"I got it from the gals in Info-Sys," James replied, smirking. "And besides, it's too hellishly difficult for your little brain to contemplate." James rose to his feet, glaring back at Adnan. "Now if you excuse me, I've got other things to occupy my time." He pushed past Adnan and a sudden spark flashed between them when his coworker grabbed his wrist. James gasped and quickly pulled away as Adnan winced.

"What the hell?" Adnan hissed, curling his hand into a fist as he took a step away.

"That's the same reaction I had with that cute redheaded girl and the captain!" James thought, hurrying past Adnan. He glanced at the overhead clock and headed out the door intending for the office park, overwhelmed by many thoughts swirling in his head. *"At least it's noon..."* James walked directly for the crater and upon approach; he made a quick cautious survey around, then took a leap, ascending for the clouds. *"If I stay high enough from the ground, the people below might think I'm some kind of large bird."* He chuckled to himself as he headed for Cedarwood. *"Who would care? If anyone did see a flying man, they'd hit up the bottle or at least a shrink..."*

Later, James flew by Allen's house that had part of the front of the house boarded up and a section of the yard cordoned off with warning tape. Spotting several dark cars parked in front and around the residence, he touched down from afar and raced forward until he was several yards away then slowed into a leisurely walk.

"He wasn't kidding about the Feds swarming his house!" James muttered. "Too bad I can't go through the back door; they have it blocked off!" Approaching the front door, James turned the handle, finding it unlocked and let himself in. "Hey, Al," he greeted as he stepped indoors.

"... More attention to detail or some big trouble starts," said a sandy-haired middle-aged man in a plain dark brown suit, skinny black tie and brown loafers who reclined on the couch, a lit cigarette in hand.

James noticed Allen across the room with his back to his visitor, mixing punch into a pitcher.

"I see," murmured Allen, "go on..."

"Um," James stammered, flushing, "I'm sorry to interrupt..."

"It's okay, kid," drawled the middle-aged man. "So, my buddy here says you tinker on computers, yeah?"

"I just make them run," James said as he approached Allen. "Al here... he's the man that builds them!"

"Both of youse smart guys," the man replied. "Tell me, do you like pushin' dem papers for some nobody company?"

"I'm just waiting on my break into Pome Corporation," James answered nervously as Allen handed him a glass of juice. "Allen here... he's got a good feeling about these things. Though they've only been on the market for two years, he feels they're going to be big some day."

"You seem like a bright kid... the both of yas..."

"Thanks, Mister, but I'll be okay, really!"

"We're happy with what we have for now," Allen murmured. "WCM pays well and they like new ideas..."

James turned into his friend, leaning in close. "Al, I need to talk to you for a hot minute," he whispered. "It's important!"

"Sure..." Allen murmured, "I need some air!"

"Where ya goin', Al?" the middle-aged man drawled as he put up his feet on the arm of the couch.

"Excuse us a minute, Mister Hilland," Allen demurred. "Why don't you help yourself to some punch?"

"Yeah, take a glass... it's good stuff!" James shoved forward the glass he held and Hilland chuckled, taking it in return.

"What, with the money you're making at WCM, you ain't got no *Chivas Regal* in the house, no *Cristal* or *Crown Royal* or anything, huh?"

"Allen doesn't have any normal vices, really," James said quickly.

Allen ushered him out into the bedroom and immediately shut the door behind them. "What's so urgent?" Allen hissed as he leaned against it, listening for external noise. James stepped away, staring down at his branded hand. "Does it have to do with The Signet?"

"I guess it does," James murmured.

"Have you come to grips yet with being the most powerful guy in the world?"

"Don't be sarcastic!" James grunted. "I just need to air this out, figure things and *talk* to somebody..."

"Really, huh?" Allen snapped, "Because if my memory serves me correctly, a few days ago, you told me to get my 'manipulative butt' off your case!"

"Come on, Allen!" James cried, turning around. "Who else can I *talk* to about this thing?"

"You keep coming to me like some therapist; I might have to start charging you!"

"You're content with me not talking about it? I told Leila and I'm not sure if she's taking it well..." Allen's jaw set and he took a step forward, clenching his hands. "Look, I haven't told anyone else, so don't worry about it!"

"That's all?" Allen said evenly, "No one else?"

"No one else."

"Not even Roxanne?"

"Roxanne?" James squawked. "Damn, Allen, what the hell?"

"What do you want me to do?"

"Tell me I'm not crazy." James sank onto the nearby mattress of the neatly made bed, holding his head in his hand. "Tell me that I'm not tripping out of my skull. Tell me that I actually met a living, breathing, alien from another planet. Tell me that I actually have a tattoo that can give me the power to vaporize downtown Petoria, and the power to lift the Porta Archway and the power to fly like some kind of caped crusading vigilante!"

Allen paced across from James. "So what are you doing hiding behind a desk at a nowhere company that is known for its incredibly high turnover rate due to suicide?" he retorted.

"Let's get this one idea straight: you could've easily left Parsons and Parker for 'greater things', whatever that is..."

"What, working for their rivals Dunn, Knoh, and Nutten?"

Allen groaned once he paused in front of James and slapped a palm against his forehead. James winced and shied away, glaring at Allen. "I'm starting to think that Signet thing is draining you of your smarts!" he snapped.

"I don't know what 'greater' things I can accomplish!" James complained as he rubbed at his forehead with the back of his hand. "This isn't like in the comic books, where superheroes are the norm!"

"So what do you *want* to do?" Allen demanded, folding his arms across his chest. "What do you think you *should* do?"

"I don't know..." James shrugged his shoulders. "Something important, I guess."

"Then figure out what it is and *do it*, Jamie!"

James blew a hard sigh. "This is tough," he grumbled. "When I finally lose it, commit me, okay?"

"Just stay out of any wars and don't start any new ones."

James snorted. "What time do you have?"

Allen pushed up his sleeve and glanced at his watch. "A quarter till," he murmured, "and your lunchtime's almost over and you won't make it back - unless..." The color drained from Allen's face as James rose to his feet, smiling slightly.

"Yeah," he declared, "I *flew* here."

"Jamie!" Allen snapped in frustration.

"It's alright, really," James said assuredly. "Thanks for listening, Allen." James turned for the door and opened it, letting out a surprised yelp when he found Hilland standing on the other side with his drink in hand. "Mister Hilland!" he cried in shock.

"Oh, um, yeah," Hilland said quickly. "I was just on my way to the bathroom!"

James glared at Hilland's back as Hilland hurried down the hall and entered the bathroom, slamming the door shut behind him. *"Right,"* James thought, clenching his teeth, *"While carrying your drink...!"*

"Do you think he heard?" Allen whispered from behind as James exited the room. James hovered from the floor, his left hand glowing in pale yellow light.

"Maybe, I don't know," James spat. "Who cares?"

"You should be careful, Jamie!" Allen hissed, glancing down the corridor. "I'm *telling* you: be careful!"

James made a straight shot through the hall, surprising Hilland as he stepped out and flew through the hole in the wall, rocketing skyward.

"Why can't Allen ever turn off the conspiracy-theorist stuff and just talk friend-to-friend?" James thought in disgust as he headed back for Parsons and Parker's office complex. *"Yeah, I needed advice and maybe some objective opinions, but not more questions!"* Landing at the crater in the office park, James made his way back for the offices, walking quickly. *"I wish this Signet thing came with an instruction manual..."*

CHAPTER ELEVEN

At five minutes after five o'clock, James placed the last file in the cabinet and shut the drawer, sighing heavily.

"It's quittin' time, Russell," Xavier called. James turned around in his chair, spotting the young man slinging a navy blazer over his shoulder as he stood at James's cubicle entrance. He pulled out a floppy patchwork applejack cap from his rear pocket and placed it over his short black hair. James noticed a pair of navy-framed reading glasses clipped into the pocket of his dress shirt.

"Yeah, I guess," James muttered and turned off his nearby word processor.

"You guess?" Xavier scoffed as James unplugged the machine. "You plan on getting too hung over tonight, or what?"

"What?" James drawled, standing.

"Look, man, you know with me and the boys, we were just kidding around," Xavier explained. "I know you're a smart guy. Hell, even that goofball Reinhold knows you're smart."

"You keep saying that," James muttered as he took his overcoat from the back of his chair.

"I hear you talking to Arikara from downstairs in Mainframes," Xavier went on. "Sometimes about girls and cars, but more about computers and various coding languages..."

"So what about it?" James pulled into his coat and sat on the edge of his desk.

"I've even *seen* that stuff you write up sometimes; might as well be Cyrillic to me!"

"Where are you getting with this?"

"Did you ever go to college for that stuff?"

James flushed slightly. "I learned SAPIC on my own, with my Commandpro 76 at home," he explained. "But when I wanted to get serious about computer programming after playing those awesome games made on the 'Pro 76, I went to the community college to learn VAFOL. The professor told me that it would be the bridge to X, one of the business languages used these days."

"Now what you just said made my head hurt," Xavier exclaimed. "It's worse with Arikara yakking about BUCOL and ALCOS... but you see, the difference between you and him is that you're not afraid to use your brain, to branch out for something better!"

"Tell me something I don't know," James muttered and stood.

"That's why you're spitting out that Orichide code on your down time, trying to master it," Xavier complained as James pushed past him, "while Arikara's slacking around in Mainframes with punch cards!" He quickly walked in step out into the dimly lit corridor along James's side.

"So what are you trying to say exactly?" demanded James.

"I'm saying that I don't know what to make of you being *here* in *this* mind-numbing joint." The two stood before the glass double doors that led to the outside as Xavier held fast to the handle, barring it from opening.

James saw Adnan standing nearby at the smoking shelter leaning against the glass wall, speaking to another coworker out of James's line of sight. "Then don't try to figure me out," he grumbled.

"Listen, I know we just barely see each other in this place, but I'm begging you, don't let P and P rot out your mind!" Xavier nodded toward Adnan's direction. "You might not see, but it's starting to affect him too! So use the gifts the gods gave you; you owe it to your own self, if not the world!"

"Thanks for the unneeded advice." James pushed against the door. "Let me out, will ya?" Xavier blew a short sigh and let go. James pushed open the door and stormed outside. "What does he know?" he grumbled as he stomped for the bus stop. "He actually wants to *be* here and yet I don't! I just need more time before I start thinking of shooting myself." James clenched his teeth when worry hit him hard in the guts.

"*What the--?*" he thought, bewildered at what just left his face. "*The stress and boredom's starting to get to me! Maybe I should try harder and get out of here while I still can!*"

In the dark of the parlor, James sat in his unzipped slacks and open shirt with his loosened tie hanging around his neck. He finished his fourth beer can from the six-pack he bought down the street at the local liquor store dubbed 'Good Times' and hiccupped.

"I'm never buying *Bristol* brand again," James moaned and shut his eyes when the walls melted and the room around him spun uncontrollably. "Even if it is a local brand and it's the cheapest around!" He grunted and wiped at his face with his hand. "Why am I drinking away my problems?"

When the dizziness ended, James opened his bleary eyes and stared at the dark television set, looking back at his reflection in the dim screen.

Crushing the can after emptying it, James let his hands flare and crushed it again, making it smaller into almost quarter-sized. James tossed the smashed metal aside on the end table and staggered to his feet.

Keeping a hand to his waistband to keep up his slacks as he shuffled to the rear door, James opened it wide and leaned against the frame, staring out into the dark evening sky.

"*I need time to think,*" he mused, "*but being this trashed totally rules out driving the coupe across the river to Altair...*"

The phone rang moments later and James went back indoors. He slumped onto his couch then leaned over, picking up the telephone receiver off the end table with a weak hand.

"Meet me at *La Luna Discotheque* in an hour," a dark voice muttered over the line. "Come alone." The line clicked before James had a chance to inquire.

"This is getting too serious!" he muttered and dropped the receiver. "That club is off the riverfront club district downtown!" Pulling out of his dress shirt and slacks, he dropped them onto the floor and returned to his bedroom.

James reached into his closets, pulled out the uniform and quickly changed. Heading back outdoors, he staggered out to his rear yard and sighed, looking out at the busy nighttime streets and the Porta Archway in the distance.

"Man, the sky is so clear tonight..." James thought. *"I wonder if I can make a break to the moon..."* He yelped in surprise when he hovered over the ground without thought and teetered forward before striking the dirt.

"Alright, Jim," he grumbled, "No flying tonight..." Springing to his feet, James took off in a run, cutting across the yard to the parking lot on the way. *"Maybe a run will clear my head,"* James considered as he focused on running, *"then I can check out this La Luna business!"*

Finding the discotheque with ease, James clenched his teeth, noticing the patrons filtering inside. Comparing himself to the club-goers, he realized he would stand out and be too easy a target. James turned away and walked down the side street, coming around the rear of the establishment.

"It's better to go around back in the case I'm being followed," he murmured, "and I have a good means of escape..."

A high whine gave James pause and he turned around, spotting a tall humanoid figure standing in the shadows away from the glare of the lamplight.

"Have you come here to die?" a low voice growled.

"You're in my way," James declared, clenching his hands that flared in yellow flame. "If you came here to get rid of me, I have to let you know something: I don't go down that easy!"

"Well, I can fix that!"

James quickly leaned out of the way of a fired shot, breaking out in cold sweat as part of the brick wall behind him crumbled. Pale yellow light quickly flared around his body.

"*All I have to do is just let the power rise even more,*" he thought, heaving for breath as he fought for control. "*Let it flow beyond my body...*"

"You are not meant to keep this power," the alien in the darkness shouted. "You have stolen property!"

"That's news to me, buster!" James spat back.

"Return it and keep your life!"

"Yeah, I've heard that before!" James shouted, growing incensed. "I got it for a reason - you want it, you take it from my cold dead hands, sucker!" He thrust forward his left hand that blazed in orange light. "Don't make me fry your butt straight to Hell!"

"You cannot control nor understand this immense power!"

"Why do you guys keep coming after me?" The energy that surrounded James increased, brightening the corridor of the alley. "I swear; I will go off *right now!*"

"You don't want to kill!" the alien bellowed. James saw the fighter come into view, wearing an identical suit in a different color with a closed-faced helmet that had a polarized visor.

"So you want to kill me instead, is that it?"

"Not just kill..."

"And then what?"

"It's to prevent war!"

"We're already at war!"

Several high-powered pulses tore into James and he screamed in terror, forcing him powering down quickly. He fell forward, stunned and shaking as he gasped for breath. James grunted when a heavy foot pressed into his shoulder.

"The Signet, Earthling," the alien above him sneered and jammed its pistol into his forehead that emitted a high whine, "or dealing with the Corpii will be the least of your problems!"

"*If it were that easy*," James thought. "*If I could just give it back and pretend it never happened, but it had, and it's still going on now! How will I protect Allen and Leila and Roxanne...?*"

"What is your answer?"

"You're wrong about me," James snarled. "Yeah, this whole idea freaks me out, but only because I'm not sure of my true power..."

"Then let the ones that understand the power have it!"

"I can't let you... Not yet, not now." The pale orange flames faintly flickered around James. "I want to know how far I can take this..."

"You won't have long, Earthling. If you insist on keeping Federation property, you *will* be hunted for the rest of your days, until the Signet is taken off your body!"

"Not unless I will it to move!" James snapped. "The guy who gave it to me, he told me that as long as I can still think, then I won't have to worry about others taking it from me!"

"Relayer, sir," a voice asked from behind, "shall we rid of him now?"

"Do it."

"No!" James shrilled and let out a cry as violet plasma blasted into him and the light that surrounded his body released, incinerating the surrounding area. He quickly rose to his feet, shaking and gasping.

"*They're dead,*" James thought, leaning against the smoking blackened brick walls in awe of the charred bodies that lay scattered around in the vicinity. "*I was lucky to contain that blast!*" Nearby, trash smoldered from half-melted canisters that formerly contained them. "*Maybe I should just give it up. It can't be safe with me of all people owning such destructive power! How many times can I keep lucking out like this?*"

"Hey, what's going on?" a voice called and James hurried into the shadows of the alley, quickly getting out of sight.

"Man, what happened here?" said a second.

"A bomb or something..."

"Yeah, something..."

"Damn gangsters... it's just not safe anymore."

"Yeah, stupid turf wars..."

James levitated off the ground and mulled over various possibilities, relaxing once the curious gawkers left the alley entrance.

"*It's dumb for me to think that I could actually be a hero!*" He clenched his teeth. "*Though Xavier was right about one thing; that I've got to use this gift. Yet, I don't know how and I don't know when I'll figure it out eventually.*" James bulleted skyward and flew for home. "*Will 'eventually' be soon enough?*" He glanced down at the rushing city lights beneath him. "*In the meantime, things could be worse...*"

CHAPTER TWELVE

After going through his usual routine at the office, James stepped off the bus, loosening his tie as he walked across the parking lot to his apartment.

"*Man, that Adnan's riding my ass tonight, making me work late!*" he thought, glancing at his watch. "*I bet he was the one that got those reports on those tapes erased...*"

Coming to a pause when he spotted Leila in her compact car singing along to heavy metal music as she played air guitar, James grinned, forgetting his earlier frustration.

"Leila, hey," he called, knocking at the window. "What song is that?"

Leila looked up, startled, and grinned as she opened the door. "*Love, Peace and Heavy Metal*, of course!" Leila replied happily. "When do you think *Incus* is going to do another tour?"

"Beats me..."

"Well, it's about time you showed up," Leila said, cutting him off. "I waited out here since thirty after five!"

"So what *are* you doing here?"

"I told you I was going to come over tonight, remember?" Turning off the battery, Leila leaned over into the next seat and pulled out a large empty canvas rucksack. "It's laundry day, or did you forget?"

"That's right," James answered and groaned. "It's the half-price Tuesday deal..." He ran a hand through his hair as his face flushed scarlet. "Sorry to make you wait; I hadn't even heard my messages yet since I had to work late tonight..."

"P and P's driving that nail into your coffin, huh?" Leila cracked. James grunted and headed for his front door. "Jamie, I didn't mean it!" she called after him.

James opened the door and he threw off his overcoat onto the end of the couch then padded into his bedroom. Moments later, he heard Leila enter, picking up his discarded clothing that he had strewn about the room.

"It's okay," James called back as he kicked off his shoes and pulled out of his slacks and dress shirt. "No harm done."

After pulling into jeans and a T-shirt, James drifted into the kitchen, searching the refrigerator for a can of soda.

"You sure you're alright?" Leila asked as she stuffed articles into the rucksack.

"I'm fine; just have a lot on my mind..."

Pulling out a cola, James nudged the refrigerator close and approached the table, taking the newspaper Leila left for him. He glanced at the headlines then turned for the classified sections, skimming the listings.

"While you're in between your ears, you mind telling me where the other brown sock is?"

"Try under the table."

"What are you looking for?" Leila asked upon bypassing.

"A cheap washing machine," James quipped, grinning.

"What, aren't I cheap enough?" Leila said wryly and drifted into the bedroom.

"No, you're too expensive!"

"Hey, how about this outfit?" Leila called and James glanced up, noticing the uniform she held draped over her arm. "Does this need to be washed or dry-cleaned? There's no care-label tag inside and I'd hate to shrink it..."

"I don't know what it's made of," James admitted, turning the page. "It was given to me." He shrugged. "I think it's related to this GEARS thing."

"What...?" Opening the can of soda with one hand, James let out a yelp as he cut his finger against the aluminum. "Jamie, what happened?" Leila cried, dropping all that she held.

James stuck his bleeding finger into his mouth, stunned. "Just nicked my finger is all," he muttered.

"But I thought you couldn't get hurt..."

"I can if the power's off, I think," James murmured, looking down at his finger. "Since it only protects me when it's *on*, I have to *think* it on. I guess I just relaxed a little there..."

"Am I that much of a distraction?"

James chuckled. "Oh, yeah," he answered.

"Right. So speaking of relaxing..." James smiled when Leila rubbed gently at his back. "It's getting kinda late to do the wash tonight."

"What do you mean?" James left her side and rummaged through his kitchen drawers.

"I can't do both mine and yours right now, Jamie!" Leila complained as he found tape and gauze to make a bandage.

"Besides, it's already a quarter to eight and the Laundromat closes at ten."

"So what about tomorrow?"

"So how about I take you out and treat you to a cone?"

"I don't know..." James wrapped his finger while Leila put the rucksack full of dirty clothing near the back door.

Leila then picked up the uniform and came around James, touching him on the arm. "I'll throw in a back rub," she said gently.

"Nah..." James murmured and his face burned when she squeezed his shoulder.

"You're so tense these days," she murmured. "How about a front rub? Sometimes those help..."

James grinned as he shut the drawer with his hip. "Okay, but I'll buy the ice cream!"

"See, isn't that easy?"

Leila headed into the bedroom and James approached the table to pick up the paper. Before he turned the page, his eyes landed on one classified that stood out, taking a quarter of the paper.

"Hey, Leila," James called as he read the article. "Check out this big classified!"

"What is it?"

"It says, 'Flying man! I wait for you every evening at the place where you burned like the sun. Desperately need you. Help me please.' Signed, 'Damsel in distress'."

"What do they mean...?"

"They mean *me*, Leila," James said seriously. "... 'Burned like the sun'. They're talking about the first time I let the power flare up."

Leila returned and stood next to James, reading the advertisement. "So you think someone saw you?" she asked.

James dropped the paper, stepping away in slight fear. "Unless *you* told someone!" he squawked.

"I didn't say anything to anybody!" Leila cried, putting up her hands. "Really!"

"*And Al wouldn't tell anyone...*" James thought, turning away. "Hey, would you mind if we postpone the ice cream?" he asked softly. "I really need to look into this and find out who this is and what they know about me!"

"It's going to be dangerous..."

"Nah, I'm a pretty smart guy, Leila!" James said, standing straighter. "I'm not just going to roll into trouble and have them hand me back my ass; I'll be careful!"

"Well, I'll take this stuff out tomorrow night and bring it over, okay?"

"Sure, thanks," James said, heading into his bedroom.

"*I shouldn't show up wearing my regular clothes,*" he thought, changing into the uniform Leila left on the bed. "*If that person saw a flying man, it's better to see me as Jim the Super Wannabe than Jim the Flying Desk Jockey!*"

"Didn't you hear me?" Leila called, cutting into his thoughts. "You have a date tonight with Roxanne. She called me looking for you when you ran late!"

"Now you tell me!" James fussed.

"But don't worry, I covered your butt and she'll see you tomorrow night."

"Thanks a million!" The front door shut after Leila and James pulled into his gloves as pale white light flared slightly around his body. "It's time to party!" He hurried out his back door, flying for Industrial Street.

"*There's the slag dump,*" James thought as he neared Industrial Street, "*or what's <u>left</u> of it after I did that supernova blast thing here two weeks ago...*" He noticed a small white sports car sitting on the side of the road, beneath a broken street lamp encased in darkness and took in a deep breath as a young woman exited the vehicle once its hazard lights came on. She sat on the small car's trunk and withdrew a book from her pocket. "*... and a girl. Maybe she's the 'damsel in distress'?*" Touching down from afar, James grunted when he stumbled forward and walked forward silently, observing. "*Play it cool, Jim. Don't mess it up!*" Getting closer so that she was in his line of sight, James swallowed hard when he saw her features in the dim lighting from the car's interior light. "*Her olive skin and red hair... not bad for someone exotic like that...*"

James cleared his throat and the young woman gasped, dropping her book. She immediately stood, clenching her hands.

"Who is there?" the woman asked in a slight clipped accent.

"*Tiny waist... even better!*"

"Who are you? You... you startled me... "

"Man, get your head out the gutter!" James clenched his teeth. *"She could have her friends clustered somewhere nearby, waiting to take you down!"*

"Silence... I see." The young woman sighed heavily. "Are you... are you the one I'm waiting for?"

"What should I do? This is getting too heavy, Jim! Too damn heavy...!"

James swallowed hard again and grew tense as his heart pound hard in his chest and cold sweat broke out on his forehead and neck.

"More silence... That tells me what I want to know anyway. Nobody just happens by here if they're not drag racers and anybody as nervous as you *must* be the man I'm looking for. I know you can fly!"

"Who are *you*?" demanded James. "What's this about?"

"Me?" The young woman laughed nervously. "Well, I'm a student at Jones University. I am just, um, interested in *flying*, you know. I'm writing a thesis."

"Get off," James growled. "I don't have time for this!"

"All right, the truth: my boyfriend put me up to this."

"Go figure!"

"Please, don't leave!" The young woman quickly picked up the fallen book. "You see, the Strategic Service Offices investigated the slag dump blast and they turned up nothing much, except one less-than credible eyewitness who claimed that a flying man blew up the dump." She waved the book she held in her hand. "A traitor in the Strategic Service *sold* that report to, uh, an enemy government headed by someone crazy enough to *believe* in *you*!"

"Yeah, I'm listening..."

"Since then, *his* 'agents', mostly students, like my boyfriend, have been staked out around here watching. Sure enough, several times they caught a glimpse of a flying man!"

"*Damn*," James thought, clenching his hands. "*No more flying over to Allen's place.*"

"So they hatched this big plan to make contact," the young woman went on. "I've been sitting out here for a *week* trying to read, getting eyestrain. I'm so glad *you* showed up!"

"What do you want?" James asked caustically.

"Well..." the young woman nervously replied as she pocketed the paperback book. "Whatever it *is*; how do you *do* what you do?"

"You wouldn't believe me if I told you." James turned away. "Look, Lady, you're wasting my time."

"I *do* have something to offer you in return," she said quickly. "I have money, drugs, anything you want! I'll even let you use me however you wish..."

"Sounds good..."

"Well..."

James took in a shallow breath as she slowly approached to where he stood. "*I can't risk it, even if she has a smoking body,*" he mused as she came closer. "No," James said firmly.

The woman paused in step. "No?" she probed.

"It's a good offer, but no thanks."

The woman ran up to James and he let out a yelp when she grasped him firmly by the arm. "You don't understand," she cried. "My boyfriend and the others... they're watching from a distance. They *know* I have been talking to you. If I do not get what they want from you, they will be *angry*! They will *hurt* me or worse-- Please!"

"Lady, this isn't what you think!" James snapped, pulling out of her grip. "It's nothing-- just a trick; a gimmick. Forget about it!"

"I'll tell them you said you'll come back tomorrow night," she called as he walked away down the street. "Please, come back tomorrow night! They'll *kill* me if you don't!"

James walked up the steps at Roxanne's house, holding onto a bouquet of various tropical flowers. He paced nervously outside the door, trying to work up the nerve to ring the doorbell.

"Man, the last time I was in such a rush to get out of here, I left that rental car behind," James thought. *"At least they didn't fine me too much since I left the keys in the door."* He blew a shaky breath and ran a hand through his hair. *"I hope Roxanne didn't put two and two together!"* James struck the buzzer. *"Don't faint, Jim! Keep it together!"* The door opened, revealing Roxanne.

"Hello, love!" Roxanne greeted and she embraced James firmly. "Are these beautiful flowers for me?"

"Yeah, yeah, they are Roxy!" James said brightly, thrusting forward the bouquet. "I had them flown in special!"

"You are too much!" she said gaily and kissed James on the cheek. "So sweet, I swear! I need to put them in water." She hurried indoors and James entered, stopping short when he spotted a young woman on the couch. The young woman tossed back her long dark brown hair as she set her handbag on the table.

"Missus Citovecca, the kiddos are in bed now," she called as Roxanne returned from the kitchen with a glass vase, setting it on the cocktail table near the couch. "Oh, Missus Citovecca, those flowers are nice!"

"*Now that's nice,*" James thought, eying the babysitter in her form-fitting yellow cashmere sweater, tight white jeans, and brown short boots. "*If I knew I was going to run into someone that hot, I wouldn't mind busting my butt flying all the way out to the Amazon to get flowers for her too!*"

"Well, my lovely boyfriend got them for me," Roxanne gushed.

"Yeah, nice flowers for a nice lady, huh?" James said, grinning.

"So, ready to go?" Roxanne asked, touching James on the arm to get him out of his thoughts.

"Yeah, sure..." James murmured and exited, swallowing hard as he tried to contain his excitement.

"*Down, Jim, don't screw this up!*" James yelled at himself in his head. "*Remember, you're with Roxy right now!*"

"So where are you going tonight?" Roxanne asked as James led her to the rented sedan parked at the curb in front of her house.

"Whatever you want..." James muttered.

"What about going to *The Lounge*?"

"Nah, not feeling like those cool cats with the acid jazz tonight," James replied as he opened the door for her. "What about the *Crazy Eighty-Eights*?"

"I'm not a head-banger or a punk rocker, James!" Roxanne complained.

"*Cracked Foxx* then?"

Roxanne stepped in and raised an eyebrow at James. "Goth music? Really?"

"So do you feel like dancing?" James came around and entered the vehicle as she shut the door and pulled into her belt. "I haven't seen you do the *Bodyrock* in a while!"

Roxanne grinned. "Yeah, it has been a good while... almost two years!"

"I think I might know a place..." James got in and started the engine.

"The *Ambassador Disco* might be a good place."

"Nice choice!"

A server with a tray in hand waved to James and Roxanne. "Are you James Russell?" she yelled over the music once she approached.

James glanced down at her and took in a shallow breath, noticing the thin young woman who wore tight hip-hugging black jeans and a light-blue halter-top. She ran a hand through her shaggy dark hair and blew away strands that fell in her narrow steel blue eyes.

"That's me!" James answered. *"She's totally foxy,"* he thought, swallowing hard. *"Keep it cool Jim, keep it cool!"*

"Levin said to give you this front row table, Mister Russell."

"Thanks, I guess."

The waitress showed them their table and the guitarist, with his raven pompadour and muttonchops wearing a white and black lounge suit, waved to them excitedly as the lead singer danced around with the microphone stand.

"Jamie, baby!" he yelled.

"Ay, Verne!" James called back, waving.

The server giggled. "Wow, you're friends with the band," she exclaimed. "So cool!"

"It helps," James said, shrugging.

"Have a good time, you guys!"

"Isn't that the guy you talked about from Central State?" Roxanne asked, taking her seat. "You said Central was a real party school..."

"It is," James answered, sitting across from her, "but they have an excellent computer programming department!" He kicked back his chair, watching the server leave to another

Across the river in Illinova County, Jame

parking lot of a lively dance club in Eas

switching off the engine, he heard heavy bas

inside.

"Before I forget," Roxanne said, touching J

before he got out, "I wanted to tell you that

acting not like herself lately..."

"What do you mean?"

"She's been moody since you took that toy

"It's, uh..." James said quickly, "Probably j

know?"

"Sure, let's forget about it now," Roxan

giving James a gentle squeeze. "Besides, you n

let's put everything aside and have some fun to

"Let's do this!" Clamoring out, they

discotheque and James recognized one of the g

the live band situated at the rear of the club.

"*Is that Verne from Central?*" he thought, bo

to the music. "*His band is good! I hope they get a*

table and taking orders. "I didn't know Verne did disco! He was such a metal head like me!"

"If disco pays the bills, you do it," replied Roxanne. "It worked for the *Brothers Giri!*" James laughed and Roxanne's expression turned serious. "Isn't that hostess a knockout?" she noted.

James stiffened once brought back to the present. "Yeah, I guess," he murmured and let the chair back onto the floor.

"What about the babysitter?"

"Don't miss much, do you?" James drawled, blushing. He took Roxanne's chin in hand. "I'm sorry, but I couldn't help but look..."

"Don't be. She's gorgeous of course, but remember; she's *only seventeen!*"

"No lying?" James cracked a mischievous grin. "Well, remind me to give her a quarter and tell her to call me in four years, okay?"

"But I'll be thirty-five then!"

"You'll still be the most beautiful woman in the world." James leaned in to kiss Roxanne. "The most perfect..." he kissed her again, "the most intelligent..." Roxanne leaned into a deeper kiss and James pulled away, touching his forehead against hers as he stared deeply into her eyes. "Everything."

"You're so sweet, James," Roxanne purred. She pulled away, flushing darkly. "But..."

"But what?"

"I have two kids, James!" Roxanne complained. "I know that worries you. When I mentioned Darlene as we came in, you seemed pained. Do they bother you that much?"

"No, it's not that..." James took Roxanne's hand. "Look, Roxy, it's not that, really! It's just... I'm a little *afraid* of them, I guess."

"What do you mean?"

"You know, the responsibility, the stress. Kids are..."

"Did someone mention kids?" a voice called from behind. James let go and looked up, spotting Verne standing before them holding a glass of rum and cola in his hand.

"Hey, Verne," James greeted, "long time, no see!"

"Dude!" Verne said brightly, "Still rockin'?"

"Still rockin' the desk at P and P."

"Whoa, and you're still not dead yet?" Verne poked James in the forehead and James laughed, pushing his hand away. "You sure that ain't no zombie, Roxy?" He quickly threw back his drink and set the glass on the table. "Look at me guys, I'm that one guy in the far back in *Powerline*'s *Horror Show* video!" He broke out into routine, shuffling about on the floor. "Arg... arg... It's a killer, a chiller... horror show tonight!" Roxanne and James laughed harder.

"Verne, you're too much!" Roxanne said.

"Yeah, so how's you like the *Funky Fresh Fellas*?"

"You guys sound alright for a disco band," James replied.

"Hey, man, it's *New Wave*, get it right!" Verne laughed and dug through his pockets. "Yo, get some drinks, dude! Have some on me!" He withdrew his wallet.

"I thought the *Funky Fresh Fellas* broke up after we all finished at Central."

"I started that computer club and this is my band, so whatever." Verne shrugged.

"Seriously though, man, I was gonna call you and I just got swamped."

"'s a'ight, Dude," Verne said and thrust forward his wallet, unleashing an accordion file of photographs that depicted his wife, himself, and a baby girl. "Check this!" he crowed, "It's my little girl!"

"You had a new baby?" James cried, astonished.

"No, doofus, my *wife* did!" Verne said, chuckling. "Now, for the other side!" He turned the wallet around. "Bam; check that! Man, it's so awesome... Her name's Bobbie Joan. Isn't she cute?"

"What, you couldn't think of a name?" James cracked as Roxanne took the wallet and studied the pictures.

Verne let out a robust laugh. "Nah, man, you know me better than that! My wife's a *Powerline* fan, Dude!" James snorted, shaking his head as Verne became animated. "Man, she's like, was doped up on that stuff and he was singin' on the radio and she's all like 'That's it! That's the name of my baby!' and I was like 'Baby, Dude, what if you popped out a boy?' and she was like 'Then you can call it Von Jani,' and I was like 'Sweet!'" Verne pumped his fists.

James roared harder with laughter, striking the table. "You can't be serious, Verne!" he said. "You like *Von Jani*?"

"Hey man, don't hate! I like rock as much as I love my metal, a'ight?" James giggled. "Dude, I *love* this Daddy stuff, man!" Verne grabbed a chair and plopped into it backwards, leaning against the back. "It's exciting stuff, you know? I mean, there's this little person that's all yours, like clay for me to mold and shape and stuff. It's gonna be awesome hellas to watch her grow up!"

"You and your wife must be very proud!" Roxanne said brightly, passing the wallet to James. "Oh, James, look at this! She's so cute!"

"How is Sheila by the way?" James asked as he glanced at the pictures. "She's hardly big enough to make a sandwich out of..."

"Dude, she's like..." Verne glanced up, trailing off. "Hold up, guys, okay?" He left his seat, walking away to another part of the club.

"Isn't this great, James?" Roxanne asked, leaning against him as she looped her arm through his. James stared at the photograph, growing chilled. "It's so awesome that he's happy about his baby!" A sever approached with a tray of drinks, setting them before both James and Roxanne.

"Yeah, but I don't know, Roxy," James murmured. "Maybe it's just *me,* or isn't it a little *weird* about the way Verne talks about molding her and shaping her... It's like 'Oh boy! I get to play like some kinda creator god!'" He shuddered slightly. "That's... well, um, scary..."

"He probably doesn't mean it *that* way, James!" Roxanne replied, chuckling. "Besides, kids need somebody responsible. I mean, what are you going to do, let them run wild?"

"No, but Verne sounds like he thinks of his kid as some kind of *toy...*"

"But if you're responsible, you put your feelings aside and do what you have to do. You keep your commitments." James set the wallet aside Roxanne placed a hand on his arm. "Now don't take this wrong, James... I'm not pushing you, but I think you'd be good at that." James turned away, catching sight of Verne holding the hostess close and speaking softly in her ear as they swayed to the music the disc jockey played.

"Would I really?" asked James. "Is Verne...?"

"I wonder what his wife Sheila would think..."

"Yeah, what *would* she think?" James muttered and gulped down his drink.

"Let's dance!" Roxanne said quickly and sprang to her feet. She yanked up James by the arm and pulled him to the dance floor, moving to the beat of the sound.

James fell back as he receded under her intoxicating spell, watching her dance alone as if she became one with the music and nothing else mattered.

"This is what I love," James thought as he snapped his fingers and tapped his foot while he bopped his head to the music, unable to get his body to dance. *"This is what I miss... watching her move, watching her groove, like she's some kind of free spirit..."*

Later, arriving back at Roxanne's house, James lingered near the door while Roxanne paid the babysitter her money.

"Thanks a lot, Gloria," she said.

"Sure thing, Missus Citovecca," Gloria answered. "Good night!"

"Walk her home for me, please?" Roxanne asked James as the babysitter came out onto the stoop. "I don't want her out this late on the streets..." Gloria crossed her arms, rubbing at them slightly. "Oh, you almost forgot your coat!" Roxanne ducked inside and returned with a lined pink parka, handing it to hand to Gloria. James put on a tight smile as he face grew warm watching the babysitter pull into it.

"Didn't mean to make you stay out too late," James said sheepishly.

"It's alright," Gloria said and walked away.

"Come back after you walk her to her house okay?" Roxanne called and grabbed James by the lapels of his overcoat, pulling him close. "We might even get to *Boogie Down Fresh*," she cooed, "just like the movie."

"*Don't do this to me*," James thought as the flush on his face turned darker. Roxanne let go and waved him away. James hurried up to Gloria's side and she smiled brightly as James put his hands in his coat pockets.

"It's really nice of you to walk me home, Mister Russell," Gloria said brightly. "I get really afraid of walking home late at night, you know? There *are* some real crazies running around..."

"Yeah, no problem, Gloria," James said, feinting aloofness. "Except that when you call me 'Mister Russell', I swear, I think my old man's following me, walking right behind me!"

"Oh... okay..." Approaching her stoop, Gloria pulled out her keys and waved to James. "Well, thanks and good night, James! See you soon, I hope!"

"Good night, Gloria," James said and walked away. "Oh, if you only knew," he muttered under his breath.

Once he returned to Roxanne's house, he tried the door, finding it unlocked and entered, closing it softly behind him. Roxanne, in a loose black camisole top and bikini briefs, sat on the edge of the couch. James cleared his throat as he slipped out of his overcoat and approached the couch, resting the coat on the arm.

"Ah, you decided to come back!" Roxanne chided. "So you *do* prefer the withered-but-worldly to the nubile-but-naive, eh?"

"Nah, her daddy chased me away with his shotgun," James quipped, grinning.

"His check is in the mail..." Roxanne lifted a leg to her head, stretching the muscle.

"Damn Roxy," James said, mildly surprised. "I didn't know you used to dance professionally!"

"Nah, I just get freaky and swing off chandeliers."

James chuckled as she stretched her other leg the same way. "Really now?"

Roxanne grabbed for the front of his sport coat, pulling him close. "Now, come here..." James took in a shallow breath as Roxanne put her arms around his neck and he put his hands to her hips, staring down into her deep violet eyes.

"What are you planning to do to me?" James asked, grinning shrewdly. "I don't mind freaky action, you know..."

"You drove me to this with those thousand-year-old eyes," Roxanne purred. "If I leave teeth marks and scratches all over your body, I'm not responsible."

James felt himself sinking and pulled away, trying to breathe. "Roxy," he said thinly, "I... I have to tell you something..." He took her chin in hand. "You know, with what you said before... Do you think I'd be good, well, you know, with kids?"

"Yes, because you'd take it seriously, because you *can't* turn your back on responsibility once you've taken it..." James turned away, pained at her words. "...which is why you're so cautious about *accepting* it, in your job with me, you know?"

"*My job, huh?*" James thought in disgust. Roxanne took his face in hand, turning him to face her.

"Why, is there... is there something you're not telling me?"

"*Responsibility,*" James mused, "*I've got to be more responsible, which reminds me...*"

"Well...?" Roxanne asked, cutting into his thoughts.

"I can't explain now," James said, pulling away completely. "Look, I've got to go and take care of something. It's going to take a while."

"Why *now?*"

"Because..." James picked up his overcoat. "There are some real crazies around."

Roxanne gasped, biting her hand and James hurried outside.

Leaving the rented car at his apartment complex parking lot, James quickly changed into his uniform and took off for Industrial Street, finding the car parked on the side of the road several yards from the slag dump.

"*There's the car,*" James thought as he touched down. "*It's pretty late, so she probably fell asleep waiting on me.*" Glancing around, James slowly walked up to the vehicle. "*I suppose it won't hurt to look... besides, it's too dark out and nobody could have seen me land.*"

The street lamp above them slowly flickered on, casting pale frosty light down on them. James peered into the car window and gasped when he found the young woman slumped over the front passenger seat with a bruised face.

"Holy--!" James yelped. "*She's hurt,*" he thought and cold sweat broke out on his forehead and neck, "*and she wasn't lying about those guys!*" Trying the door, James clenched his teeth as it clicked, unable to open. "*Damn thing's locked!*"

His left hand flared in golden light and James yanked with all his might, ripping off the door with a crash. He tossed the removed metal and glass aside and reached in, pulling the woman out.

"Oh," the young woman moaned as James put her down on the ground. "You came back... thank my stars..."

"Easy," James said gently as he knelt beside her, "it's all right now."

"When you didn't come by midnight, my boyfriend... his friends... they beat me up. He said if you didn't come by dawn, he would *kill* me!"

"The bastard!" James sneered, glaring off into the distance. "Where's that son of a bitch?"

"He's insane! Please, help me... They're close by..."

"I'll get you away from here," James said, cupping her face in hand. "Trust me."

"No, you don't understand," the woman pleaded, "Somehow they will find me and kill me. You *must* give them what they want, please!"

"But, I can't!"

"All right then; take me away from here! To your place perhaps?" Brushing her cheek, James froze when he noticed it smeared and stared down at his fingers in shock.

"That's not a bruise!" he thought, slightly puzzled. *"It looks like makeup!"* James quickly let go, forcing the young woman falling back onto her rear, stunned. *"Jim, you idiot, you walked straight into a set-up!"*

"What's wrong?" the woman asked as James turned away horrified. He immediately put up a hand, shielding his face.

"She's studying me!" James jumped to his feet. *"I need to get out of here!"*

"If you don't give them what they want, *many* will be murdered!" the young woman screeched. "One for every day until you give up your secret!"

"Forget it!" James shouted.

The woman pulled out a handgun from inside her jacket and released two shots, forcing James to stagger back, astonished. "You're bulletproof too?" she cried. "Good, fantastic!"

"You little--!" James roared, rushing forward as the power quickly flared around his body. He snatched the semiautomatic pistol out of her hand and grabbed her by the collar of her jacket, then paused as she laughed darkly at him when her clothing smoldered in his hand.

"Go ahead, kill me," she said defiantly. "It won't matter; my friends have been watching. They have all the proof they need!"

"Damn you!" James threw her back and crushed the gun, exploding it. He took a leap, hovering several inches above the ground and clenched his brightly burning hands. The power that blazed around his body turned from gold to white as his rage intensified. "Get out of here before I really get pissed off!"

"You stupid idiot!" the woman shouted at James, shaking her fist at him. "Sooner or later, you are ours!" She grabbed for his foot and James nudged her back, forcing her falling back on her rear.

"That's never going to happen!" he declared and levitated higher from the ground. "Besides, I'm my own person and nobody runs me, got it?"

"We'll see about that!"

James took off skyward before she could say any more, flying for home. "*Great, Jim,*" he admonished himself, "*this is just great...*"

Entering his apartment once more, James pulled out of his jacket and gloves and shuffled into his bedroom. He sat on the edge of his bed, growing cold and numb as he kicked off his boots then chucked all the articles into the corner as a heap on the floor. Hearing a creak, James quickly stood as footsteps neared his bedroom door.

"Hey," Leila said as she leaned against the frame. James raised an eyebrow, noticing she wore his bathrobe.

"What are you doing here?" James demanded. "And why are you wearing my clothes?"

"I didn't think you'd mind... Remember, I did your laundry," she reprimanded. "I've got a spare key, or have you forgotten?"

"Yeah, that's right..." James slumped on the edge of his bed, sighing heavily. "Yeah, thanks, I owe you like a million favors!"

"No problem," Leila said, fingering the ties of the robe. "Besides, you look beat. What's the matter?"

"Long story..."

"You can tell me."

"You know that damsel in distress?" Leila nodded. "They saw my face; they saw what I could do!"

"Man, that's harsh..."

"All of a sudden, this is a lot more complicated than I thought..."

"You can handle it, Jamie," Leila said cheerfully as she came around the bed. "You always have it under control." James followed her with his eyes, watching her slip out of the bathrobe and dropped it to the floor, revealing her nude body from underneath.

"*A lot more...*" James thought, coming out of his pants.

PART FOUR
TEST OF WORTH

The telephone rang, taking James out of his fog. He turned over and his legs and feet became tangled in the sheets. James reached blindly for his night stand and picked up the receiver.

"What?" he moaned.

"Come over right now," said Allen's voice over the line through static. "This is important!"

"What the hell? It's like how early...?"

"It's a quarter to five," Allen snapped. "It's important, please..."

"What's this about?"

"Hilland..."

"Damn it, Al!" The line cut off before James could say more and he sat up with a start, incredulous.

"This can't be happening," he thought. Glancing over at the other side of the bed, James found mussed sheets and Leila absent. *"This can't be happening, Jim. What if that story that girl told you was for real?"* He felt the panic rise as he numbly exited out of bed, stomping for the shower. *"What if those damn Feds finally caught up with you? What if they're torturing Allen right now? What if...?"*

James thought no more about it as he washed and threw on a sweatshirt and jeans, then headed to the front of his apartment to take his car to Allen's house in Cedarwood.

Pulling up a block away, James parked at the curb in front another house and walked the rest of the way to Allen's home. He entered through the usually unlocked garage door and made his way inside, finding Allen sitting in the parlor situated in the lone chair in the center of the room.

Allen appeared deathly pale as he gripped the arms of the chair. The skin around his bony knuckles appeared strained as he dug his nails into the fabric. Nearby the agent Hilland paced and smoked a cigarette, agitated.

"'Bout time, kid," Hilland grumbled. "I was thinkin' of wastin' him if ya dint show up 'fore seven. I's got stuff to do, ya know...?"

"What's this about?" James asked apprehensively.

Hilland took a slow drag then blew a puff of smoke over his head, pointing ahead at Allen. "My buddy here says you can't get hurt, yeah?"

"What's it to you?"

"Prove it." The agent withdrew a pistol with a silencer attached and pointed it at Allen's head. "Or youse gonna see yer friend become head cheese!"

"Al!" James cried.

"Please, Jamie," Allen pleaded, "just tell him the story!"

"Okay, I, um..." James felt as if the air in his lungs slowly leaked out as he told the story of what happened to him two weeks before.

"Yeah, space aliens and all that jive," Hilland drawled, "and youse want me to believe that junk? Huh, ain't buying it!"

"Al," James wailed as Hilland pulled back the hammer. "What should I do?"

"Show him!" Allen screeched.

"Yeah, show me," Hilland growled. "Dis the 'show me' state, yeah? So youse gotta *show me* or his brains are gonna show *real nice* and pretty all over dis white carpet 'ere."

"With what?" James snapped.

"I already bought some stuff wit' me," The agent said, gesturing toward the table where a bag of tools situated next to a bottle of whiskey. "Pick somethin' and have 'im get to whackin'!"

"Damn it, Al...!" James growled and clenched his hands as faint white light flared around them.

"He's been following you, Jamie," Allen hissed as he got to his feet and approached the table. "I told you to be careful, but did you believe me?"

"Sit yer ass down, monkey!" Hilland barked and clamped a hand on James's shoulder, forcing him into the chair. "Youse clowns gonna show me what's dis game ya got goin', got it? I'm sick of bein' laughed at by my mates, man; teasin' me 'bout boozin' too much, sayin' there ain't no flyin' man, that there ain't no man strong enough to twist metal and whatever!" Hilland came around, standing before James.

"And then what?" James snarled, glaring up at Hilland, sneering. "What if you find out you can't kill me?"

"Everybody's gotta weakness!"

Allen picked up a mast ax and crept up behind James.

"You'll never figure it out, pig!" James spat.

"What you say?"

Allen slammed the blade over James's head with much effort, letting out a yell. The metal cracked, with the resulting force causing Allen to stagger back, dropping the ax in stunned silence.

"You heard me, punk," James hissed and grunted when struck with the pistol.

"This whole thing is *so* impossible," murmured Allen in awe, "that even *seeing* isn't believing..."

James glanced up, rubbing at his head. "Huh?" he murmured. "Trying to give me a haircut, aren't you? I think your razor's a little dull."

"Stop jokin' 'round, clown!" Hilland shouted, striking James again. "I still don't believe it!"

James spat blood onto the carpet. "Keep this up," he fussed, "and you *might* just kill me!"

"I just tried to split his head open like a watermelon!" Allen hollered. "What more proof do you need?"

"Get the cutting torch," Hilland commanded. "Let's see if his freaky ass can burn!"

"But we don't have any tanks to use this welding tool..." Allen whimpered as he dug around the bag.

"There should be a butane one in there," Hilland barked. "Get to it!"

Grabbing for the small torch, Allen adjusted the valve, releasing a shot of blue-white flame.

"And then what?" retorted James. "If I can't get burned..." Hilland's eyes widened as Allen put the high-intensity flame to James's hand.

"This doesn't hurt either?" Allen asked, dumbfounded. "Can you even *feel* it?"

"Well, I can feel that it's *hot*," James answered, glaring at Hilland, "but it doesn't hurt..."

"So, youse guys sayin' that nothin' can hurt him?" Hilland cried as Allen turned off the setting valve on the torch.

"*Nothing* can hurt me," James said evenly as he narrowed his eyes, "only if you make me lose my concentration, but I'm not going to give you the satisfaction!"

"Oh my god," Hilland shouted, pointing the pistol at James, "you're a friggin' freak!"

"Shoot me, I dare you."

Allen let out a panicked cry in sheer terror as Hilland unloaded the entire round contained in his pistol. Allen gripped his hair, heaving for breath.

"Oh my god," Allen cried. "Jamie, he just *shot* you! He just shot you like fifteen times!"

"Relax, Al, it's no big deal," James said coolly as he rose to his feet. "Let's show Mister Hilland his way out, will ya?"

"Out, right..."

"Get away from me, you freak!" Hilland thundered when James approached. Hilland backed away, shuddering in fright.

"Get the hell out!" James roared and hovered several feet from the floor. The light blazing around his hands turned from red to orange.

"Your ass is goin' down, boy!" Hilland cried and he raced out the room.

James descended back onto the floor and Allen moaned as he dropped onto the chair, completely spent.

"Jamie, they've been at WCM, asking everyone about me," Allen mewed. "They're destroying me, trying to get everyone to turn against me!"

"What do you want me to do, Al?" James grumbled. "Turn myself over to them?"

"I don't know..."

"But you believe me, right?"

"I want to, but, you know..." Allen blew a heavy sigh. "It just sounds too far out; with space aliens and flying saucers... it's too unlikely!"

"But *look* at me!" James yelled, gesturing to his chest. "Look at my shirt, damn it! It's riddled with bullet holes and I'm not even bleeding!"

Allen winced, drawing up his knees. "I'm getting too old for this, Jamie," he said softly. "Don't make me go through this!"

"Don't let those damn Feds get to you," James said in irritation. "Come out to P and P's office park after work, okay? Meet me there at the offices at five and I'll show you myself!"

"Okay..."

James stormed out through the front door, returning to his car that parked a block away.

Later that morning, James flew over to the office park where the crater was located.

"*Here we are,*" he thought as he touched down and stumbled forward, then quickly righted his stance. "*This is the area where I fought the second alien and his gang...*" Glancing around, James found scorch marks on the ground and broken limbs in the trees. "*This is where his ship was hidden... What more evidence do they want?*" Kicking at gun fragments embedded into the earth, James glanced down at his watch. "*I gotta get to work before they think about firing me.*" He walked away in determination. "*I will prove to Allen that I'm not a liar! I* can *fly, I* can *deflect bullets; that's real and he knows it! He shouldn't let those Feds rattle him!*"

Returning to the offices, James entered and headed down the corridor where his department was situated. Adnan, in tailored navy suit that had a blue rose pinned to the lapel, blocked the doorway. His frizzy strawberry blond hair hung back in a loose ponytail with several loose strands falling into his eyes.

"Good morning, Adnan," James said politely.

"Good *evening*, Mister Russell," Adnan sneered and shoved past him.

"*What's his problem?*" James wondered as he watched him storm for the elevators. Turning away, James entered the cubicle farm. "Hey, Xavier," he greeted, "Hiya, Reinhold!"

"'lo, Russ," Xavier called from his cubicle.

"Ho, Russell," Reinhold called back from near the mimeograph machine.

"What's up with Adnan this morning?" James asked as he headed to his desk and pulled out of his overcoat. "Too chilly for him?"

"Mister Carellis says he wants Adnan on Department 616 tomorrow," Xavier answered, "and you too, Russell!"

"Me?" James yelped, surprised. "Isn't 616 programming and development?" He set up his processor and turned it on, then began typing reports from his 'in' box.

"Yeah, it is," Reinhold called, kicking the machine. "Me and Ecks sent that Orichide stuff up to Carellis and he wanted to see for himself! They ordered a Pome from those guys and they wanna see you in action!"

"Guys...!"

"You ain't even got your stuff together?" Xavier exclaimed. "You'd better hustle, man!"

"Yeah, whatever," James muttered. "*Like that matters*," he thought.

"Hey, Reinhold," Adnan called as he returned. "Go get us some breakfast, will ya?"

"What's the occasion?" James asked as Adnan entered his cubicle.

"A little celebration," Adnan answered, leaning against the archway.

"Yo, get the usual and make sure they fry some onions with those taters," Xavier called as Reinhold left the office.

"Who's buying?" James asked.

"Reinhold," Adnan answered, smirking.

"Damn it, you guys!" Reinhold squawked in the corridor.

"So, what do you want?" James asked coolly as he typed.

"I saw you," Adnan said softly.

"Yeah," James grumbled, "everybody does."

"I saw what you can do."

"Right..."

"And I know we're the same."

"I doubt it."

"Listen to me..." Adnan approached, closing the lid of the keyboard. "You only get one chance at being hero, catch my drift?"

"So?" James grunted and folded his arms across his chest. "Maybe I don't feel like it. It messes up my nightlife, you know?"

"Just wait..." Adnan grinned and James leaned back as the power glowed around his body.

"*There's something going on here,*" James thought, watching Adnan leave his desk. Opening the keyboard of the word processor to reveal the monitor, James returned to task and noticed that he typed faster than usual. "*Huh, with the power on, I can use my speed even for boring stuff like this.*" He grinned as he hurried along his paperwork. "*I'll save an hour doing this the quick way, since that GEARS machine thing says I have double my base speed. The guys would never notice I'm not typing at my usual seventy-five words a minute!*"

After finishing typing his papers, James grew chilled when Reinhold returned later, gasping for breath.

"Yo, you guys, you wouldn't believe it!" Reinhold said excitedly. "The diner was just robbed, right before I got there!"

"What?" James yelped and turned in his seat, facing Reinhold who stood in front of Xavier's cubicle across the room.

"Yeah," Reinhold said quickly, "three greasers clocked old man Machiavelli on the head with a tire iron and grabbed the cash!"

"How bad is he hurt?"

"Don't know... *real* bad!"

"Man, I wish I'd been there," James murmured, clutching the edge of his desk.

"Nothing you could have done anyhow, Russell," Xavier said softly. He picked up the bag of food Reinhold held and glared at it. "What's this, dumb nuts?" he growled.

"Insta-Breakfast!" Reinhold said brightly.

"*You're wrong, Xavier,*" James thought, clenching his teeth. "*I could have done plenty, but here I was, busy typing some useless files!*"

"While some of us have more important things to do," Xavier said as he returned to his cubicle, "why don't you and Russell haul more beige boxes up to Department 3126?"

"Man, why do Records need more computers from out of Mainframes?" Reinhold grumbled. "Those suckers must weigh at least twenty-five pounds each!"

"They're fifty each," Adnan said as he appeared near James's cubicle. "Now get a move on!"

James rose to his feet, glaring at Adnan. "What do you want with me?" he snapped.

"I'm sure you won't have any problems with it, Russell," Adnan replied caustically.

"What's that supposed to mean?"

Adnan grinned. "I'm sure you know."

"Out of my way, you freak," James grumbled and pushed past Adnan.

"I can't believe this," Reinhold complained as he stormed out, "the torture he puts us through!" James followed him as they headed for the elevators. "Why don't Records just update their computers instead of using the old ones?"

"Mainframes handle the archives, which need faster and better equipment," James explained as they entered the cable car and headed downstairs. "Since Records will need older stuff to keep track of basic files and retrieval. They're good for at least five years…"

"It's just Adnan hates flat-bread muffins and egg, that's all!" Reinhold grumbled once the doors opened and they entered the corridor of the lower levels.

"*What another great waste of this power,*" James considered as he waited until Reinhold left with one unplugged computer, carrying it to the elevators. Stacking two computers that were set aside from the others in his arms, James flew upstairs before Reinhold came off the elevator and set them up in an empty office that had a note of intent taped on the door.

After work, James exited the glass doors, spotting Adnan at the smoking shelter, speaking to another employee from the building. Avoiding his line of sight, James headed for the parking lot where he spotted Allen's old car and approached, finding it void of its driver. Heading for the office park, James stuffed his hands in his pockets, shuddering against the cool October breeze blowing through him.

"At least payday is a week from now," James mulled, *"and even if I blow twenty bucks at the grocery store, I still owe Leila that hundred she loaned me..."* He sighed heavily, looking up at the looming gray clouds. *"So it's going to be muffins again for lunch next week if this keeps up! What do I have to do, knock over a liquor store or two?"* He paused, hearing voices nearby. Taking a small leap forward, James hovered over the ground, following the sound of indistinct talking.

"Sorry, I'm late," James heard Allen say.

"I don't mind," said another voice of a man James didn't recognize.

"I know it's pretty dangerous out here, but this was the only place I could think of," Allen said nervously. "I need to make this quick, since my friend is getting off work soon."

"So, which one is your friend?"

"James Russell. His employee badge is JR-703, he works mainly in Department 387, and though he rides the Bi-State bus, he sometimes drives an old model green coupe... don't know what year it is, though."

"That's fine," said the stranger. "I need a challenge." James found Allen and a tall young man with a walrus-style moustache and a head of curly light brown hair. The stranger wore mirrored gold aviator sunglasses, a heavy bomber jacket and slacks with riding boots.

"*Allen's selling me out!*" James thought and clenched his hands as the power quickly flashed around him. "*What is that, some cop, some undercover agent...?*"

"So, what's this thing called again?" the mysterious young man asked as he pulled out a miniature notepad and pencil to write down items of importance.

"The Signet," Allen answered. "I don't know much about it, just as much as he told me. Thanks for listening to me, Mister Menotti."

"Yeah, no problem," Menotti answered as he scribbled notes. "Look, I'll keep a close eye on him, trust me."

"The hell he won't!" James muttered as Allen walked away.

Pocketing the notepad and pencil, the man named Menotti withdrew a revolver, scanning the area. James left his place to descend silently behind Menotti, hovering close behind him. He clamped a hand on his shoulder, only to get cold steel on the back of his head as Menotti froze.

"Say nothing," a voice hissed in James's ear.

"Forget it!" James growled and rocketed skyward, leaving the scene before Menotti could turn around.

CHAPTER FIFTEEN

Landing on his haunches with a bang, James dented the hood of Allen's car and Allen screamed in terror, clutching the steering wheel in fright.

"What the hell, Jamie!" Allen wailed.

"I should say the same to you!" James shouted.

"What are you talking about?"

"You traitor! You lied to me, you son of a--!"

"Hey, I'm only trying to protect you; he's on our side!"

"Liar!" The golden light quickly blazed around James's hands. "Give me one good reason not to punch a hole in your windshield and drag you out here like the piece of crap you are!"

"Leila called me at work and told me to tell you something came up and to meet her at Diana's Diner, okay?"

"Which one?"

"The one off Highway 367."

"Fine!"

"Hey, don't you want a ride instead of using up all that energy to fly over there?"

James glared at Allen and looked up at the darkened sky. "Just this once," he muttered, getting off the hood. "After that, anything goes, okay?"

"I'm sorry, Jamie," Allen murmured as James entered the vehicle and slammed shut the door.

"Shut up!"

Arriving at the diner, James slammed the door with a bang and stormed inside without acknowledging Allen. Upon entry, he found Leila at a booth, staring out the window.

"Hiya, Leila," James said brightly, "I hope you don't mind taking the bus back... Allen gave me a ride."

"It's okay," Leila said warmly. "I drove here."

James slid in the seat next to her. "So, what's so important that you want to talk to me about?" he inquired.

"First, let's get some ice cream and then I'll tell you."

"That's right, I owe you one." After the server approached and they made their orders, Leila suddenly grabbed the lapel of James's overcoat and pulled him close.

"Don't look now, but right across the room is that guy," Leila whispered. "He's been following me around at work..."

"How can he even get in at the radio station?" James hissed. "I thought you had to have special clearance!"

"K-SHO sometimes doesn't check everybody," Leila murmured. "But I swear he's pretending to be a janitor or something so he can go through my stuff! It's making me paranoid..."

"Is he with the guy that Allen's talking to?"

"What guy...?"

"Don't know..."

"Is it about that Signet power?"

James quickly flailed his hands, frantically looking around to see if the mysterious patron across the room in the booth overheard them. "Hey, shush," he uttered in a low tone. "Don't say that out loud!"

"Hey, I don't think he heard us anyway..."

The server arrived with their meals and Leila let loose her grip.

James sat back in his seat, relaxing slightly. "Well, let's get some food in," he said in a normal tone. "I'm paying, okay?"

"Then I should order the most expensive thing they have!" James nudged Leila and she giggled, nudging him back.

"What's with you having dessert first, then dinner?"

"To mix it up a little!"

Biting into his ice cream, James glanced over at the mysterious dark-haired young man in the leather coat and driving cap, reading the newspaper.

"*I don't like this...*" James said to himself.

The young man stiffened and looked up, his deep-set brown eyes locked onto James's intense gaze. James swallowed hard and looked away, shaking off a cold chill that settled in his bones.

Two hours later, after pulling up into the Verde Court apartments, James got out of the car and leaned over the passenger side door. "Say," he said, smiling faintly, "thanks again for dinner."

"What are you thanking me for?" Leila asked. "Besides, *you're* the one that paid for it all!"

"Well, just thanks for hanging out with me, is all! I owed you one, you know?"

"You deserve to be happy." Leila shut off the vehicle. "You're the best person I know."

"Oh, stop!" James pulled away and headed for his apartment steps.

"Really, Jamie!" Leila continued as she exited her car and followed him. "You never have a bad word about anybody and are always glad to see me, no matter what."

Tossing his keys aside on the nearby end table, Leila pulled off James's coat and held it.

"Really," James probed, grinning as she shut the door behind them, "you think so?"

"Yeah, no conditions either. You're nice and just happy when you're with me and that makes me happy too."

James pulled out of his tie and blazer. "Well, you know what else makes me happy?"

"What?" Leila blushed slightly and pulled out of her jacket then set both coats onto the nearby table.

"That body of yours!"

"Eek!" Leila cried as James lurched forward. He grabbed her by the waist and swung her around. "Put me down, you animal!"

"Okay, alright," James said and yanked off her sweater, chucking it overhead. He placed her on the couch and Leila giggled as she unbuttoned his dress shirt. "Did you know your body is like a map?"

"Really?"

James kissed her on the throat, going downwards her chest and stomach. "I see London, I see France..." He blew a raspberry into her side, forcing Leila to squeal and giggle.

"That tickles!" she cried.

"Ah-ha, Liechtenstein!"

"You're going to get it," Leila warned and pulled off his shirt. "I'm going to pin you down!"

"Hell, those guys who wrestle at the Park Plaza can beat you!"

James laughed and wrestled with Leila on the couch, forcing her into a fit of giggles.

Some time later, James reclined on the couch in his T-shirt and boxers while Leila danced around to the music that blared on the record player in her underwear. He fanned the plastic film photographs, making the colors appear.

"How can you do that?" James asked, mesmerized.

"You just move, slowpoke," Leila answered as she snapped her fingers.

"I can't dance for the life of me!"

"Oh, so the former all-star high-school gymnast doesn't know a few moves?" Leila teased. "Breakdancing should come easy to you!"

"I have a tin ear for music," James said, grinning. "That's why I'd rather headbang instead!"

"It doesn't matter what *kind* of music, you just find the groove and move to it!"

"How is it you can dance to *Centrifugal Nous* and *Jockstrap* and then do the same thing for *Regent* and your über-fave, *Incus*?"

"Like how you try to dance to *Diadem Meridian Amour* and *Rockbox*! You just do it!"

James blew a raspberry. "For one, those two bands are completely different!"

"My point exactly!"

"Do something dirty and sexy for me," James declared, picking up the instant camera. Leila giggled as she struck a suggestive pose. "Say '*Tracheophyte*'!"

"Oh my god, you listen to *Tracheophyte*?" Leila yelped, falling into a fit of laughter. "*Albescent Serpent* and *Venomous Toxicant* are cooler than that!" The camera spat out the photograph and James fanned it.

"Ooh, I like this one," he said after glancing at it. "I'm sending it directly to *Hedonist*!"

"Let me see!"

"Nope!" James quickly jumped out the way once Leila grabbed for it. "It's not done developing yet!"

"Aw, come on!" Leila grabbed his free arm and twisted behind his back, forcing him onto his knees.

"Damn girl," James yelped, wincing. "Where'd you get those moves?"

"Chop-socky films," Leila declared and took his wrist to pull closer. "Aw, Jamie, why'd you take that picture? I'm too fat..."

"You're pretty damn hot stuff to me!" James looked up, grinning wolfishly. "You know, I don't mind getting beaten up by you..."

"You're so dirty!" Leila let go and scooped up the other photographs on the floor that depicted them goofing off with the camera.

"You're so neat," James said as he rose to his feet. "You like me back, right?"

"Of course I do, dork."

James chuckled as he grabbed Leila by the waist and pulled her close. "Prove it." She kissed him on one cheek and patted the other with her free hand. "That's it?" James complained. "Don't kid around!"

"Yeah, that's it! I gotta save up." Leila grinned. "Besides, if I gave you everything, you'd die right here, right now!"

"You know, that sounds like a good idea..."

James froze and Leila gasped when they heard a sudden knock at the door.

"Were you expecting someone?" Leila whispered as James pushed her away.

James approached the door, forcing golden light flaring in his left hand. "Who is it?" he barked.

"Roxanne," Roxanne's voice called from the other side.

"Oh, crap," hissed James as Leila hurried into her clothing.

"It's cool," Leila whispered back.

"In a minute," James called.

"Later!" Leila said softly and hurried out the back door.

The flush on James's face spread to his ears once he opened the front door as Leila stepped out.

"Hey, Roxy," James said nervously, "what brings you over this way so late?"

"It's only a quarter to ten," murmured Roxanne. "Were you in bed? I didn't mean to wake you!"

"No, I wasn't..." James opened the door wider. "Come in!"

"I'm just..." Roxanne sighed heavily, looking down at the floor.

"What's the matter? You seem upset..."

"I don't know how to say this."

"Come out and say it." James shut the door and ushered Roxanne to the couch. "Look, anything you can tell me, I can handle it."

"Something's wrong, James... a *lot* of things. I know you don't want to be tied down, but..."

"Roxy, we've been down that road like a million times!" James fussed and took her hands into his.

"I know," Roxanne said sadly, "and I'm not here to go through it again."

"So, what is it?"

Roxanne leaned against James, rubbing her fingers against his palm. "It's, well... lately, things have been *different* between us, like something had *changed*..."

"I'm still the same guy you met two years ago, Roxy!"

"Maybe it's my fault, especially lately, worrying about Darlene. She has been having trouble in school and has been moody and difficult..." Roxanne blew a disconcerted sigh. "Basically, she hasn't been herself since the night you took that toy gun away from her. You still haven't told me what was that all about!"

"Well, um…"

"You haven't told me much of *anything*, James, not of anything recently, either!" James stiffened when Roxanne grabbed for his left hand that had the Signet tattoo marked on his palm. "I hardly ever see you and you're never home when I call and you've been acting strangely altogether…"

James clenched his teeth. "What do you mean by that?" he murmured.

"Like this tattoo, for instance… It's just not *like* you to *do* something like that." Roxanne ran a hand through her hair, fighting tears. "I used to feel so *close* to you, but now, sometimes I don't even *know* you!"

"Well, it, um, isn't a tattoo," James muttered, rising to his feet. "It can come off, yeah, with some… uh, special soap. Look, Roxy, I'll get rid of it right now, okay? Wait here." He hurried to the bathroom and looked down at his glowing palm.

"*Can't I will it to move?*" he thought. "*Is it the same as thinking about flying like Ubermensch and up I go?*" James turned on the tap, running the water. "*The Space Guy had me touch his hand and somehow it moved, so if I want it to move, it should!*" He pulled up his shirt and touched his right pectoral, furrowing his brow as he thought hard. "*Move, damn it! I hope this works…*" James felt warmth leaving his hand and radiating throughout his chest. "*Good, I did it!*"

Shutting off the water, James pulled down his shirt and returned to the parlor where he left Roxanne who stood before the couch, clutching her purse. "Hey, look, Roxy!" he said, holding up his hand. "All gone now, see?"

"Oh…" she muttered.

"It was just a novelty shop thing, you know?" James prattled on. "I don't know why I picked it up. It was just a crazy whim to waste some quarters..." Roxanne sighed heavily, unanswerable. "Um, Roxy, you okay?" She whirled around, smiling brightly as she placed a light hand onto his chest.

"Yes, I'm just fine," said Roxanne in false cheer. "I was... just lost in thought."

"You sure you're okay?" James asked gently and ran a hand through her hair.

"I'm just a little tired too... It's getting late, so I should be getting home."

"Okay," James said dejectedly. "I'll call you soon. Is tomorrow okay?" He leaned in to kiss her and she turned her head, forcing James kissing her cheek instead.

"Don't worry about me," Roxanne murmured. "Good night, love."

Letting her out, James leaned against the door, blowing a hard sigh. The record player cut off as the record wound to a stop, filling silence in the room.

"*That was weird,*" James mused. "*Oh well...*" Approaching the couch, James stiffened when he realized where she stood. "*She was standing right <u>here</u>... where I left the pictures!*" Picking up the photograph of Leila posing suggestively for James, his face burned in embarrassment. "*Oh crap...!*"

He dropped the photograph and fell back onto the couch abruptly as if his legs turned into jelly. Ripping off his shirt, James glared at the tattoo that glowed dimly on his chest.

"What is somebody like *me* doing with this thing?" he moaned and threw his head back, rolling his eyes at the ceiling.

He grunted in disgust. "Space Guy," he grumbled, "you really picked a winner..."

CHAPTER SIXTEEN

Driving up to Allen's house in Cedarwood, James parked across the street under a broken streetlight and hurried up the porch. Knocking on the front door, he waited for an answer, only to get none. Letting himself inside, James let out a yelp when a baseball bat crashed over his head.

"Damn it, Al!" James screeched as the lights turned on.

"Why are you here, Jamie?" demanded Allen. "It's after midnight!"

"I couldn't sleep," James grumbled, rubbing at his sore head. "I didn't want to bother Leila and I was out for a drive..."

"Right... Want some coffee?"

"So, why are *you* awake?" James shut the door as Allen set the bat aside and headed for his kitchen.

"I salvaged some perfectly good hubcaps at the car wash," Allen answered. "You know I go hunting for abandoned stuff on Trash Night and at car washes!"

"Why are you so nervous otherwise?"

"Why are you so tense otherwise?" retorted Allen. He poured water into a kettle. "It's about the same thing, this whole mess with The Signet."

"I just wish someone could rob a diner right in front of me so I can do something *useful* with this power," James moaned and plopped onto the stool at the kitchen counter.

"I was thinking about the story you told Agent Hilland," Allen murmured as he placed the kettle on the stove and turned on the burner. "At first I thought that the first alien and the second alien were the same guy giving you some kind of test to prove your worth in handling the Signet, you know?"

"But that doesn't make any sense…"

"I know, but then later, I realized that I can't really believe the whole concept of aliens and saucers and ray guns… Any of it's going to be out there in the open until you bring concrete proof!"

"I was going to show you until I found you talking with that Menotti guy!" James snapped, bristling. "But you *have* to believe me! You were *there* when that alien blasted the side of your house! You *saw* the second alien put that pistol to your head, ready to blow out your brains! Even Roxy saw one of his guns!"

"No, all I saw was an explosion shatter my patio doors and some bright flashes of lights," Allen said slowly. "Nobody except *you* saw the concrete evidence of extraterrestrials. Until you produce any solid proof, I can't--I just can't--!"

"Damn it, Allen!" James roared and slammed a fist onto the counter, cracking the surface. "I know the bodies were incinerated from that fight, but the Space Guy left me that machine, that GEARS thing that you touched yourself and felt *in your own hand*! He even left me a suit that's tougher than *any material on Earth* and that I can show you too!"

"Real, however obviously, where it comes from, is open to question," Allen said softly. "It just boils down to one thing: something happened to you and now you can do amazing things."

"But why *me*, Al? Why does it have to be me? Why not you? Why not some other jerk?" James gripped his hair in frustration and tugged at it firmly. "I don't feel like I'm living up to this thing; I feel like I'm not worthy, not smart enough, not *good* enough..." James blew a defeated sigh. "I don't know what to do. What *should* I do?"

"What should *any* of us do?" Allen retorted and took a pair of mugs from the cabinet above the sink. "What should we do with the powers that we have?"

The kettle whistled and Allen picked it up, pouring the water into the cups then filled them with instant creamer, instant coffee and sugar.

James rose to his feet, grinding his teeth in anger. "What the hell is wrong with you, Al?" he snarled. "Something's wrong with you... you *changed*! You're starting to sound like some armchair hack psychiatrist, *not* my friend!"

"I haven't changed," Allen said gently and passed a cup of coffee over to James. "I'm still your friend. It's just that there are some things I can't deal with right now..."

"What did Hilland do to you?" James murmured.

"Nothing!" Allen shouted and stormed away.

James sipped his cup of coffee, wondering why his friend acted differently than he remembered. Moments later, he heard Allen shouting and items breaking. Leaving the kitchen,

James found Allen in the rear yard, slamming the broken mast ax onto a cord of wood, barely splitting it down the middle.

"What are you trying to do?" James asked.

"You son of a--!" James quickly leaned out of the way when Allen tossed the mast ax at him, crashing the weapon through the window. "You either help me split wood for the fireplaces," Allen bellowed, "or get the hell out!"

"You need to work off some of this stuff, Al!" James groused. Allen chucked the cup of coffee at him, whipping back his head from the force as the mug bounced off. Wiping at his face with his sleeve, James glared at Allen who stormed back indoors. "Better be glad I can't feel anything!" he yelled as the door slammed shut behind Allen. James drove a fist into the wood, splitting it in half. "Because of you, Allen Jontei, my life is even worse! Some friend you are!" James continued punching into cords of wood, splitting them into smaller sections.

"It's a quarter to four in the morning," Allen called. Stepping outdoors, he found James wavering, struggling to split more wood once his strength receded. "Come on, that's enough."

James wearily staggered to his feet and Allen put an arm around his waist, aiding him to his car.

"I still hate you," James grumbled.

"Be lucky today's Saturday," Allen murmured. "I wish you could stay at my house and I'd love if it that did happen, but I don't want you to be an easy target for those Feds!"

"Yeah, so they can cut up on me!"

Placing James inside his car, Allen clamored into the other side and started the engine.

"You can pick up your car in the morning..."

James groaned and looked out the window of the passing scenery while Allen drove. Easy listening music played softly in the background on the radio, drowning out his depressing thoughts. "*Who should I call about this?*" he thought. "*There are aliens in Petoria! They're going to take over Earth if I don't do something...*"

Once Allen aided James inside his apartment and put him on the couch, James fell on his side, snoring.

Waking up several hours later, James grabbed the telephone directory and researched numbers to call.

"Let's see, *United States Government Offices...*" he murmured as he turned pages. "Hm... *Air Corps, Department of the Air Reserves...*" His finger went down the listing until he found the one he wanted. "Here we are, *Petoria Office of Public Affairs*. I'll try them all!"

Taking the phone, James dialed the number and waited until someone picked up the line.

"Recruiting office," said a gruff voice on the other side.

"Oh, sorry," James said dejectedly, "I wanted the office of public affairs."

"Yeah, that's us," the voice drawled. "What can I do for you?"

"Well... look, this sounds strange, but..." James blew a shaky sigh. "I had an encounter with a UFO and..."

"UFO?" the voice squawked. "Hold on, please..."

James glared at the receiver when the man on the other side broke out into laughter. "At least cover the damn mouthpiece!" he shouted and waited until the officer on the other end calmed then picked up the line.

"Hello? Yeah, well, um, we can't help you with your, er, um, problem, but I'll give you a number at the Stanfield Air Corps Base. Maybe they can do something..."

James grunted as he wrote down the number and then searched the directory for the Space Systems Division. After repeating his request, he clenched his teeth when declined.

"Well," said the secretary, "we used to be in charge of *Project Green Book* but that was years ago. We don't investigate UFO's anymore. Sorry."

"But...!" James glared at the receiver when he heard a click. "If petty bureaucrats can't help, maybe I could try talking to the President..."

Placing the receiver back onto the cradle, James hovered near his window, staring outside into the cold October morning.

"*I know there's no point in barging through the front gate,*" he mused. "*The Secret Service guys would start shooting at me the moment I landed on the porch. Even if I sneaked in through the roof or a window, those house guards would be on my butt like white on rice...*"

James touched down and grabbed his overcoat draped on the edge of the couch. He pulled into it and walked outside, going down the streets of North Petoria.

Hours later, James walked inside a bar and took a seat at an empty booth.

"What's yer poison?" asked the tender as he wiped down the counter.

"I'm not much of a drinker..." James murmured. "*I can't afford it,*" he thought sourly.

"You look depressed, Son. What's yer problem?"

"Nothing really..." James answered.

"Listenin' to troubles is my specialty." The tender filled a glass of water and ice and handed it to James. "Here, gargle them pipes and let me hear it."

Gulping down the drink, James stared down into the glass of ice. "*What should I tell him?*" he considered. "*This whole thing with aliens; it sounds like straight out of a comic book or some pulpy science fiction story...*"

"Well...?"

"I'm writing a book about this average guy that's pretty keen with electronics," James said softly, "and aliens from outer space show up to give him this awesome power." He blew a short sigh. "So after a while, the average guy decides to turn himself over to the President, since the power gives him super strength and speed and able to shoot fireballs and stuff..."

"Fireballs and stuff, yeah?"

"Yeah." James idly ran a finger around the lip of the glass. "He thinks it's just too strong a power for some ordinary guy to have, but his heart is in the right place and he wants to help people with it..."

"Really, huh?" drawled the barkeep. He stroked his chin, thinking.

"So that's where I'm stuck." James swirled the ice in his glass. "Should he turn himself in or try to do the vigilante super-hero thing?"

"That's an easy one," said the tender. "If he went with the Government, first they'd freak out of course. After that, then if he seemed like a peaceful fella, then they'd get *real* friendly..."

"What do you mean by that?"

"First they'd talk him into fighting terrorists and commies and stuff for them, then after they get all that outta the way, then they'd talk him into getting tested at their labs and stuff, not wanting to believe he was really for real."

"What would he do then?"

"He'd have to keep proving and proving himself, to show them it ain't no trick."

"That sounds tiring..."

"Yeah and finally when they're convinced that he's for real and it ain't no gimmick and that he can *really* do all that super stuff you say he can do..." The tender made a slicing sound as he ran a hand across his throat. "Then they'd kill the poor bastard in his sleep."

"What?" James cried. "Why'd they do that?"

"You know, all those tests are to secretly find his weakness." The tender leaned in. "Look, kid, the guy would be too dangerous to keep around. Too much power can go to anybody's head, superhero or not!" The barkeep chuckled as he filled a glass of his own to down. "I know these Government guys, hell, I used to work for them back when them senators and politicos was tryin' to get at them commies. They'd be afraid your guy would try to take over if he got too power-hungry, or get miffed over something and use some monument to harpoon some aircraft carrier." He chuckled heartily. "I *know* these guys. They don't like people with power they can't control for themselves."

"Thanks," James muttered and pushed his seat away. "How much for the water?"

"On me."

James stalked out, exiting into the evening air. *"I wish there was somebody I could talk to,"* he thought as he headed down the sidewalk. *"Allen's out of the question, the backstabbing jerk... Leila's the only other person I trust, but lately things have been getting too weird between us. I could tell Roxy, maybe she should've been the one to confide in at the start!"* James ducked behind an alley of a building and rocketed for the sky, speeding for the Pomaderris area.

Touching down in the rear yard of the Citovecca home, James grunted when he hurtled over onto the ground and slammed onto his back. Groaning when he rose to his feet, he hopped the fence and came around the front, then jumped the porch and knocked on the door. Moments later, Gloria the babysitter answered, smiling warmly at James.

"Hot damn," James thought, swallowing hard as he took in her outfit consisting of a form-fitting black pullover sweater, white pipe-leg jeans, and black short boots. *"She's so...!"* He cleared his throat. "Oh, hey, Gloria," James said nervously. "Is Roxy out?"

"Hi, Mister Russell... I mean, James!" Gloria said, blushing slightly. "Missus Citovecca's at the hockey game with one of her girlfriends."

"Didn't know she was much of a Bluenote fan," James murmured. "Oh well..."

"Hey, James," Gloria said brightly as she unlocked the screen door and pushed it ajar. "I already put the kids to bed. So, do you, um... want to come in and watch teevee with me?"

"*What the--?*" James thought as he face grew warm and he stepped away, sucking in a shallow breath. "*What's this?*"

"I just popped some popcorn and everything!" Gloria interjected.

"Uh, thanks, but... I'd better not," James said slowly, forcing out the words. "Maybe some *other* time, okay?"

Gloria smiled. "Promise?" James nodded wolfishly. "Great! See you later!"

James quickly turned away, forcing his feet down the steps. "*Why did I say that?*" he berated to himself as he walked away. "*I'm just glad she couldn't see my interest behind this overcoat I'm wearing!*" James blew a heavy sigh as he headed down the street. "*You gotta remember, Jim, she's seventeen, and she's the damn babysitter and if Roxy ever caught you, you'd be having frank and beans for dinner!*" He shuddered. "*Man, if she was that upset over pictures of me and Leila goofing off... but that body!*" James looked skyward. "*Maybe I should hang around and wait for Roxy to get back. I really need to talk to her...*"

He glanced back at the house and hovered near a tree, taking a seat on one of the heavy low-hanging branches to watch the shadows of the parlor move about within.

"I can always daydream..." James murmured.

Four hours later, James checked his watch, grumbling to himself.

"Where *is* she?" he griped. "The game must have ended at least two hours ago or so... Even if she stopped for drinks, it shouldn't take *this* long! I hope nothing major happened to cause her to be out this late..."

Noticing a car slowly coming up the street and park before the Citovecca home, James clenched his teeth as a middle-aged man in a dark brown suit exited and walked around the passenger side, opening the door.

"I had a very nice evening," Roxanne said as she stepped out, wearing a shimmering hot pink sequined cocktail dress with red flats.

"Is it over?" asked her suitor as he led her up the porch steps, "or may I come in?"

"Hm..." Roxanne sighed as she sifted through her clutch purse for her keys. "Not tonight, okay?"

"Okay," said her date. "I'm very glad we met. I'll call you tomorrow."

James ground his teeth and the power flashed around his body as he watched the middle-aged man lean in and kiss Roxanne on the lips.

"*Where did she meet him?*" James wondered, clenching his hands. "*Not at the game like she said in that dress! That* girl _lied_ to me!" After the middle-aged man returned to his car and drove away, jumped down from the tree, hovering several inches from the ground. The energy that surrounded him began to taper and James blew a heavy sigh. "_What am I getting angry for? What did I expect to happen? What right did I have to expect?_" He grunted and his feet touched down onto the ground. "_I've been nothing but a noncommittal skirt-chasing jerk! Of course she's going to go after someone much older, more mature!_" James turned away, stomping in the opposite direction.

He walked the streets for some time and looked skyward at the cold heavens that had pale stars dotting the landscape. "_Now what...?_" he mused. "_I can't go home and I can't crash at Allen's place to drink away this lousy feeling. My stomach's in knots and I can't sleep even if I tried..._" James levitated slightly off the ground. "_I'll just drift, like my life and wander and hope I run into something, anything..._"

CHAPTER SEVENTEEN

After floating over the Jonas County area, James came to a pause when he heard screams of terror.

"What's going on?" he wondered as he came across a large parking lot where many patrons ran away from a twenty-four-hour supermarket. *"This is the all-night Wally World... It's too dark for them to see me land..."*

James grew confused as to why they were running away once he touched down. When he saw no fire, he rushed up to one woman that huffed for her car and grabbed her by the arm, only to get his face struck by her purse.

"Let me go!" she wailed.

"Hey, Lady, wait a minute!" James cried. "What's wrong? Why's everybody running away?"

"I don't know," she moaned, pulling away. "I'm just scared. Please, just let me go!"

James loosened his grip, watching her hurry for her car. *"Weird,"* he mused as he walked for the store. James came to a pause as a thin young woman with shaggy dark hair and narrow steel blue eyes wearing tight stonewashed jeans and a bright violet trench coat exited the department store with bags of groceries. "*Huh, <u>she</u> looks pretty calm! Didn't I see her somewhere before...?*" Walking in step behind her, James felt himself break out into a cold sweat. "*Holy...! I gotta get out of here!*" He struggled to keep his stride as he felt himself take uneven steps. "*I need to run... but...*" James came to a stop, watching her load the groceries calmly into her vehicle. "*No! What's going on with me? That's crazy to freak out when there's no reason to...*" He sighed as the woman entered her car and drove away. "*There's nothing to run from, unless you've got a tired-looking woman.*" James took a small leap and hovered above ground as the fear he felt subsided. "*That's too bizarre to leave alone. I don't know why I suddenly got <u>scared</u>... I can't be, <u>shouldn't</u> be afraid of <u>her</u>! She didn't have a gun, or anything else that could possibly harm me. Still...*" James flew forward, following the mysterious woman's car. "*Maybe I'll just follow her and see what happens...*"

Watching the car stop along the riverfront in Carolus County, James descended and kept his distance as he watched the young woman take the bags and walk over to a gazebo.

"*Now this is a strange place to stop,*" James considered, following as close as he could to stay out of sight.

"Darren," the woman called. "Darren, where the hell are you?" James gasped when he noticed his coworker Adnan appear from the darkness, clutching a lit cigarette in hand. "Where the hell is Mister Levin?" the woman snapped. "He was supposed to be here by now!"

"*Levin?*" James thought in horror. "*I hope it's a different one than the one I know...*"

"Look, Mika," Adnan grumbled. "I don't know where he went and I don't care!" He grunted when slapped across the face by a heavy hand.

"It's *Miss* Woodrow to you, you brat!" hissed Mika.

"Whatever!" Adnan reached for the food and she kicked him back with her foot.

"Not until you get Mister Levin back here; you're not eating!"

"Stupid old cow!" Adnan groaned. "Just gimmie my cigs and I'll be out of your hair! I don't gotta eat!"

"Why won't you behave?" Mika snapped, shaking her fist. "You make me mad again and I won't hesitate to torture you!"

Adnan shrank back at the threat. "Okay, okay, gimmie one cig and I'll try to find him!" A pack of cigarettes floated out of the bag of groceries, with the paper and cellophane removed by invisible hands. James's eyes widened as he watched one filtered tip slide up on its own and float over to Adnan. He took it and tucked behind his ear then walked away. "Mister Levin!" he called, "Hey, Mister Levin, where'd you run off to now? We got food and stuff!"

"Don't make me sorry for bringing you along, you punk!" Mika called after Adnan. "I'll send you back to *The Facility* in the morning if you cross me!"

"He's probably sorry for running into us, especially *you*, is that right?" Adnan yelled. "Ah-ha, there you are!" James cringed as a pained cry came out into the darkness. "Now come over here!"

James clenched his teeth as he watched his old college friend in jeans, sneakers and padded short jacket thrown forward by a spiked whip, forcing him bowling over at the woman's feet.

"That's Verne!" James thought as Verne groaned in pain. *"I know that rockabilly-wannabe anywhere!"* James panted weakly for breath, inundated by fear and anger as Mika bent down over Verne, cupping the man's face in her hand. *"Where did Adnan get that whip...?"*

"Thought you could run away, huh Mister Levin?" Mika cooed. "I bet you're exhausted, aren't you?" Mika stroked Verne on the head. "You're going to be my dog!"

With a flick of her wrist, Verne let out a cry once thrown into the air and crashed into the nearby river by invisible forces. He thrashed in the water before sinking moments later.

"Time to make my move," James muttered as Adnan returned, sitting on the gazebo's steps and rifled through the bag of consumables. "Hey," he barked. "What are you doing?"

Adnan dropped all that he held and quickly rose to his feet as dark green light surrounded his body. "What do you want?" he sneered.

"Who are you?" commanded Mika.

"I want you to leave my friend Verne alone," James snapped. "He's got a wife and kid to worry about!"

"He's got obligations," Adnan declared, "with *us!*"

"You're not hurting anyone else!" James spat.

"Darren, let him take his friend home," Mika said as she took a seat on the gazebo's ledge. "You never told me he had a family!"

"He never said anything about it!" Adnan squawked. "With the way he was all over you--!"

"What were you two planning?" James cut in.

"Nothing..." Mika said nonchalantly and folded her arms, looking away.

James grunted when the overwhelming fear returned. *"There it is again!"* he thought. *"That same strange sense of dread I felt at Wally World!"* James took a hesitant step backwards. *"Calm down, Jim. There's nothing to be afraid of. That pixie can't hurt me unless I panic..."*

"Well?" Adnan said irritably.

"I'm trying," Mika grumbled, glaring at James.

"Don't lose it, Jim!" James yelled inside his mind as he ground his teeth. *"Keep it under control! But that terror, the sheer force of it - it's still gnawing at me...!"*

"Maybe I can help?" Adnan asked, rubbing his hands together deviously. "You know he works with me at Parsons and Parker. I don't like this punk at all..."

"Maybe..."

"How is she doing this?" James wondered as he stood his ground. *"I can't believe it. There can't be..."*

"Come on, Mika!" Adnan begged. "Please, gimmie a shot; I can make him go away!"

"Oh, all right, you brat," Mika grumbled, "But if you get us in trouble..."

"Yeah, yeah..."

A sudden crash came from behind and James whirled around, finding Verne tearing across the sands and barreling for him, letting out a battle cry.

"What's going on here?" James thought as he jumped back from a fiercely glowing fist aimed for his face. *"How is this*

possible?" James thrust forward his own glowing hand, forcing Verne yelping in surprise once struck in the chest with a hard palm slap. "*Amazing! Verne's a lot stronger than a guy his size should be, or even <u>my</u> size!*" James grabbed his shirtfront and lifted Verne overhead who continued to snarl and claw at him. "*She's still at it, clawing at my self-control...*"

"You're a tough one," Mika declared, "are you?" The small woman jumped down from her seat and stomped up to James.

James glowered down at her with narrowed eyes, grinding his teeth as she glared up at him. "*There must be some rational explanation on <u>why</u> they're like this,*" James wondered and threw down Verne. Verne grunted as he tumbled backwards onto his side in response, stunned, with the breath knocked out of him. "Look, Lady," James snapped. "How do you *do* that?"

"I don't know," she replied.

"Did someone *give* you this power?"

"You tell me."

"Was it some *Starguard* or *Space Defender* lookin' fella?"

"You look at too much telly, Russell," Adnan said, smirking.

"No matter how hard I try, you won't *budge* at all!" the young woman snapped. "That's *very* unusual!"

"This is pathetic, Mika!" Adnan shouted.

Mika threw back a hand and Adnan grunted when thrown aside with force. "Know your place!" she barked. "Mister Levin, you're letting me down! Now get back over there!"

"Look, Lady, I'm warning you," James stated and clenched his hands that glowed in golden light. "Cut it out already!"

"You're not going to hit little old me, aren't you?" Mika teased.

"I'm seriously considering it." James let out a wail in pain when a heavy stone crashed into the back of his head. "Hey!"

Another weighty blow slammed into his head and James staggered forward. He turned around, blocking another attack with his arm and screamed when the bone snapped from another hard blow. James stumbled reward, stunned when he faced a muddy and soaked Verne who had granite-covered fists. Verne threw a powerful punch and James faltered when rammed into his arm and chest, throwing him to the ground with force.

"*He's trying to kill me!*" James thought as he scrambled to his feet and ran back. "*He's going to kill me!*"

"Come on!" Verne roared and stomped the ground, forcing deep tremors rattling through James.

Taking a hesitant leap, James hovered unsteadily in the air. "*Gotta get outta here,*" he thought and the light flickered around him. "*Take off! Damn it Jim, don't let the power fade, not now, not now!*" James again screamed when a heavy fist banged into his back, throwing him forward. "*I can't fly! Not now, not like this!*" He struggled to get up and wavered when repeatedly struck in the head and back. James shrieked as the stone fists tore into his coat and into his skin, rattling him.

"Stay down!" Verne thundered and his punches became harder.

James wailed louder in pain, cowering and covering his head with his hands as the pain seeped into his muscles and his bones crunched from pressure.

"*No!*" James screamed in his mind as the pain and fear became crushing to his psyche all at once. "*Got to get it back calm down catch my breath just need another second come on...!*"

"Yes, get rid of him!" Adnan cheered from offside.

"He'll be a very good pet, do you think so, Darren?" asked Mika. "Much better than you!"

"Hey," Adnan squawked, "what's that supposed to mean?"

"*Just another second!*" James thought as he struggled to get up, only to find that his body refused to respond. Verne screamed over him, his punches becoming harder, more intense, tearing into his skin with sickening cracks. "*He's on top of me, can't let him hit me like this... gotta move; move, damn it, Jim! Move, get out the way; roll out!*" He let out a throat-grating scream when the granite fists turned into lead, whaling into his body with heavy metallic crunches.

"Yes, yes!" Adnan cheered. "That's the spirit!"

James screamed again, much louder than before when the fists targeted his head and all sound turned diffused. His vision washed out from color to red, and then changed to grayscale. He became one with the pain as the gray-tinted world turned white before fading to black, followed by silence altogether.

CHAPTER EIGHTEEN

James moaned when bright light flashed in his eyes and a low drone buzzed in his ears. A blurry form stood before him in tan and dark brown amid the murky world.

"... Right...?" a voice called from far away.

"What...?" James groaned and staggered to his feet, only to fall back and met the earth once more.

"Are you all right?" the hollow voice asked again. Slowly James's hearing began to clear and he heard the faint chatter from police radios.

"Hey, Son," another voice called to James. James slowly turned his head when another officer approached. "What happened out here?"

"Got into a nasty fight," James grumbled and ran a hand through his hair. He sucked in a pained breath through his teeth. "*My bones should be broken,*" he thought. "*What happened...?*"

"Can you get up?"

"Yeah," James muttered, "gimmie a minute..."

"We had calls that there was some screams out here..."

"Yeah..." James slowly sat up. The officer extended a hand and James brushed it aside as he slowly rose to his feet. He staggered about, trying to find his footing. "But I'm cool now."

"So who was it that beat you like that?"

"I still got everything," James mumbled. "They didn't steal anything..."

"Probably a gang initiation thing," grumbled the secondary officer from offside. "They clocked this unsuspecting kid here just cos..."

"Yeah," James grunted and rubbed at his throbbing temple, "just cos..."

"Don't be walkin' these streets at night, Son," said the officer closest to James. "It ain't what it used to be."

"Yeah, thanks..."

"Need a ride home?"

"I don't live too far."

"Alrighty."

James shuffled away, following the tracks on the sandbar near the riverfront while trying to track down his attackers. After the officers left and James finished combing the area, he approached a tree and struck it in frustration.

"Not a trace!" he screeched, slamming a charged fist into the side of the trunk. "I can't find them *anywhere*!" The tree shattered from impact, blowing wood shards everywhere. "If I could *kill...*!"

James decimated what remained of the tree and grew exhausted once his strength receded. He dragged his sore body to a bus stop and waited for the next bus that came.

Staggering back for the Verde Court apartments after a lengthy bus ride and several transfers, James entered his apartment and tossed his keys and wallet aside on the end table near the couch.

"Ow..." he grumbled and shut the door then pulled off his clothing, shucking them to the floor while making his way to his bedroom. "Never felt this sore in my life..." Along the way, he flipped on the television that blared out the early morning news. Heading into the shower, James turned on the tap and leaned against the wall, relishing the hot water pelting at his back. "I'll feel better once I tape up after this..." He later grew relaxed as the steam flooded him in the darkness.

The telephone rang moments later and James groaned, not wanting to leave his place of comfort. It kept ringing, only to cut off when the answering machine picked up. The telephone rang again and finally, after reluctantly turning off the water, James left the shower stall and shuffled to the phone then picked pick up the receiver.

"Yeah?" he grumbled.

"Hey, Russell," Xavier's voice said over the line, "man, sorry to be calling you like this."

"Xavier, what's going on?" James asked, stunned. "Why... how did you get my number?"

"Man, somebody hacked into P and P's security department and we need some coders to fix the hole," Xavier said. "I can't get a hold of Adnan anywhere, and you seemed like the next logical choice!"

"Look, Ecks, I don't do ALCOS or BUCOL, okay? Tell Mainframes they can sit on it!"

"Dude, it's all in SAPIC, something you're really good at!"

"Which SAPIC?" James snapped. "There are different ones!"

"Man, how the hell am I to know?" Xavier cried. "Look, if they're all similar and come from the one source, with different variations, you should be able to figure it out!"

"Ecks, come on..."

"Look, if you can save P and P's ass, they'll pay you *triple* of what you're getting and you might move upstairs to a better department!"

"Don't play around."

"I'm serious, Russ," Xavier said evenly. "They're freaking out and need it done before Monday!"

"Alright, I'll be there in two hours..."

"You sure you're all right?"

"Yeah, just had a hard night..."

"Man, I wish I had the time to party like you do! I just can't afford it..."

"Don't worry, Ecks, it's not all that great."

James hung up the line and sighed, staring back at his reflection in the mirror. He faced a worn-down and bruised young man with broad shoulders, thinning shaggy blond hair and weary blue eyes.

"Now I gotta go to work in a couple of hours," he mused, *"so there's no sense in sacking out now..."*

Leaving his room, James padded into the kitchen and opened his refrigerator, revealing spoiled milk and deli meats, spotted cheese and hard bread. At the bottom shelves were several cans of soda.

"If I had time to enjoy some coffee, I would," he muttered and grabbed a can of cola. "I've been so busy; I never got around to cleaning this fridge or buying groceries and stuff..."

James shut the door with his hip and popped the tab,then gulped down the cold drink and returned for his bedroom. Heading for his closet, James opened it wide and set aside his soda can on the nearby dresser. He pulled out the bench press set he had folded within and set up the bar with weights, then returned into his kitchen, withdrawing several rolls of elastic bandages from the kitchen drawer. After wrapping his chest, torso, shoulder, wrist, and arms, he went back to his bedroom, standing before the weights.

"*Before I get cracking in front of a computer monitor,*" he considered as he cracked his knuckles, "*there's something else to do with the power off...*" He picked up the weight and struggled to lift it off the floor. With each repetition, James found to his horror that his breath became thinner and his muscles shook from pressure. "*Damn, can't even do fifteen at twenty-five pounds... I really lost some muscle!*" He dropped the weight and plopped on the bench, wheezing for breath. James glanced back at his reflection in the mirror across the room and frowned at what he saw. "*Never noticed I had flab around my middle before either...*" The phone rang again as James took up the weight once more, struggling for lift number sixteen. The answering machine picked up the call and beeped.

"Hey, Russ, it's me," Xavier's voice said as the machine recorded. "They're talking about time and a half, but you might work yourself up to ten bucks an hour if you salvage the mess, fifteen if you can fix the hole and twenty if you can find the one who hacked into the system. Arikara's been called in too and he's using this as an opportunity to move on up. You owe it to yourself, Russ to get out of 387. I mean it. Hell, I'll even order pizza and coffee for you if it means you'll get outta this dump. Well, I gotta go and get to the office. See you there!"

James blew a hard sigh, thinking about the events from three weeks before.

"*I don't know why I got this power, or why that alien chose me,*" James mused after twenty lifts and set down the bar to readjust the weight in which to press. "*But it doesn't matter. I got it and I've got a choice. I can be worthy or not...*" James grunted as he lifted the heavier weight over his head, restarting his counting at one. "*That's the same choice I had <u>before</u> the Signet. Like Nadine said, we all have powers and we all have to decide what to do with them. It's just that now, I've got <u>more</u>...*" The phone rang again and James cringed as he heard Adnan's voice on the machine.

"I hope you feel good, Mister Russell," Adnan's voice sneered. "But there is no point in advancing. You will be put behind me..." Adnan chortled darkly. "If I can't beat you down, then I'll just have to show you up!"

"*Until now, I've been playing games with myself...*" James ground his teeth, feeling his arms shake from the pressure and searing pain. "*I've been 'proving' to myself every which way that I'm not 'good enough', with Roxy, with Leila, at Parsons and Parker... all to 'justify' backpedaling, laziness, and exploiting the power for petty, selfish things.*"

James let out a cry and dropped the barbell, heaving for breath as the pain clawed through his arms and back, turning his stomach sour. He held his head in his hands, fighting tears and nausea as his phone rang once more.

"Me again," said Xavier. "Reinhold's looking for you; he's freaking out. We're at the office and all your stuff's cleared out. You're not thinking of pulling the trigger, are you?"

James growled and grabbed the barbells, readjusting the weights. He lifted again, disregarding the intense agony in his joints.

"I'm not going be rid of that easily!" James shut his eyes as tears ran from them. *"Tonight was my big test with this power, and I couldn't even keep it up! In the movies, the hero always got a second shot at the villain. What if I don't see that punk Adnan again or that weirdo chick with him? What if I don't even find out if Verne's okay...?"*

James wheezed for breath after twenty lifts and put on the heaviest weights he owned, slowly lifting them. He struggled to move as the telephone rang, cutting into his thoughts.

"You have what I seek," a new, strange, voice hissed and echoed over the line amid heavy static. "I am prepared to wait... but I will find you. Will you be set for battle?"

James grew chilled after he finished the last of the lifting. "You need to even the score, Jim," he muttered to himself and wiped away the heavy sweat that drained down his face and neck. "You need to get ready... You *survived* for a reason, with the universe giving your goofy self another chance to kick back these aliens that threaten the planet! There is only one planet Earth, and I need to fight to hold onto it! I *am* the right guy to have this power if I *want* to be." He slammed the barbell onto the floor, gulping for breath. "Twenty reps at forty-five pounds... Damn, I need to get back with it!" Standing to his feet, James glared back at his nude, bloodied and bruised reflection. "Look at what they did to you, Jim," he snapped as he pointed at the mirror. "Get it together!" James sucked in a shallow breath through his teeth as the pain coursed through him and he shut his eyes, running a hand through his hair, moaning. "I'll never be weak again, not for long," James grumbled and stood straighter as his eyes snapped open, looking intently at his reflection. He clenched his hands at his sides, unleashing golden flames. "Never again!"

PART FIVE
CROSSING THE LINE

James groaned when knocking at his front door brought him out of the realm of sleep. He groggily sat up and pulled into his jeans that lay on the floor nearby and padded to his parlor.

"Who is it?" James called as he rubbed sleepily at his eyes. "Man, don't you know how early it is?"

"C'mon, Jamie, it's me, Leila!" his friend called back from the other side. "Let me in, will ya?"

"I wanna be left alone," James griped. "Let me catch up on my sleep... it's still early and I've a few hours you know!"

"I brought a present over for you, Jamie," Leila teased. James smiled slightly and opened the door, then met with a crushing hug. "Congrats, Jamie!" she said happily.

"What's this for?" James yelped as he staggered back, stunned.

"I heard what awesome work you did for P and P!" Leila pulled away and dug through her purse then pulled out two small wrapped boxes. "Here!"

James chuckled and caught the gifts she tossed to him. "I did my best," he replied, blushing.

"Well, it's good enough for a promotion!"

"What? That's news to me!"

Leila pushed the door closed and headed past James into the kitchen, pulling out of her coat and tossing it into an empty chair along the way. "So what eats you have in here...?" she murmured, fishing through his cabinets.

"Where did you hear about my promotion?" James asked as he took a seat at the kitchen table. "What did you get me?"

"I heard it from Xavier when he stopped by the station," Leila answered as she pulled out a carton of eggs and milk. "He won tickets to see *Airesculptor*..."

"What's this... a mini flashlight and a compass?" James murmured after opening the small gift boxes.

"Well, yeah," Leila said and rolled her eyes. "For navigating when you're flying around like a ghetto wannabe Ubermensch!"

James laughed and left his seat, hugging Leila from behind. "You're too nice to me!" he murmured and nuzzled her neck.

Leila blushed and quickly set the eggs and milk aside on the counter. "Cut that out," she squawked, giggling as she pushed his roaming hands away. "Stop feeling me up!"

"We've got some time, huh?" James said and kissed her on the side of her neck as he unbuttoned her blouse.

"We have to get to work soon, especially *you*, Jamie!" James levitated slightly off the floor and Leila gasped, and then laughed brightly as he took her with him toward his room.

"It's early; we have a while!" James kicked the door shut and dropped Leila, landing her on the bed. She let out a squeal as he pounced on her. "Rawr!"

"Eek!" Leila cried and fell into a fit of laughter as she wrestled against James.

Exiting the shower, James dried off and padded into his bedroom to catch Leila at the side of the bed, setting the receiver back in the cradle with a perplexed look on her face.

"What's the matter, Leila?" James murmured and wrapped the towel about his waist. "You're looking kinda down..."

"Xavier called and wanted me to tell you about coming over to meet his new girlfriend out in Moline," Leila answered. "He wants you and Roxanne to come out to the *Limelight*."

James cleared his throat, surprised. "Come on," he said uneasily, "you gotta be kidding me!"

"You're acting like something's wrong with the whole idea! What is it about you and Roxanne?"

"What about her?"

"Well..." Leila made motions with her hands, and then dropped them into her lap, sighing heavily. "Do you think it's over with her?"

"Oh, that sort of thing, huh?" James murmured, taking in a shallow breath. "Yeah, I really blew it this time. I mean, she's *already* seeing some *other* guy!"

"Is it because of...?"

"Nah, not cos of you, Leila!" James ran a hand through her hair and cupped her face in his hand, forcing her to look up. "I'm a jerk, I'll admit to that. Besides, I couldn't keep up and I'm just not that good with kids, you know?" Leila took his hand and squeezed it firmly. "So, what Ecks gotta say?"

"Other than inviting you and Roxanne over this evening?"

James blew a hard sigh. "Why me?"

"If you don't want me to come..."

"Yeah, come with me. It's going to be awkward anyway if she shows up with her new boyfriend..."

Leila grinned. "Yeah, and I can show off my new dance moves!"

"Right, like you can dance!" James took off the towel and snapped at Leila with it.

Leila squealed, quickly rising to her feet. "Much better than you, Mister Golem!" she teased.

"I have you know that I was king of the dance floor back in the day!" James crowed.

"Only in your head, wannabe!"

"Whatever, but I can legg with the best of them!"

"We'll see that at the *Limelight* tonight!"

"Yeah, bring your skates!" James snapped at her again with the towel and she ran out of the room, giggling.

"Oh my god, James," Leila called from the next room, "It's a quarter to eight; you'd better boogie!"

"Damn..." James hurried into a pair of slacks and grabbed a dress shirt from the rack in his closet.

"It's payday, Ladies," Adnan announced as he entered the cubicle farm with numerous envelopes in hand, "so read 'em and weep!" He tossed an envelope on James's desk as he bypassed his cubicle and James glared up at him.

"Got downgraded to Robinson's job, Adnan?" James teased as he snatched up the envelope and opened it with the edge of a pen.

"Robinson's out sick with Mono," Adnan snapped back. "Did you give it to him?"

"Thanks a lot," James grumbled as Adnan smirked and left. He glanced at his paycheck, mildly surprised. *"Huh, I got a raise,"* James said to himself. *"They must really <u>want</u> to keep me here!"* He grinned. *"At least I didn't get a gift certificate to some truck stop diner like last pay rise..."*

"Alright," Xavier crowed, "I'm rich!"

"Man, I don't know what you're all excited about, Ecks," James said as Xavier came to his cubicle archway, smiling brightly. "You make even *less* than I do! Hell, you can't even get *married* and support a family on *this*."

"Hey, tonight I'm gonna blow it on pizza, gas, and maybe a show. It's my birthday today!"

"Well, well, happy birthday!" James left his desk and gave Xavier a friendly jab on the shoulder. "And one for luck!"

"Why are you so uptight?" Xavier asked, pushing up his reading glasses that threatened to slip off his nose. "I'm glad you decided to come back to work with us though..."

"What are you going on about?"

"You cleared out your desk earlier..."

"I'm fine, really," James said quickly. "I, er, well, needed time to think."

Xavier grinned. "Well, who said I was getting married *now*?" He gave a dismissive wave to James. "I've got plenty of time to waste some bucks on that. Right now, it's all about *partying!*"

James chuckled. "That's what life's all about, huh?" he teased.

"You bet your bouncy booty!"

James chuckled and shook his head. "Get outta here!"

"Yeah, I got a bonus, guys!" Xavier exclaimed as he left James's cubicle. "Russ and I totally kicked ass patching up that hole the other day!"

"Can it, Xavier!" Adnan carped.

"Aw, give the kid his props," Simmons called. "He's gonna go places!"

"Not Reinhold," Xavier said, "he loves us too much!"

"Stop it!" Reinhold whined as the others laughed. "You guys play too much!"

"*I don't know about him,*" James thought as he pocketed his paycheck, "*but I know I need to do something now before I die in here!*" James opened the drawers of his desk, finding his personal belongings thrown in haphazardly. "*At least whoever cleaned out what little crap I have in here put it back!*" He touched the desk calendar that was still in the box. "*By January I'm gone, for sure.*" James shut the drawer and grabbed his stack of papers that needed filing and set about finishing the remaining work he had.

Exiting the offices of Parsons and Parker at the end of the workday, James heard someone call his name and whirled around, spotting Xavier waving at him.

"Hey, Russ!" Xavier called. "Where you going?"

"Home, Ecks, where else?" James replied. "Gotta get this bus if I'm going to make it."

"Catch a ride with me, will ya?"

James shrugged his shoulders. "Sure, I can save the change..." He followed Xavier who headed back indoors. "I thought you were going home?"

"Well, I realized I forgot my keys!"

"So excited that you can't wait, huh?"

Xavier blushed and chuckled. "Man, this girl I'm with is totally foxy..."

Entering the office, James paused in step, spotting Adnan at a terminal. Adnan had a stack of forms next to him as he typed away and his blazer lay draped on the back of his chair. Adnan, who wore his hair down with his tinted glasses perched atop his head, had his tie loosened about his collar and the sleeves of his dress shirt rolled up at his elbows. "Extra work, huh?" James quipped. "First you're doing Robinson's job, now Mitchell's?"

"No thanks in part to you," retorted Adnan.

"I can't help it if I've got the skills to break free from here."

"Then congratulations are in order," Adnan said icily.

Xavier walked by, tossing his keys in his hand. "Let's go, Russ!" he chirped.

"Laters," James said and Adnan raised his fist.

"Pick a finger," Adnan growled.

James made a mock salute and walked out with Xavier. "Hey, Ecks, do you know what's with Adnan these days?" James asked as they walked out across the parking lot. "He's been acting a little off to me."

"Well, he's been working really hard, is all. He wants to get out of Clerical Processing just like the rest of us."

"But you seem pretty content."

"I know I'm not that bright, but at least where I'm at has stable pay, a raise every year, the occasional bonus and a comfy job that's not too hard or too easy either. Hell, managing databases is all right by me. I kinda like it..."

"But you're shuffling papers *all day*! How can you be fine with *that*?"

Approaching a small two-door flatbed sedan, Xavier opened the passenger side door for James then went around for the driver's side. "It pays for service on my Grenada," Xavier said simply.

James entered the car and pushed back the seat. "Jeez, Ecks," he griped, "you sure know how to pack it in."

Xavier chuckled as he started the engine and shifted gears.

CHAPTER TWENTY

"Hey, why are we stopping here?" James asked as Xavier pulled into a quiet neighborhood. "This isn't your apartment - I thought you lived out on Grandview."

"This is my mother's house," Xavier answered as he stopped in front of a large pale blue ranch-styled house with white trim. "She called me at lunch about getting a letter from the draft board this morning, so I promised her that I'd check it out."

"I'll wait in the car," James said and folded his arms across his chest.

"It's all right; come in with me, okay?" Xavier cut the engine. "She can get a little overbearing..."

"She's that scary, huh?" James joked and stepped out of the car. "I need to stretch my legs anyway..."

Xavier exited, shut the door with his hip and headed up the walk, tossing his keys in hand.

"It'll only be a second, promise," Xavier said assuredly to James as he came across the yard and knocked on the door. Hearing no answer, Xavier used his keys to enter.

"Surprise!" voices called from inside. Xavier cried out in shock and staggered back outside. James hurried up and grabbed Xavier by the arm before he fell back down the steps.

"Are you all right?" James asked and looked in the doorway, seeing several people clustered inside. "What's this, some kind of party...?"

"Mom, what's all this?" Xavier cried, peeling away from James.

"Happy birthday, Boris!" she called and Xavier blushed darkly as the crowd sang the birthday song for him.

"I can catch the bus..." James said and Xavier grabbed his wrist.

"No, please, stay," Xavier pleaded. "I'd really like it..."

"But...!"

"Please, for me?" James nodded and Xavier let go. "Oh boy; this is really a surprise!" Xavier said brightly as he entered. James followed behind, shoving his hands into his pockets as Xavier introduced everyone to him. "Russ, this is my mom, my dad, my sister Cora and her husband Peter..." He shut the door behind him.

"Hey," James mumbled and extended a hand, shaking hands to those Xavier named.

"Everybody, this is James, a coworker friend of mine."

"How are you?" exclaimed a robust middle-aged man with a slightly thick accent as he took James's hand and firmly pumped it. "Quite the grip there, eh?"

"Yeah, ouch..." James said and winced. He felt slightly removed as Xavier chatted candidly with relatives. "Heya, Missus Xavier, Cora, Peter..." He gave a slight wave in their direction and followed Xavier toward the dining room table where a cake rest.

"Mom made the cake," Cora said wryly as she pulled out a large knife, "so don't worry about choking on the dryness."

"You guys!" Xavier exclaimed and turned to James. "Care for some triple chocolate cake?"

"Sure, I'll take a slice." James answered. He leaned against the wall, watching Xavier's family chat to him while his sister cut the cake and handed out slices on saucers. The doorbell rang moments later and Cora left the room to answer it.

"Boris," she called, "your girlfriend is here!"

"Goody!" Xavier said brightly. "This'll complete my day!" Cora returned with a young woman who had long dark brown hair and striking gray eyes, wearing a pale yellow form-fitting sweater, tight white jeans, and black calf-high boots. Xavier left his seat and gave her a firm hug, spinning her about the room. James choked on his bite of cake and dropped the plate he held, quickly banging a fist into his chest.

"You all right, Russ?" Xavier asked as he set his girlfriend down on her feet.

"Gloria!" James exclaimed once he caught his breath.

"Oh, hey, James," she said, waving shyly.

"You two *know* each other?" Xavier asked, turning to him.

James quickly marched over and grabbed Xavier by the arm, pulling him aside. "Do you know how *old* she is?" he hissed.

"Yes, seventeen going on eighteen!" Xavier whispered back, rolling his eyes. "I'm only two years older than she is!"

"You're nineteen?" James said, stunned.

"Twenty now," Xavier corrected. "I tested out early." He shrugged. "I wanted a chance to get out into the world early and get my Grenada worked on some more... Office work seemed like the easiest there is."

"I don't believe it...!" James let Xavier go and Xavier joined the others. The doorbell rang again and James's unease intensified as Roxanne came in, holding several bags.

"I brought gifts," she said brightly.

James set his jaw at the sight. "*I don't believe it!*" he thought incredulously. He immediately rose to his feet, knocking back his chair.

Xavier turned around, startled. "What's wrong, Russ?" he asked. "Bathroom's down the hall..."

"I gotta get going," James said. "Do you know where I can use a landline?"

"In the kitchen."

James left for the kitchen and picked up the receiver on the wall then quickly dialed a number. Before he could put the handset to his ear, he paused as Roxanne entered the kitchen.

"James," she said coolly.

"Roxanne," James replied in kind. "What happened to your date?"

Roxanne blushed lightly and turned away. "Oh, him..." she murmured. "I didn't know that you knew."

"It wasn't like you were exactly hiding him."

"He had to work late and Gloria wanted a lift."

James hung the receiver into the cradle when he heard a tinny voice saying 'hello, hello' over the line. "Didn't know she was dating Ecks," murmured James.

"So you work with him at Parsons and Parker?"

"He's a good guy, knows his stuff." James leaned against the wall. "Look, Roxy--"

"I'm not staying long anyway," Roxanne cut in. "The kids are with another sitter and I don't really like the new one."

"Yeah..."

"James--"

"I didn't really expect to see you here," James said quickly. "I'm just kinda shocked, is all."

"Well, Gloria invited me to come with. It's a small world, huh?"

"It's not like I don't want you here but..." James folded his arms across his chest and stared down at the floor. "I'm just... well, you're seeing someone else and..."

Roxanne placed a hand on his elbow. "It's okay," she said softly. "I know you want your freedom, but I'm stuck... I really want to be free too and you know that's never going to happen."

"Well, er..."

"Is the idea of a package deal making you balk?"

James snorted. "Roxy, come on!" he protested.

Roxanne squeezed his arm slightly. "James, I love you," she said softly and James blew a short sigh.

"Roxy, I'd love to talk about it," he said irritably, "but not here, okay?"

"So, what about later tonight?"

"Busy making sure Xavier doesn't kill himself at the rink tonight. How about tomorrow?"

"I have a teacher's association meeting then."

"What about Saturday?"

"I have a date..."

"Oh, right..."

"Sunday then?" Roxanne smiled slightly. "I know you're not the churchgoing type."

"Yeah, lapsed Baptist and all that..."

"All right then, I'll see you." Roxanne left the kitchen and James picked up the phone, dialing the number once more.

"Hello?" a voice said quickly after the first ring.

"Leila, it's me," James answered. "I'm sorry I made you wait almost two hours..."

"It's okay," Leila replied cheerfully. "I bet you had a good reason."

"Well, I'm stuck at Xavier's place. They're throwing him a party and everything!"

"And you didn't invite me?" Leila teased. "You know I love a good party! So, is it *Mioler* or *Breyer*?"

"He's not twenty-one yet, anyway. Let's save that for next year!" Leila giggled. "Anyways, meet us at the *Limelight*, okay? I know I promised to pick you up..."

"I'll be there." About to hang up, James heard Leila's voice call for him. "Hey, James..."

He put the receiver to his ear. "What is it?" he asked.

"I thought I heard Roxanne over there."

"Yeah, about that..."

"James, you ought to let her go. She's too high-maintenance for you!"

"You think so?"

"You're bending over backwards for this girl. I don't know how messed up things are between you two, but if you have to work *that* hard, then maybe she's not a good fit for you."

"Leila, I don't know what to say..."

"We can hang out later and have some fun tonight, if you're not too tired. You know I'll do anything for you, Jamie."

"Yeah, well... Thanks, I suppose." James hung up the line and went to the sink, leaning against the counter. "*Man, that's just too much devotion,*" he thought as he gripped the edge, trying to catch his breath. "*It's not right for me, not good for her...*"

"Hey, Russ!" Xavier called and entered the kitchen with a saucer in hand. "Let's get going! We need to dance off this cake!"

"Yeah," James replied, glancing up, "about the mess I made..."

"Don't worry, I got it."

"Well, I wanna save a slice for Leila."

"Oh, sure thing!" Xavier went through the cupboard, searching for foil and a paper plate.

James straightened as Xavier's father entered the room.

"You're good friends with my son, no?" the older man asked.

"We're okay," answered James. "He's a good guy."

"I was getting concerned. He always had his nose in books; never took up a sport. I was worried he was getting soft."

"Dad," Xavier whined, "I'm right here!"

Xavier's father laughed robustly. "I'm happy for you, Son!" he said gently. "When you brought in your handsome friend here, I was very worried the worst was happening. But then, you brought in that nice girl... you have good taste!"

Xavier laughed out loud and James blushed darkly in response.

"You mean...?" James started and Xavier laughed even harder. James chuckled nervously, wincing when Xavier slapped him on the back, hawing.

"So my fears are nothing but," Xavier's father continued once Xavier left the room. "You make sure he keeps a hold on that yummy creature, yes?"

"Er, I'll try."

"Let's go, Russ!" Xavier called. "I got her piece wrapped up."

"See you now, Boris!" Xavier's father called as James left the kitchen and joined Gloria and her boyfriend at the door. "Have fun with the dancing and shaking your booty!"

Gloria giggled and the three headed outside. "Do you think there's room for me in the back?" she asked as they crossed the yard.

"It's only a coupe," Xavier explained. "You'll have to squeeze in the middle."

James cleared his throat, growing overwhelmed as they returned to Xavier's car and Xavier and Gloria entered first. James came in last, shutting the door. "Tight fit, huh?" he cracked.

"Don't worry," Gloria replied and James's face burned bright scarlet when she patted his knee, "you're not crushing me."

"Good to know," James murmured and turned away, staring out the window as his face grew warmer.

Xavier started the car and pulled out the driveway. "This is really great," he said cheerfully as he drove. "This is the best birthday ever!"

"I didn't know that it was," James murmured.

"I hope you're not embarrassed by what my father said."

"Oh? I'm just a little flattered is all."

Gloria giggled when the flush spread from James's face to his ears. "Well, he *is* very handsome," she interjected.

"I sometimes get hit on by guys," James admitted, "but I don't swing that way."

"There's nothing wrong with that."

"Yeah, Ecks, nothing wrong with that at all…"

CHAPTER TWENTY-ONE

"Tell me something, Ecks," James said as they sat at the table with pizza and sodas, beneath the blasting dance music streaming from a speaker above them. Xavier glanced out at the skating rink and waved at Gloria who waved back before performing a triple axle. Leila zoomed past, spooking her and giggled when she fell. She came back around to lend a hand and Gloria chased after her, laughing.

"Yeah, Russ?" Xavier murmured and sipped his soda.

"You like Gloria a lot, yeah?"

"Yeah, she's so sweet, man. She's foxy to boot and I'm just still in shock that she's into a nerdy guy like me."

"You're no geek, man; you're a helluva smart guy."

"She might like someone different, you know?" Xavier shrugged his shoulders. "I try not to over-think it and enjoy the moment. She might get restless and move on to some handsome fella, so I gotta enjoy what I have now."

"So *are* you going to settle down with her?"

"I'm all for it, but she's not. I know she thinks I don't know, but I don't want to hold her too tight now."

"But if you hold on too loosely, you'll lose your grip."

"Don't get too personal, okay?" Xavier sighed heavily. "So, do you have girl trouble of your own?"

"A little, I guess..." James rolled his eyes. "Roxy wants me to move in with her and settle down. All or nothing it seems like."

"Then why not go after her? She seems nice and well-adjusted!"

"Well, the thing is that she's got two kids. Their daddy got whacked in the war and whatever she told me, and I'm afraid I can't be their new daddy. I'm not a right fit for them."

"Then what about your buddy, Leila?"

"Man, she loves me like a rock. No questions asked, but..."

"She's a bimbo, huh?"

"Ecks, come on!" James grumbled. "She's *not* like that! She's helluva smart like we are, but I don't know if computers turn her on like it does us."

"But didn't she go to Central with you?"

James nodded. "That's how I met her." He blew a wistful sigh. "She's the best person I know. It's just, well... I just feel *bad* cos it feels like I'm just *using* her."

"Well, when she doesn't want it any more, she'll move on." Xavier looked at James over his reading glasses. "Save yourself the guilt."

"I don't know..."

"I've read plenty of relationship books, Russ, and my advice is this: forget Roxy, stop worrying about Leila and get on enjoying life." Xavier pushed up his glasses that threatened to fall off his nose. "We only have one shot at it, you know? So let's get as much out of it as we can."

"I guess you're right..."

"Of *course* I am! So why not find yourself some stranger and live it up like it's your last day here on the planet?"

James glanced at Xavier warily. "Are you *sure* that soda's not spiked?"

Xavier laughed in response.

Moments later, Leila skated up to them. She leaned over the wall and grabbed a slice of pizza that rest on the table between James and Xavier. "This is great," she said between bites. "I haven't done this in a few years!"

"Yeah," James exclaimed, "We were getting stupid at Central chugging beers all night!"

"Hey, Xavier, your pal claims he was king of the disco floor back in high school!"

"Let's see it!" Xavier said brightly.

"Not on the skating rink," James replied, blushing. "I don't do roller disco... it's hazardous for my health if you know what I mean."

Leila and Xavier giggled.

"I thought you could legg with the best of them!" Leila teased.

"When I was still into gymnastics, I could!" James retorted.

"Now you're sounding like an old man," Xavier interjected and Leila laughed harder.

"There's the dance club next door!" Leila said happily. "Let's see you work it, Jamie!"

"Yeah, Jamie!" Xavier chimed in. "It's my birthday! Please?"

"Fine by me," James replied, standing. "Who can resist such a pretty face?" He pulled against Xavier's cheek and they all laughed. "C'mon Leila, I'll need a partner for the Rope Hustle!"

"I don't even know what that is!" Leila squawked.

"I think all that booze we did in Central fried your brain!"

Xavier waved at the rink area. "Let's go, Gloria," he called. "We're going dancing!"

"That's swell!" Gloria called back and skated over.

Xavier pulled at James's sleeve. "You're going to have some deep competition," he said excitedly. "She's a hell of a dancer, Russ!"

James grinned. "We'll see about that!"

James lost himself in the beat of the sound and the flashing of the strobe lights, dancing with Leila for hours between fast and slow songs.

"Man, oh man, Jamie!" Leila said once a slow song came on and she collapsed into his arms. "How do you keep going like that?" He ran a hand through her hair, grinning wolfishly. "Whoo, if I keep this up, I'm going to need a break!"

James chuckled. "If you can't keep up with my dancing, then how will you keep up later tonight?"

"You're so bad," Leila said, giggling.

James raised an eyebrow. "So you're on for tonight?"

"We'll see!"

After the latest song ended, Leila excused herself for the restrooms. Another slow song came on and James stiffened when slender gentle hands wrapped around his waist.

"That was fast," he said, mildly surprised as he unlaced the arms that held him. "Did you change your mind and get a drink instead?" Turning around, James gasped when he faced Gloria instead. "Hey, Gloria!" he cried. "Where's Ecks?"

"He's just taking a break," Gloria murmured as she wrapped her arms around his waist.

James grunted, keeping his arms at his side. "You sure he'll mind me dancing with you?" he asked nervously. "I'm sure you heard all the rumors about me..."

"He's not a jealous guy, James." Gloria placed her head on his chest as she held her hands at his back, pulling him closer.

"Don't hate me if I act... well..." Gloria chuckled when James tentatively placed his hands on her hips and they swayed to the music.

"Why are you afraid to touch me?" Gloria asked.

"No, I'm not at all...!" James swallowed hard. "Hell, as far as I'm concerned, that smoking body of yours was *built* for roaming hands..."

"You're such a sweet talker," Gloria teased. "Keep it up and I might just fall for it!"

"Don't tease me," James moaned.

"I'm not a heartbreaker, promise."

"So you've always noticed..."

"I've seen the way you try to undress me with your eyes."

"If I act on what I'm feeling right now," James said softly, "Ecks will hate me."

"If you act on what you're feeling before my birthday, you might get in trouble!"

"Don't mess around with older men," James murmured in her ear. "You might get hurt."

"I'll keep that in mind." After the song ended, Gloria peeled away, leaving James standing in the middle of the dance floor.

James watched her as she headed back to the table where Leila and Xavier were occupied conversing over drinks.

"*She's gonna be trouble*," James thought as his face burned. "*A hot mess of trouble...*"

Later that night, James stood on the stoop of his apartment with his door ajar. Holding Leila close, he kissed her on the cheek and she pressed against him, relishing his touch.

"I thought it was Ecks's birthday," James murmured and grinned wolfishly as he kept an arm around her waist. "Don't start something you can't finish..."

"I won't be starting anything," Leila teased, "because there won't be anything." James stroked her face and she pulled away, blushing darkly.

"Please?" James pleaded. "You're hurting me here!" He stiffened when Leila groped him.

"Call it a special gift for getting that promotion!" Leila cooed. James groaned when she let go and pressed a finger against his nose. "Now let me get home so I can catch up on my sleep!"

"Spend the night, please," begged James, "please?" Leila peeled off his large hand that held her and kissed the tips of his fingers lightly. "You promised!"

"See you later!" Leila let go and gave a firm whack on James's rear once she slipped out of his grip, then returned to her car parked in the lot.

James waved and went inside his apartment. He shut the door and leaned his forehead against the paneling, letting out a shaky sigh as he clenched his hands.

"Why is it I feel guilty?" James thought. *"The sex is great but I can't get Xavier's words outta my head! I need to forget about Roxy... I'm not the guy she's looking for to settle down with anyway."* He left the door and returned to his bedroom. After peeling out of his coat and clothes, James fell onto the mattress and covered his head with the sheets.

"I'm so disgusting. Leila lets me use her too much and I just let my stupid fool self take advantage!" Turning onto his back, he stared up at the ceiling. *"So, what is this wild bachelor doing this Friday night? James the slime ball would've been back out the door, cruising the South Side for a pick-up. But no, I'm lying in here, fighting the sheets thinking about Leila. I'm sitting here while my stomach's tied up in knots and doing back flips freaking about Roxy's date tomorrow!"*

James turned over on his side and glanced at the clock, noting the time. *"After three in the morning! Maybe my body's trying to tell me something, like bringing me some kind of message from my subconscious... like I'm not nineteen anymore and have to grow the hell up."*

James sat up, gripping the sheets. *"I'm twenty-five... I need to settle down, but to do that; I need to make more money. The question is how to go about it..."* The telephone rang moments later, scattering his thoughts. James picked up the receiver. "Yeah," he grumbled, "it's me."

"Just letting you know I'm home," Leila replied on the other end.

"Take care; good night." Hanging up, James glanced down at his chest that had the insignia of the Signet on the right pectoral.

"*Maybe with this Signet,*" James mused, "*I can make money...*" He sucked in a shallow breath as everything hit him at once. "*I almost forgot--! The gun I took away from that girl - my fingerprints must be all over it, <u>embossed</u> even despite the gloves and crunching it to bits!*"

James groaned and bapped the heels of his hands to his forehead. "*And my stupid fool self just <u>dropped</u> it, left it behind! What was I <u>thinking</u>?*" James got out of bed and walked to his window, staring out from behind the blinds. "*They must have that gun and might be looking for me, right now, this instant! They're out there, probably <u>watching</u> me...*"

Leaving the window, James pulled into a pair of loose-fitting jeans and went out through the back door. Taking a leap, he landed on the roof of the apartment and sat on the edge, looking out at the dark sky sprinkled with stars.

"*I don't know who or what else might be hunting me too,*" wondered James. "*Right after that weird Space Guy gave me the Signet, he vanished and then that other alien attacked me, like some sort of Space Cop... How do they tie into Roxy's little girl acting so weird and being brainwashed and stuff?*"

James lay back, blowing a heavy sigh in the chilly November air. "*How can I even <u>think</u> of a future with Roxy as long as I've got this thing? As far as I'm concerned, I'm a walking <u>target</u>, a potential destructive force to everyone involved... a <u>danger</u> to anyone close to me!*"

CHAPTER TWENTY-TWO

James sat up with a start when bright light shone in his face. Landing with a hard thud, he looked around his surroundings, trying to figure out where he was.

"That's right," James muttered, "I fell asleep out here on the roof..." He glanced around before taking a leap down and returned inside his apartment. "I guess the cold air doesn't bother me since I tend to run *warm*..." James blew a disconcerted sigh. "I need to get away for a while, maybe clear my head somewhere."

Sifting through his drawers, he came across the map and flashlight, remembering that Leila gave it to him and figured he ought to put it to good use. James headed into his closet and pulled out the mysterious uniform that enabled him to fly faster than normal and not worry about ruining his regular clothes.

After changing, James pocketed the map, flashlight, and the handheld device that chirped when he picked it up. Leaving his apartment, James headed for the rear of the complex, searching around for any source of life. Taking a leap skyward, he made a straight shot south.

"And we have takeoff!" James whooped. "Man, I can never get tired of this flying stuff!"

As he flew over various towns, many thoughts swirled in his mind. *"I might as well enjoy this for all it's worth,"* he mulled, *"and use this damn power for everything it's got, cos it's causing me enough grief as it is!"* Catching sight of a beach with no people around, James touched down and surveyed his surroundings. *"Looks like I got a decent beach to myself!"*

James giggled as he stripped down to the nude and ran into the ocean for a swim, taking a dive into the clear blue depths.

"I wish Roxy was here... I just can't get that girl out of my mind! If the Signet's going to stand between me and Roxy, why should I keep the power? I could easily give it to some other poor jerk."

Spotting a whale, James quickly surfaced and treaded water, watching the whale's fin splash the water above him.

"Dude!" a voice cried and James whirled around, spotting a surfer riding a wave several yards away. "Check out those whales, man!" James grinned when he saw more fins appear and several whales splashed as they dove from beneath the water, playfully jumping around James and the surfer who sat on the edge of his board, paddling in the water. "Whoo!"

"I know!" James called back. Turning away, he continued treading water.

"I probably still have my doubts," he mused. *"The old James Russell wouldn't be out in the middle of the Pacific or something playing around with a crazy surfer dude and these hunker whales!"*

Breaking away, James swam back for shore, cresting out of the water. Planting his feet on the soft sands, his face flushed scarlet as he stepped forward, spotting a young woman with long frizzy peroxide blond hair sitting on a towel next to his articles. He shielded his eyes against the glare, noting that she wore a hot pink and black zebra print bikini, rose-colored mirrored aviator-style sunglasses donning her face and had long tapered nails colored hot pink.

"Is this a mirage?" James asked.

"No, it's not warm enough for that," she called and adjusted the large pink hoop earrings she wore.

"So, I'm not dreaming?"

"Sorry, you're not."

James dropped his hands at his side, suddenly realizing where he was. The flush on his face burned hotter when the woman smiled back at him.

"Enjoy the swim?" she replied.

"Er, hand me my shorts, will ya?" James said sheepishly. The young woman grinned as she picked up his boxers and tossed them to him. "So, um, I know this is a strange question," James said once he caught his underwear, "but can you tell me where we are?"

"You're at a beach," the woman answered, smiling as James hurried into his shorts.

"I mean, *what* beach is this...?"

"Why would it matter?" the young woman shrugged. "You won't be able to find it on any map..."

"So is this some kind of *private* beach?"

The blonde chuckled, waving away James. "You know, I haven't heard that 'little boy lost' line in months!"

"Um, well..." James stammered and the flush on his face grew darker as the young woman expressed amusement.

"Relax, it worked!" she said gaily. "So sit down and tell me why you're all disoriented and stuff."

"*Man, she's so forward!*" James thought, sitting next to her on the towel. "*She wouldn't believe it that I really _am_ lost!*"

"So you're here for vacation too?" she pressed and James nodded.

"Just the weekend," he murmured, drawing up his knees.

"I'm here for the winter myself. Oh, by the way, my name's Brandi."

"Heya, Brandi," James greeted and gave his name in return. He lent a hand and she took it, shaking firmly. "*With a grip like that...!*" James noted.

"So what are you escaping from?" Brandi asked.

"A worldwide shipping and receiving company," James replied.

"What do they ship?"

"Gadgets and doodads."

Brandi fell into a fit of giggles. "Well, I don't do a lot," she said. "My father's head of a corporation and that large house with all the glass on the hill is his."

"Is your father here on vacation as well?"

"He's in Madrid right now and I have it to myself until this weekend when he gets back." She touched James on the knee. "Care to join me?"

"Sure, I'd like that." James grinned wolfishly. "Seems it's my lucky day!"

"Why not?" Brandi rose to her feet. "Come on, I'll show you around."

James gathered his clothing and noticed a tattoo on her left thigh. *"What a strange marking,"* he wondered. "Hey," James said, "that tattoo you have there... What is it?"

"Oh!" Brandi blushed and quickly picked up the towel, shaking it out. "It's nothing important," she said and wrapped it around her waist, "just a wash-off."

"Hm..."

James was astonished by all the high-end electronics he found inside the beachfront house. "This is amazing," he said, surprised. "What does your dad do?"

"He dabbles in the occasional sound recording," Brandi replied.

"Oh really?"

Brandi's face flushed scarlet. "Want a sandwich or something?" she said instead.

"Soda's fine." Leaving the parlor, James peeped into other rooms, checking out their interior. Coming into one room that held computer equipment of different brands, James glanced back out into the corridor then entered the room, giving the machines a closer examination. "There's all sort of stuff in here," he murmured, "WCM, Astori, Commandpro... even a Pome!" Spotting a small beige machine, James grinned. "Her dad's got a Shellacker too! What does he do with all this stuff?"

"James?" Brandi called. James quickly stepped out into the hall, bumping into Brandi who held a plate with a sandwich on it. She let out a yelp as the glass she held in hand sloshed the drink, spilling the punch on herself and the floor. "What are you doing in my room?"

"What?" James cried and thrust a thumb back in the direction of the room. "All that computer stuff is *yours*?"

"What!" Brandi scoffed. "You thought I was some dumb blonde, huh?"

"No, never crossed my mind!" James took the sandwich and the glass from hand. "Sorry about that."

"I was going to take a shower anyway..." Brandi smiled and prodded James in the chest with her finger. "I have you know, I'm pretty capable in making machines talk."

"Really?"

"You'll see once I get into something more comfy."

James stared after her wolfishly as she padded into the bathroom. *"How comfy are we talking?"* he thought.

"Oh, by the way," Brandi called and poked her head out the door. "Your clothes are in the wash."

"Thanks!" James called back and headed into the kitchen. He took a seat at the stool in front of the dining table, eating his sandwich in silence and enjoyed the morning surf outside the large bay windows.

James happily talked to Brandi most of the day about computers and programming languages, also in admiration at her skills as a fellow programmer when she showed him her work on a video game she developed.

"I can't believe you made this," James said after he finished testing the program. "This is really awesome."

"I have an idea for a game I've been thinking about," Brandi said, "though I'm afraid the computer processing power isn't up to spec to what I want it to be."

"Well, I'm decent in utilizing memory," James replied and turned his chair around, facing her, "and executing programs with small footprints."

"Do you think you can help me out with this project?"

"Sure. So what's the game about? I love playing and breaking them. That's how I got into programming on the Commandpro. I'd get the magazines with the code in the back and always tried to figure how to make it better!"

"I guess we're on the right track."

James watched Brandi leave the room and grinned. *"She's smart and really hot to boot,"* he thought. *"I can so drop Roxy for this chick..."*

Moments later, Brandi returned with a stack of dot matrix papers and set them down next to the desk. "This is what I have for the game so far," she explained. "Right now, it's titled 'Urban Superhero'."

"Sounds interesting..." James nodded thoughtfully. "Go on."

"This game is about a guy or gal who wakes up from having nightmares about being experimented on. They find out that they have at least one super power and spooky agents are knocking on their door, so they'll have to keep the agents away and use the power to their best advantage."

"Sounds like a game I'll play." James crossed his legs in the chair and cupped his chin in hand, watching Brandi talk animatedly while she paced.

"I have ideas for letting the player choose who they want to be... like choosing your gender which has certain advantages and disadvantages, like speed and strength."

James nodded. "That's different," he murmured.

"Then a starting power," Brandi went on, "and making decisions, either good or evil, that will determine which power is opened to you as you progress."

"I can help with that."

Brandi paused in her pacing and turned to James, surprised. "How?"

"Well, I've seen your graphic designs and they're really good... on a Commandpro no less! I'll help with programming and story since I had ideas of a superhero game of my own."

Brandi folded her arms across her chest and grinned brightly with heightened interest. "Let's hear it."

"Well, this Joe gets approached by aliens and he's got strange fire-like powers. Right now, I'm struck cos Joe has no clue on what to do next."

"So your Joe is stuck with devastating powers and he's busy walking around crying about it?" Brandi let out a robust laugh. "Well, Mister, I see a hole in the story right there!"

"And what's that?" James crossed his arms, pouting slightly. *"I can't help it if I have no clue what to do with this damn thing,"* he thought irritably.

"Joe wants to be a hero, right? So have him look in the newspapers for potential crimes that haven't been solved."

"What about newscasts?" James asked.

"That too; he's gotta develop his rep somehow!"

"What kind of jobs you think he can handle?"

"It's random whether the job he chooses has a high difficulty. So he's gotta be smart and able to shift abilities depending on the situation. He might have to get ingenious if say, he happens on a bank robber with ice powers that can easily burn him out."

James snapped his fingers as he leaned back in his chair. "I like your way of thinking already!"

"So my thought is while he's building a reputation and respect as he's fighting small local crimes, the agents are watching him, getting information and hoping to use them for their own ends..."

"Like an intergalactic war?"

Brandi clapped her hands, pleasantly surprised. "That's so cool!" she said cheerfully. "Having Joe involved in an intergalactic war would *really* test his skills! That way, he can see if he's truly worthy of keeping the power."

"Tell me about it!"

CHAPTER TWENTY-THREE

After talking most of the night over coffee and writing notes, James retired to the master bedroom while Brandi stayed up, programming on the computer. He woke up feeling warmth next to him and turned over, glancing at the clock.

"*It's later in the afternoon,*" James thought, sitting up. "*She's now getting to bed?*" Stepping out of bed, James grabbed his pants draped on the back of a chair and pulled into them, then slipped into his boots that rest nearby. He walked down the hall and stepped into the next room that had a soft hum emitting from it. "*Huh, she left a computer running.*"

Entering the room, James examined the floppy disks left lying about and picked up one that had a label titled 'test'. He put it into the computer and typed the text it needed to run the program's boot sequence.

"*It's her 'Urban Superhero' game,*" James noted. "*Let's see what she has so far...*" He grew disturbed after playing a new game, sensing having recognized some of the events in the program. After finishing the level, James removed the diskette and turned off the computer. "*Have they run into her too?*" He sighed heavily as he left the chair. "*I have to find out!*"

Returning to the bedroom, James searched his pockets for the device and paused when he realized it wasn't there. "That's right," he muttered, "she washed my clothes!" James left the room, searching for where it would be. Hearing a chirp, he whirled around, trying to locate it. "Come on... beep again." Hearing the noise once more, James rushed for the sound and found the GEARS unit resting on the kitchen counter. He then opened it, washed by the glow of the screen in green text.

SECONDARY SIGNET IN RANGE

"Which Signet is it?" James growled, punching buttons.

"James?" Brandi called.

James pocketed the device and returned to the bedroom. "Yeah?" he said and leaned against the doorway. "Why are all the curtains shut in this place?"

"I'm a vampire," Brandi joked. "I work all night and sleep all day. Also, sunlight just kills my beauty sleep." James chuckled and approached the edge of the bed, plopping down. "What's the matter...? You don't look too happy."

"Well, I've got a lot on my mind, is all," he murmured and glanced up at Brandi who smiled faintly in return, running a hand through her hair. *"You haven't touched me at all last night,"* James thought. *"I think I know why..."*

"What do you have on your mind that's weighing you down?" Brandi asked.

James leaned closer and Brandi gasped, pulling away. "But you like me," he said softly, "... don't you?"

"Yeah, I do," answered Brandi. "It's so unreal... almost like it was too much to hope for."

"I'm over her, if that's what you're worried about."

"Not just that..."

"Then what is it?" James took Brandi's chin in hand before she could protest more and kissed her deeply, only to get a mild shock in return. Suddenly James felt as if an external force drained the breath from his body and the world around him fell at his feet.

"James...?" Brandi's worried voice called from afar. "James!"

"What...?" Opening his eyes, James found Brandi standing over him in the brightly lit room.

"Are you okay?" she asked.

"Yeah, I'm fine..." James sat up, holding his head. "What happened?"

"You passed out, is all," Brandi said nervously. "Maybe you ought to eat something before you go."

"I'm craving orange soda."

"I'll get it."

"Why would I pass out like that?" James wondered as he watched her leave the room. *"It's probably related to that weird tattoo she's got... I wonder if she's got a Signet too."* Brandi returned with a frosted glass of orange soda. *"If that's the case, why didn't I have a reaction as quick as I did when I touched that cute redheaded girl...?"*

"Here you go," Brandi said brightly, handing him the glass.

"Thanks," James said gratefully.

"Are you sure you're all right?"

"Just a little out of it," he murmured and took the drink in hand. "You know, with someone as foxy as you are, why aren't you having guys lined up outside your door panting and wishing they'd be in your bed?"

"Because I'm like uranium," Brandi drawled, grinning. "They never come back."

"Nah, you're not like that."

"So you want to do anything later today?"

"Oh, you really don't want to know what I have planned."

Brandi's face flushed in response. "I don't know if I can accommodate you," she murmured.

"I have to get going soon anyway." James downed the drink and handed her the glass. "Thanks for letting me hang out with you."

"Look me up sometime, okay?" Brandi took the glass.

"Do you live around here?"

"No, I'm from Newport Beach."

"Okay, Brandi from Newport Beach…"

"Brandi Hyatt, and that's Brandi with an 'I' at the end."

"Got it."

Brandi left the room and James got up from the floor, fishing for the remainder of his clothing.

"*I wonder if I can easily 'get over' Roxy*," he thought as he dressed. "*I do want to be with someone, I admit to that, but I don't know who to choose.*" Approaching the sliding door in the parlor, he glanced back at Brandi in the kitchen, cooking. "*I have to make a choice. Why does it have to be so hard?*"

James sighed and he slipped outside, walking around to the side of the house.

"Jim, you're a hopeless romantic!" he grumbled under his breath.

Overlooking the beach, he spotted surfers out on the water. They appeared to be only the ones out there for the day, and too far away to see someone take off in flight. Looking toward the heavens, James took a leap and bulleted skyward, heading for home.

"I need to do <u>something</u> with this power," he mused. *"I was given this thing for a <u>reason</u>, and I'm not giving it up. I <u>will</u> show those folks that I <u>am</u> made of tough stuff, of the right stuff, and <u>nothing</u> is going to stand in my way! First thing, I'll tell Roxanne..."*

Arriving back at his apartment, James picked up the newspaper left on his porch step and entered, heading into his kitchen. He tossed the paper aside on the table and opened the refrigerator, taking out a can of soda. Popping the tab, he took a long drink then set it next to the paper, set on searching for suitable clothing to change into. Entering his bedroom, he struck the answering machine on his nightstand, listening to messages as he browsed through his closet.

"James, it's me," Roxanne's voice said on the tape. "I know I promised to call Sunday, but I have a church function that's going to be late tonight. Someone invited me."

"Well, that's unusual," James contemplated, *"for her to be busy on Sunday for a change... I'll probably stop by and check*

what's up." The machine beeped and another voice came through the system's speakers.

"Hey, Russ," Xavier's voice said. "I'm just ringing you up to tell you thanks for the awesome party. You're not a bad fella to hang with. Let's hang out again sometime, okay?"

James grunted when he found nothing fitting to wear. "I need something for nighttime crime-fighting," he muttered. "If I'm gonna be this hack wannabe superhero, I can't be found running around at night. Last thing I need is the cops on my butt!" The device in his pocket chirped and James took it out, glancing at it.

TEKNICS NEEDED

"What the hell is *that,*" James growled, "you stupid machine?" The screen changed, showing more data.

TEKNICS
[Tactical Equipment Kernel Network: Immaterial Creation System]:
A SET OF INTERCHANGEABLE CARDS GIVING THE TEK DEK VARIOUS ABILITIES TO AUGMENT THE TEK JACKET AND FORCE HELMET.

"TEK Jacket and Force Helmet... is that what I found?"

Hearing his doorbell ring, James set the small machine aside and hurried to the door to answer it. Upon opening, he found a delivery carrier on his porch, holding a box.

"Delivery for James Russell," the carrier murmured.

"Delivery on a *Sunday*…?" James said, surprised. "Aren't you guys usually watching the game or something?"

"*Delivery Express* delivers any time day or night," the carrier answered, "and any day of the week."

"Do I have to sign for it?" James asked, raising an eyebrow.

"Yeah, gotta sign."

"Next you'll be asking for a thumbprint too!" James griped and frowned when the carrier passed a clipboard to him. He scribbled his name on the paper with an attached pen on a chain.

"Have a nice day," the carrier said politely then handed over a small box.

"Get outta here," James grumbled as he snatched the box away.

"Whatever, you jive-ass turkey!" the carrier groused and stomped down the steps.

James grunted and kicked the door shut. "I don't remember ordering anything…" He murmured and glanced at the box, searching for a return address. "There isn't any…" Opening the box, James found several metallic diskettes within a gold case, labeled 'cards'. "Now what's this?" Returning to the parlor, James picked up the small machine that beeped loudly and a small hatch in the back opened. "Huh, it takes these weird cards or something?"

Placing a disk marked with a diagram of a pentagram circled in blue into the hatch, violet electricity emanated from the machine as a high whine resonated. James cried out when the light surrounded his wrist and the violet electricity turned to gold. The suit and boots he wore changed from red and black to completely black. James approached his bedroom mirror and grinned.

"Awesome," he said to his reflection and pocketed the small hand-held computer. A belt appeared around his waist with a small hard case that held the stout diskettes in place and a harness materialized around his thigh that held the compact hand-held computer. "Now we're talking!" Leaving his mirror, James headed into the kitchen and took apart his newspaper, reading the articles.

CHAPTER TWENTY-FOUR

After pouring over the classified section, James came across one that caught his eye.

"Ah-ha!" he muttered to himself. "Now *this* looks interesting... 'Flying Man, I grow weary waiting for your appearance. Meet me tonight the same place as before. Cooperate and you will be rewarded handsomely. Fail to do so and the blood of innocent lives will be on your hands. The choice is yours.' Nice..." James chuckled to himself. "Well, isn't *that* cute, those spy friends of mine are *looking* for me... They're probably behind the little package that got sent here - It's just too convenient!"

James put the paper aside and headed for his bedroom, searching for a mask to put on. After rummaging through the drawers, he then sifted through his closets for a ski mask and the red helmet with a black visor rolled out of the closet.

"This thing...!" he thought, mildly surprised, *"I almost forgot I picked it up that day when I found the suit!"* Putting it on his head, the helmet fit loosely. *"This thing is two sizes too big!"*

Bright gold light flashed and the helmet shrunk down, fitting him perfectly. A slight buzz of violet electricity surrounded the helmet and it too changed to all black. Flipping up the visor, James grinned at his reflection as he passed the mirror.

"Now we're in business," he said triumphantly. Flipping it back down, James bounded out his back door, taking to the sky.

"They must know who I am in part, having sent that package," James considered as he flew to the intended destination. *"But the article said 'Flying Man', so it might mean they might not know who I am* exactly, *so there might still be time for me to make the offensive."*

Flying over a quiet neighborhood, James slowed when he spotted Gloria walking home. *"Roxy must be home tonight, might as well check in on her."* Touching down near Roxanne's home, James came around the side of the house. *"It's not even midnight, so if Roxy's home this early, then that must mean her church thing didn't go so hot."* Taking a small leap, he levitated in the air and floated up for her bedroom window. *"Can't help myself... gotta see if she's really alone."*

Peering into her bedroom window, James flipped up his visor to better see inside and found the bed empty. Touching down, he stepped carefully to the parlor window. Catching sight of Roxanne speaking to a young man in soft tones, James swallowed hard when he watched them exchange kisses.

"Oh man, they're on the couch--!" James clenched his teeth. *"Kissing... making out?!"*

"Ouch, you're hurting me," Roxanne suddenly cried.

James clutched his hand into a tight fist that flashed dimly in orange light as the two sank into the couch cushions. *"That jerk's hurting her!"* he thought, clenching his teeth.

"Not so rough, Darryl," Roxanne complained.

"Sorry, my dear," answered Roxanne's date. "Is that better?" Roxanne giggled and James turned away, wheezing for breath.

"What the hell's wrong with me?" he admonished himself. *"What am I doing here? I've gotta get outta here... can't stand this crap!"* James flipped down his visor and ran away from the home before taking a bounding leap for the sky. *"Roxy found someone else, so I know where she stands with me now."* James bulleted forward, with steadily increasing speed as he flew for his intended mark. *"There's no use in telling her my secret. She'd probably think I was nuts. Anyway, enough about her, I've business to take care of! They said 'the same place as before', so the meeting place must be the slag dump off Industrial Street..."*

Flying overhead at his target destination, James reduced his speed, easily spotting a stout compact car parked under a street lamp that had several reserve fighters nearby in the immediate distance.

"For spies, these guys aren't that bright, using the same setup as before," James mused. *"They'll need more imagination than that. Last time, I was curious to find out how they found me and how much they knew, so I talked to them like some kind of idiot and let that girl get a good look*

at me, not to mention my fingerprints on her gun." Touching down several yards away out of sight, James crouched low to observe them. "*I'll wait until they get tired of hanging around for me to show up and follow them to their lair...*"

After several hours, the reserve fighters left their spot and headed back into the car with the woman who slept behind the wheel. Upon awakening, she started the vehicle and James took flight, flying over them. Later after several miles of trailing them, he noticed they headed toward a college dormitory.

"*Huh, we're in Midtown,*" James considered as the car parked into the lot. "*So these guys go to school here at Petoria University...*" He followed them, watching the group file into student residence. James then flew around the building, spotting one of the rooms lighting up and peered into the window, finding several young adults speaking to each other.

"*Wish I could understand what they're saying... They don't look like they're from around here, not even from any other country. Something's just off, just like that cute girl driver...*" James blew a heavy sigh. "*I know they're not talking about a field trip to the Botanical Gardens!*"

Watching the students approach a desk where many papers lay scattered, James blew a hard sigh, feeling at a loss on what to do next.

"*Now what, Jim?*" he wondered, "*Break in there and bust their butts? What would that accomplish besides giving me some satisfaction?*" James gasped when several more young men entered, carrying a heavy trunk. Setting it on the floor, they opened it, revealing high-powered weaponry. "*Holy -!*

These kids aren't playing around! Those guns might not be worth beans against me, but I'll need another idea..."

Leaving the window, James came around to rear where they left the car parked and tore open the trunk, revealing more weaponry inside.

"Jackpot!" James whooped. Making note of the license plates, he hurried for the public telephone across the street and made a call.

"Dispatch," said the operator.

"Yeah, I'm here at the university in Midtown," James said. "I think we got some terrorists here posing as college students..."

James took off his helmet and joined the curious crowd who gathered outside the school while police officers carted away the suspects into a large holding van.

"What happened?" James asked to no one in particular.

"I heard that the cops got an anonymous call about a car full of guns," replied one bystander.

"I heard they had to get a warrant to search the house first," said a second.

"I heard they just swooped in and raided the place, finding all sorts of bombs and guns and stuff!"

"Yeah, the cops said they're these really dangerous terrorists and they're gonna be questioning everybody about them!"

"So," James said, "what about these terrorists?"

"Nobody knows who they are..."

James walked away and when far enough, he put on his helmet then took flight.

"That worked out pretty well," he thought, grinning. *"With any luck, I'll get to find out, along with the rest of the world, who these strange so-called terrorists are!"*

A loud beep interrupted his thoughts and James searched around as another chime assaulted his ears, louder and higher in pitch than before.

"What the--?" He instinctively clamped his hands over his ears as the loud whine forced him out of the sky. *"What's with this noise?! How can I make it stop?"* Falling fast, James yanked against his helmet that suddenly became stuck. *"Come on; come off before I die out here!"*

"Entering battle mode," a mechanical voice said in James's ears. The gloves, boots, and suit he wore turned metallic and a sudden blast in the chest propelled him backwards.

"What the--?!" James squawked as he tumbled head over heels, slamming into a building below. Looking up, he spotted several fighters in similar suits and helmets like those he wore, though wielding large rifles.

"Tell us," a voice snarled in James's head amid static, "friend or foe!"

"What?" James cried. *"Does this thing have a receiver and transmitter?"* he thought wildly.

"I repeat," grumbled the voice, "friend or foe?"

"I'm neutral!" James yelled as he struggled to get out of the debris containing him. "Why? Who wants to know?"

"You are wearing Federation armor and must be of the Resistance; therefore you must die!"

"No way!" James wailed. Finally working free, he thrust forward a hand that blazed brightly in red flames. "You want a fight, I'll give you one!"

"Death to the Resistance!"

The radio transmission cut off and the fighters immediately fired their weapons. James flared in bright orange light and released a fireball from hand, striking one directly. The force of the incinerating blow knocked his opponent out of the sky. He quickly dodged return fire and bulleted ahead.

"I need to get them out of city limits," James thought. *"This won't be easy, fighting in the dark like this..."*

Several more fighters appeared before him with plasma swords drawn and James came to a halt, kicking one back to use as a springboard, flying up over them.

"What the hell?!" he yelped. "I can't contend with that!"

James quickly dodged and turned out as the three fighters caught up with him. He darted away, avoiding their swords that hummed and burned when they made contact.

Grabbing one by the sleeve, he slammed the fighter into the other, knocking him away, only to get smashed over the helmet by the third with his plasma blade, cracking it. James gasped for breath and kicked the fighter back, releasing another flaming sphere to quell him.

"If they keep this up," he thought as he rocketed for the stratosphere, *"I'm a dead man!"* James glanced back, spotting the four fighters coming directly behind him. *"Come on, follow me... I think I got a trick that might stop you!"* Reaching the highest point where ice began to form on his suit and helmet,

James pushed himself until his breath began to thin and the world around him flashed in red. *"Just a little more...."*

Coming to a dead stop, James watched the other fighters move on before snapping back completely covered in ice and falling back down to earth. He flew after them, yanking out a plasma sword that burned out from one of the frigid fighter's frozen hand and jammed it into a secondary combatant that appeared on his side, impaling him in the chest.

"You leave me alone," James screamed, "got it?" He grabbed his enemy by the throat and hurled him as far as his enhanced strength could take him. Descending fast, James struck earth hard in the middle of a field, spent and aching.

Hearing boots crunch across dead vegetation, James spotted a tall warrior wearing a similar suit he had, dressed in brown with a blue stripe down the side of the arms and legs and wearing blue gloves and boots. The helmet, brown with a blue visor, reflected James's image back at him as he looked up.

"Come here to finish me off?" groaned James. "Look, just lay off the flying man, okay? I'm not powerful enough for you guys. Just lay off the spies and the lackeys... I'm no good at this."

"You did fine work," said the mysterious masked fighter. "I'm surprised, by the little in which you neither know nor understand..."

"Wait," James said, sitting up, "are *you* the one who sent me those weird card-disk thingies?"

"You will need to utilize the power of the TEK DEK effectively in order to defeat your enemies, which are numerous."

"It didn't exactly come with an instruction manual!"

"The instructions are inside your helmet."

"Okay, what...?" A loud chirp came from nearby and the mysterious stranger unclipped his box on his thigh, withdrawing the compact computer called the TEK DEK. He sifted through his belt and took out a card.

"The TEK DEK or Tactical Equipment Key Data Engine Kernel is a powerful addition to this GEARS - the Genetically Enhanced Armament Restructuring System," the mysterious fighter explained. "The Signet you were given is the most powerful, destructive weapon we have. I need you to use it wisely and use it well. It is the only defense we have against the Directorate."

"Wait, you mean you're related to that Space Guy I first met?" James shook his fist at him. "You know he's dead, man! Those assassins got to him, so how do you think I can fight them; how is that even possible?"

"I don't have time to explain..."

"Why give me something so dangerous that these people are willing to *kill* me over it?" James yelled. "Look, man, you've got the wrong guy!"

"If you wish to rid of this power, then find me and defeat me in honorable combat. Otherwise, The Directorate will erase you permanently."

The mysterious fighter flipped the hatch of the TEK DEK with his thumb, slid out the old card and dropped in a new one, forcing the machine glowing in copper light.

"Wait! You've got a lot of explaining to do, buster!"

"Like I said, I don't have much time..."

The gold light surrounded the mysterious fighter's body and large blue steel chain appeared looped in the fighter's hand that had a hooked blade on the end. The fighter held the heavy handle of the chain in his free hand and the chain glimmered in violet light. With a leap, the stranger took off skyward, disappearing into the dark expanse of sky.

"The Directorate, huh?" James grumbled as he got to his feet and heard more explosions in the distance. "He's probably cleaning up the others to keep me alive... There's no way I'm flying back home with a cracked helmet like this." James started the long walk back to his apartment. "At least it's a ten-mile walk... I think..."

Coming through the front door, James kicked it shut then pulled out of his cracked helmet and set it aside on the end table next to the couch. Stripping out of his clothing, he entered the bedroom and checked his answering machine along the way, only to find it indicated no messages.

Yawning as he padded into the parlor, James switched on the television and sat on the floor in his socks and underwear, watching the morning news cast. James turned up the volume as the reporter came on the screen and began speaking.

"... KSTL News has learned that the Petoria University students arrested early this morning at their residence in

Midtown are members of a radical and extreme terrorist organization, simply known as 'The Directorate'. Police say that an anonymous caller gave them the tip that led them to the largest cache of illegal and highly-powerful weapons ever found in Missoula..."

"This is wonderful stuff!" James said happily, switching off the television. "Now back to Regular Jim, the office guy..." He left the room and changed his clothes for the day.

CHAPTER TWENTY-FIVE

After finishing filing for the first half of the day, James left his cubicle and caught Xavier taking his sport coat as he left his desk.

"Hey," James called, "are you catching lunch for the office?"

Xavier paused and turned to James, grinning. "Sure," he replied. "Want to come with me?"

"Why do you do this?"

"Gives me exercise." Xavier shrugged. "Also, it gives poor Reinhold a break."

"Yeah," Reinhold called from the rear of the office. "About damn time!"

James chuckled and followed Xavier out into the corridor.

"James," another voice called, "what are you doing?"

"Crap, it's Mister D'Arcy," James groused under his breath and turned about-face. A thin middle-aged man with thinning hair and glasses who wore a dark baggy suit that almost swallowed his slight frame approached James.

"I need to speak to you for a moment," said D'arcy upon approach.

"Go on without me," James said to Xavier. His coworker nodded and headed out the front doors alone.

"I'm glad to have caught you before you sneaked out," D'Arcy grumbled. "The manager wants to see you in his office immediately."

"What the hell?" James spat and walked reluctantly behind D'Arcy "It's bad enough I got the office supervisor on my butt, but the office *manager* on top of it?" Entering the large office, he faced a hefty bald man wearing a suit that fit him poorly, smoking a cigar.

"Here's the man you requested, Mister Vashon," D'Arcy announced.

"Yeah, whatever," grunted Vashon, puffing smoke through his nose. "Get outta here, D'Arcy." D'Arcy scoffed and stormed away, slamming the door behind him. Vashon waved at James. "Come right in, Ritter."

"It's Russell, Sir," James murmured and approached the chair on the other side of the oak desk in which Vashon sat behind. "You wanted to see me?"

"Whatever," Vashon snapped. "Reinhold told me you're a good guy and that you work hard. You know I care a lot about that."

"Yeah, so...?" James clutched the back of the chair.

"I'm thinking of giving you a shot a sales, you know, have a chance to make some *real* money. What do you say?"

James stepped back in shock. "W-what?" he stammered. "Did I hear you right?"

"So you want the position or not?"

James clenched his teeth, stunned. *"Sales? He wants me in the <u>sales</u> division?"* he wondered. *"That's barely moving up a notch on the totem pole!"* James shoved his hands into his slacks pockets. "I thought you'd give me a job in Securities," he said softly.

"That's just a one time deal," Vashon grumbled. "It took three guys to patch that leak. Maybe if you did it yourself,,."

"I'm better than this!" James thought angrily as he clenched his hands. "What does Mister Carellis think of this?" he asked timidly. "I'm good enough to be in the Securities Division!"

"Carellis thinks you're going places, that's why he recommended the Sales position."

"Is Carellis out of his mind?" James yelled in his head. *"I've got no choice... Carellis can hire or fire anybody in that pool and he's my only chance for recommendation!"* James sighed heavily. "Sure," he said dejectedly. "I'd like the sales position, Mister Vashon. Thanks for being so generous."

"Smart boy," Vashon said, chuckling. "Yeah, come Monday, you're moving down the hall to the glass corridor!"

"Thanks," James said while giving a fake smile and walked out of the manager's office stiffly. After shutting the door behind him, he shuddered. "Ugh, that lard butt gives me the creeps," he muttered and stomped down the hall. "Vashon has no idea *how* computers work, let alone knows how to *use* one... Probably only knows how to turn it on and off!"

Entering the office, James approached the lanky young man with a sandy mullet and pale brown eyes in an ill-fitting suit that hung off his slender frame, typing labels on an electric typewriter. "Hey Reinhold," James called and waved as he approached the young man's cubicle. "A minute, will ya?"

"Sure," Reinhold said as he finished typing then glanced up. "What's going on?"

"I didn't interrupt you, did I?"

Reinhold chuckled. "Nah," he said and pushed away from his desk. Leaning back in his chair, Reinhold placed his hands behind his head. "I'm just doing my usual."

"Did you tell the boss about my work?" James asked and sat on the edge of Reinhold's desk.

"Yeah, and Carellis also. Why?" Reinhold shrugged. "Just wanted to give you a leg up outta this dump," he explained. "I see you come in everyday, tired, not wanting to be here. You leave here, tired, not wanting to be here. It's on your face, Russell. This place is grinding you down."

"It gets my bills paid."

"But don't you have dreams?"

"A little..."

"So get outta here and get on the ball!"

"Well, I didn't fare any better. Vashon has me in the Sales Division now."

"Which side?"

"He didn't say..."

"You'll probably be with Shellacker. They need more guys."

"Shellacker Corporation...? You really think so?"

"Shellacker's the new shit, man. They'll be onto something. Have you seen their specs?"

James grinned. "Yeah, you got a point."

"Look, if you make a thousand sales, you get one of their computers free to take home." Reinhold nodded. "You'll work your ass off to offset the cost, but it's a sweet deal."

"Huh, never had a Shellacker before..."

"Just trying to help."

"Thanks for caring so much."

"It's a step up. Keep putting your hand into jobs that'll get you noticed and you'll finally be free from here!"

"That's if I get any news from around the water cooler."

"Look, Russell." Reinhold leaned forward. "I make peanuts here cos I know I don't have the mad skills like you got. The only thing I got going for me is being a damn pencil pusher!"

"Yeah, it's a step up from being a gofer like Simmons."

"I just know what's hot from what folks are putting their jack down on." Reinhold leaned back and folded his arms across his chest, grinning. "Those other computers are kicking around for a while, you know? They're gonna be better than the microcomputers we have now."

"How would you know?" James said incredulously and scoffed. "You can't be that much older than me!"

"By five years, man," Reinhold said and rolled his eyes. "That's old enough!"

"So what are you trying to say?"

"So if you can write stuff to make them run, you'll be rich!"

"You think so?"

"You can't do it stuck in this joint, Russell."

"Thanks." James shook his head. "I never thought you'd have something so profound to say."

"Hey, I make *acting* stupid look like an art form." Reinhold chortled. "Remember if you just smile and nod a lot and don't open your mouth, folks *think* you're smarter than what you *really* are!" James chuckled as Reinhold got to his feet and stretched. "But speak up for yourself, Russell! You can go farther than me." He tapped James lightly on the chest. "Hell, I'll probably still be here in my sixties, still typing and filing and not much else!"

"I'll keep that in mind."

"Well, if you get sick of the place, there's always a Parsons and Parker's rival, Dunn, Knoh, and Nutten."

"That's if I don't kill myself first."

Reinhold grinned. "Now you're too smart for that!" He gestured with his thumb toward the door. "I'll be back... Just gonna let the kids off in the pool."

James nodded and slipped off the desk as Reinhold left the cubicle. He felt ill as he returned to his own cubicle and withdrew the copy paper box he had under his desk.

"Why is it I don't feel any better?" James thought as he started the task of depositing the contents of his desk inside. *"Why is it...?"* As he sorted, he heard a transistor radio turn on and muffled voices coming from a slight field of static.

"Hey, you guys," Simmons suddenly called, "There's been an escalator collapse at the Memorial Center!"

"For reals?" Mitchell called back, aghast.

James listened to the reporter over the air as Simmons turned up the small radio he had on his desk. "You know what," he said and put the box aside, "I've gotta step out a minute..."

"To where?" Simmons asked as James passed his desk.

"Where you're not going to be!" James spat and headed out the office, bumping into Xavier who held several bags of freshly cooked food. "Hey," he said, mildly surprised.

"I heard Reinhold tried to get you out of this crummy job," Xavier said, smiling as Reinhold exited the nearby restrooms and returned for the office.

"Yeah, he's been here long enough," James cracked.

"Hey!" Reinhold squawked, glaring back at James. "You callin' me old, man?"

James put up his hands in mock surrender. "You said it, not me."

"Kick rocks!"

"Pound sand!" James shot back, grinning.

"Screw you, man!" James chuckled and crossed his arms as the other coworkers clustered around Simmons's desk teased Reinhold when he entered the clerical pool. "Stop hassling me!" Reinhold snapped.

"We can't help it, old man," Mitchell teased. "You're ancient compared to us!"

"I'll show you how old I am when I'm kicking your ass!"

Xavier smiled and shook his head. "What a bunch of yahoos," he said and James chortled. Xavier then pushed up the navy reading glasses on his face with a finger. "Wouldn't it be nice to get a good job where you wouldn't have to get your hands dirty?" he asked.

"Er, yeah..." James answered, shrugging his shoulders.

"Reinhold said that someday you might wanna settle down or something, but you have to move up in the world, you know?"

"I know; I want to amount to something."

"Then don't stay here to do it."

"What about Dunn, Knoh, and Nutten?"

"I doubt they're any better!"

James felt at a loss for words as Xavier walked past him and approached Reinhold's desk, placing a sack directly before him.

"What's this?" demanded Reinhold.

"Remember Reinhold," Xavier said seriously. "This is what a *real* lunch looks like!"

The other men in the office laughed as Reinhold's face reddened.

"Guys, stop picking on me!" Reinhold complained. "You all suck major!"

"Oh, what do you know about that?" Adnan piped up and Xavier suddenly let out a hearty laugh.

"Argh, you guys are so dirty!" Reinhold fussed and struck the side of his desk with his fist. "Get outta my face, Xavier, before I break it!"

James shook his head and he headed for the elevators. "*Everyone's giving me advice*," he mused as he walked down the corridor. "*Am I really wearing my disdain of this place on my face?*" Approaching the elevators, once the doors opened, James struck the button for the top floor and stepped in, waiting as the doors hushed close.

Moments later, the cable car stopped on the next floor. The doors opened, revealing a young woman with long dark hair pulled up into a bun. James's gaze lingered on her body, noting the pale blue blouse, navy skirt with matching pumps and blazer that hugged her body.

"Good afternoon," the woman said politely.

James nodded, unable to vocalize. *"Dangerous curves,"* he thought, staring at her reflection through the mirrored doors. *"Slippery when wet, I bet..."*

James clenched his teeth and glanced away as his face burned. He shifted on his feet uncomfortably, growing overwhelmed by the woman's proximity and her flowery perfume. Once they reached the top floor and they both stepped off, James eyed her carefully, falling several paces behind while they walked in the corridors. He breathed a sigh of relief when she stepped into an office and he headed for the stairwell that led to the roof.

Pulling out the TEK DEK from his pocket, it chirped and displayed data scrolling on the screen.

INCOMPATIBLE SIGNET IN VICINITY

"What the--?!" James yelped when he read the text, and then did a double take on the message. He heard the door open and whirled around, spotting the young woman stepping out. She let out a cry in surprise and quickly stepped back. "Hold on--!"

James quickly grabbed hold of the door, flinging it open and took her by the arm, only to get a spark between them. Pulling away, he sucked in a pained breath when his hand burned.

"She's got a Signet too!" James thought as the mysterious woman pushed him aside and hurried down the steps. He raced after her, reaching the lower level stairwell. Getting to the door

in the downstairs hall, he pushed open the exit and searched the corridor, finding no trace.

"Tell me where she is!" James growled and glanced down at the TEK DEK's screen. It highlighted a vector map of the building's corridors with a dark blue dot moving down and James signified as a red dot. "She's taking the stairs..."

Bursting through the stairwell door, James took a leap off the banister, soaring downwards. The TEK DEK chirped and James grabbed the railing to hop over and charged up the steps as the woman came down. She let out a cry in surprise and pushed James away, throwing him against the wall.

"Wait, Lady!" James wheezed and the woman backed away up the steps in fright.

"Just leave me alone!" the woman cried.

James grasped for her arm again and reversed her, only to have his hand burn in response. He immediately let go, sucking in a pained breath through his teeth as he clenched his singed hand. "Why did you run?" demanded James.

"Why are you chasing after me?" retorted the woman.

"Why are you here?"

"I should ask you the same!" The woman pushed past James, slamming him into the wall. "Just back off!"

"Who gave you that Signet?" James hissed, glaring down at her.

"None of your business!"

"You can't save people with that ability, whatever it is..."

"You probably can't do any better!"

"Don't follow me!"

"I have no reason to!" The woman pushed James aside and stormed out the stairwell.

James sank to the floor, exhausted. He glanced at the TEK DEK he clutched and found a profile on the screen.

SIGNET NAME: TERROSA (IN USE)

SIGNET PRIMARY ELEMENT: EARTH

SIGNET BASIC ABILITIES:

RADAR

AWARENESS

BASE STRENGTH X2

BARRIER

GEARS: INACTIVE

MOLECULAR STRUCTURE: HUMAN

DEFAULT MELEE WEAPON: NONE

DEFAULT PROJECTILE WEAPON: NONE

DEFAULT AUXILIARY WEAPON: NONE

TEK DEK: ACTIVE

TEKNICS LOADED: METAL ARMOR (INACTIVE)

ALIGNMENT: NEUTRAL (RESISTANCE FORCES PENDING)

"Those aliens recruited her?" James wondered, stunned. *"I need to get on the ball with this; it's more serious than I thought!"* He blew a hard sigh and rose to his feet, pocketing the hand-held microcomputer. *"She probably freaked out on me because those Space Cops probably tried to get her like they did me... I need to warn Leila and Roxy. I can't be around them with all this going on!"*

Hurrying upstairs, James searched for a pay phone in the hall, eventually finding one near the cafeteria. He picked up the receiver and suddenly grew uneasy as he dropped in several dimes then dialed a number. "Hey, Roxy," James said once the line picked up.

"James!" Roxanne said in surprise. "Why are you calling me...?"

"I have to tell you something important."

"What's this all about?"

"Can I come over later tonight?"

"What brought this on?"

"It's a long story and I'll tell you all about it later. I want to tell you a little secret about myself that'll explain a lot of what's been going on with me lately."

"You're not secretly on the down low, are you?"

"What?" James squawked.

"If you're seeing other men, I totally understand..."

"Roxy, it's not that!" James cried. "I know I'm good looking, but damn, it's not that at all!" He blew a heavy sigh. "Just, please, let me come over tonight so we can talk!"

"Fine, but if you're seeing other men, I don't want to see you again."

"What if it was other women?" The line cut off and James stared at the receiver in disbelief. Grunting, he hung up the phone.

"*Now to take care of something else...*" James said to himself. "*Pity anyone who crosses me!*"

He hurried down the corridor and burst outdoors then made his way for the excluded part of the park before taking a jumping leap.

CHAPTER TWENTY-SIX

Touching down in an alley, James groaned when he struck the ground and the pavement cracked beneath him. "Gotta work on my landings," he muttered. "Tend to push myself too hard when I'm rushing..."

James pulled out of his blazer and ran down the cobblestone street, exiting into cold winter sunshine. Catching sight of the large building that housed the sports stadium across the street, James noticed numerous police cars, fire engines and ambulances surrounding the front of the structure.

Timing the passing cars, James sprinted across the street, ran around the bus station and over the light commuter rail tracks.

"Hey," James called to no one in particular as a crowd formed offside. "What happened here? I heard over the radio there was some kind of collapse..."

"There are more of those Directorate terrorists inside!" said one onlooker. "I don't know why they'd come to the Memorial Center, or to Petoria for that matter!"

"Our city's mainly industrial," said another. "We've got that bullet plant and airplane factory..."

"Yeah," said a third, "especially with all those other places with army contracts and Parsons and Parker's contracts with their various computer manufacturers, we're a huge target!"

James clenched his teeth. *"They're trying to draw me out,"* he thought. *"That last call... they said to give it back or people die!"* He shuddered and took a hesitant step back. *"I'm not ready for this! I can't reveal myself now... but I just can't let people die either!"* Turning away, James hung his head and slung his blazer over his shoulder, walking for another area. *"Who am I kidding? If I went in now, then everyone would know for real!"*

James aimlessly walked around for several blocks, growing more deeply depressed as he became lost in his thoughts. *"Why am I here?"* he wondered. *"It's not like I'm breaking things off with Leila... so why do I still feel guilty?"* He then later approached the radio station and entered through the double glass doors. *"I really need to start being completely open with Leila and stop hiding everything. I want to keep her around; she is my best friend... I think..."*

Standing near the stairwell, James stared up at the high vaulted ceilings and blew a short sigh. *"I need to be totally committed... but then what's the point of Roxy other than a good screw and yet she's weighed down with the kids?"* James grunted and looked down at the floor. *"She's forgotten about me and I can't be a daddy for the kids. Besides, kids scare me anyway."*

James turned and paused in step when he saw a young woman with long curly blond hair wearing a black leather miniskirt, electric blue halter-top, and ankle-length black boots exit the elevators. She pulled into a large heavy, gray wool overcoat she had draped over her arm as she headed outside.

"That reminds me... Brandi..." James ran up the stairs for the offices.

"Hey," a voice called, "what are you doing here?"

"What?" James said and turned around, spotting a security guard in the corridor.

"You shouldn't be here if you don't have a pass," the guard said upon approach.

"I'm picking up Leila Gibson for lunch."

The guard snorted. "Yeah, kid, they all say that!"

"Tell her James Russell is here, okay?"

"Yeah, and wait downstairs while I do that!"

James grunted and headed for the steps. When he heard the guard's footsteps growing distant, he took a small hop and hovered over the floor as pale red light surrounded his body.

Peering around the corner, James watched the guard enter another room, then floated down the corridor and peeked into the window that faced the hall.

Inside James saw Leila sitting at a desk that held a large turntable, with one hand to a headphone while the other covered the microphone that rest nearby. The guard spoke animatedly to her and she suddenly brightened. The guard then shrugged his shoulders and turned away for the door. James immediately panicked and quickly hid behind the door as the guard exited.

"Yo, kid," the guard called and looked down the corridor on his right, then his left. "I owe ya an apology..."

The guard headed for the stairwell and James caught the door before it closed. He stepped down softly onto the ground and entered the room.

"James!" Leila said happily upon his arrival. "What brings you by?" She sniffed the air. "Did you just iron your clothes or something?"

James chortled. "I decided to visit you on the job!" he answered, "and no, I didn't iron my clothes. You know most of it's permanent press!"

"You're gonna melt your clothes if you're not careful!"

"Right..." James walked around, inspecting stacks of records, eight-tracks, cassette tapes and compact discs shelved on the walls. "So what's it like working for K-SHO?"

"All I do is take requests and play stuff depending on the hour and the day of the week." Leila shrugged. "Sometimes I mix music..."

"Don't tell me you're a turntablist!"

Leila grinned. "I enjoy it," she said. "It gives my poor brain a break!"

"A break from what?"

"You know I took up computer, radio, and television repair at Central, Jamie!"

"I forgot with all the partying we did," James said, grinning sheepishly.

"Well, on the side, I fix stuff and trying to keep updated with the times makes me want to smack my head on the desk!" Leila chuckled. "Anyways, I love music and I love making it more awesome."

"That's great," James replied. "At least you weren't cursed with a tin ear like me! I hear stuff on the radio and think it's one band and it ends up being someone else completely different!"

Leila laughed. "If you mix up *Incus* and--" She held up a hand as the current song ended and put on her headphones. "Alrighty music players and player haters," she announced into the microphone. "I have a special friend here in the studio who doesn't believe my awesome skills at spinning records! So who would like to hear me play? Call in now and if I get ten requests in a row, I can prove how awesome I am!"

James chuckled. "You're being silly!" he said.

The phone next to Leila immediately lit up. She leaned over and punched a button. "You're our first caller!" she said brightly.

"Yeah, I love your work," said a voice. "I want to hear a *Powerline* mix!"

"Which songs?"

"Any of them!"

"Cool..."

More lights began to flicker on the phone.

"Wow, it's like a tree on the festival of lights!" James exclaimed as Leila answered more calls.

"Hey now, tenth caller, we're waiting on you!" Leila said. "We have three requests for *Powerline* mixes, some *Incus* and *Birds of Black Metal Prey* and four requests for *Brothers Giri*, and *Aztec!*"

"Why such goofy mixes?" James asked. "*Aztec* and *Brothers Giri* are totally different, as well as *Birds of Black Metal Prey* and *Incus!*"

Leila giggled. "It's a challenge." The phone began to flash and Leila flipped the switch. "Come in, tenth caller," she answered. "What would you like to hear?" Static came over the line. "Hello, tenth caller?"

"You must not care what we do to others in your town," a dark voice growled over the air. "Then if hurting innocents does not move you, then we shall hurt those close to you."

"Hey!" James yelled as Leila blanched. He reached forward and yanked up the microphone. "I had enough of you calling my house, but don't you *dare* threaten my friends!"

"If you were half the man you say you are, you'd save them, but instead you left them alone and took advantage of the chaos to leave... So give up the weapon and let those that are worthy keep it!"

"Punks like you have an excuse for everything!" James shouted. "So you want to meet and fight? You got it!"

"Name your place."

"The Riverside Mall at midnight!"

"If you do not appear, then scaring up security will do..." Dial tone flooded the air.

"Er, let's jump to commercial," Leila said and quickly struck a button. "Jamie, what's going on?" she asked as James set down the microphone. "Please, tell me!"

"It's those Corpii, these kind of space assassins," James answered and turned away, clenching his hands. "They work for the Directorate, some kind of terrorist group."

"What do you mean, 'space assassins'?"

"I don't have time to explain it all here, so I'll tell you after work, okay?"

"Sure!" Leila grabbed James by the wrist. "Please be careful out there..."

James smiled warmly and pat her on the head. "Pick me up after work, okay?"

"Sure!"

PART SIX
THE RECKONING

James spent the afternoon placing contents from the copy paper box on his desk in his new office and going over the paperwork that detailed his new duties. When five o'clock came, he grabbed his overcoat and exited the room. James heard the TEK DEK chirp in his pocket and glanced around, spotting Adnan coming down the corridor.

Adnan wore a heavy dark green overcoat over a tan suit that had an orange carnation pinned to the lapel. As he entered the hall, he loosened his black and orange striped tie from around his neck.

"Going somewhere, Russell?" Adnan called.

"Why does it concern you?" James retorted, pausing in step.

"Hold up a minute."

"What do you want?" James demanded once Adnan approached.

Adnan withdrew a pair of violet tinted sunglasses that rest atop his head and ran a hand through his frizzy strawberry hair that hung loosely down his back.

"I heard you're meeting some shady people at the Riverside Mall tonight," Adnan replied and put on the glasses, grinning.

"Why are you bothering to wear sunglasses at night?"

"Because I'm awesome like that." Adnan pushed James back by the chest, pressing him against the wall and leaned forward. "You've been *real* unsupportive lately, Russell," he snarled. "One of these days you're going to trip up..."

"Unsupportive of what?" James spat.

"I'm *telling* you to pick a side," Adnan sneered. "You want to be on a winning team, don't you?"

"I'm not working for the Directorate if you're a part of them!"

Adnan chortled and pulled away. "So I see we actually have a clue." He poked James in the chest with a firm finger. "We've forced your friend to join our side, so if *that* doesn't make you change your mind..."

"You leave Verne out of this!"

"It's too late!" Adnan clenched his hands that glowed dimly in green light. "I'm going to handicap your ass for tonight's battle. You're going down!"

"You're nothing but hot air!" James dropped his coat and took a step forward as golden flames flared around his hands.

"Really?" Adnan withdrew the carnation he had pinned to his lapel and it glowed brightly in brown light, transforming into a black spiked whip. "If you throw a fireball at me, you'll burn this place to the ground and they'll find out for sure, won't they?"

James clenched his teeth, growing incensed as Adnan chuckled and walked away. "You punk!" he shouted after him.

"I don't think you're going anywhere tonight!" Adnan said darkly and suddenly turned, striking out with the whip.

James immediately jumped rearward and grunted once slashed at and cut across his chest, ripping the fabric. He staggered back, clutching his torn shirt.

"This *feels too weird...*" James thought when he felt a strange burning sensation chew through his chest. "*It's like something's crawling on my skin!*" James gasped when green threads suddenly appeared from his wound, quickly binding around his body. The tightening strands made him lose his footing and forced him down to the floor. "*What is this, wire?*"

"Aw, you fall down and go boom?" Adnan chided and stepped up to James. "If you try to burn through that, it'll burn everything else around you."

"You piece of trash," James growled. "I'll kill you!"

Adnan kicked James in the chest and James grunted in response, glaring back. "Though our Signets are incompatible since Fire burns Wood, if you're going to fight with the weapon, you'd better choose a good location to hold a battle if you're trying to keep your secret under wraps." Adnan perched down to James, baring his teeth. "I know you're not stupid, Russell. So seriously think about what you're getting into!"

"So you're going to leave me tangled up like this?" James snapped.

"Why not?" Adnan chortled and rose to his feet, slipping the whip around his shoulders. "You're cute this way."

"You bastard!" James wriggled from his binds, trying in vain to break free.

"The harder you struggle, the tighter you're bound," Adnan explained. "It'll dig deeper, drawing blood, and more of the threads will appear, wrapping you tighter and tighter until you suffocate and die."

"Will these things fade?"

"I don't know..." Adnan shrugged his shoulders. "No one's ever lived to tell me."

"So only you can release them?"

"I can, but I choose not to." Adnan laughed and walked away.

"Hey!" James yelled after him. "Damn you, Adnan! When I find you, you're gonna hurt so bad!" He seethed as his binds became tighter and dug into his skin. "Help!" he called once Adnan left his line of sight. "Help! Anybody!"

Moments later, Xavier and Reinhold left the offices, talking animatedly to each other. As they exited through the double glass doors, a tall young man with a walrus-style moustache and a head of curly light brown hair entered, wearing mirrored gold aviator sunglasses, heavy bomber jacket, black slacks, and brown riding boots.

"*That's Menotti!*" James thought, slightly relieved and repulsed. "What are you doing here?" he insisted once the young man approached.

"Keeping an eye on you," Menotti snapped. "What else?"

"Why are you following me and investigating me?"

"We study *all* Signet wielders," Menotti explained.

"And who's 'we'?"

"The good guys," Menotti replied vaguely. He snapped his fingers and a red saber formed in hand that burned hotly, cackling in orange energy. "We look for those who hold Signets to study, to help and strengthen them and if they're ready, join us for the eventual war that's bound to happen."

"So there's *more* out there like me?"

Menotti nodded and he quickly slashed at James, burning his binds. "More than you can wrap your head around," he answered.

"So, you *force* people to join you?" James sat up and Menotti's saber of light dispersed.

Menotti snorted in response. "We don't force anyone to join the Resistance," he clarified, lending a hand and James took it, getting pulled to his feet. "Only the Directorate forces people. We let the Signet wielders join us if they *want* to join us."

"That's nice to know," James murmured.

"Well, it's better to fight for someone who welcomes you than forces you." Menotti dug through his pocket and produced a business card. "Here, take this. You might want to call us later if you need any extra help."

James took the card and glanced at it. "*The Center*, huh?" he muttered. "Why so inconspicuous?"

"We don't want the Directorate to find us now." Menotti grinned. "Now, do you need a ride anywhere? I can drop you off."

"It's okay." James picked up his fallen overcoat and pulled into it. "I have a friend picking me up."

"Good."

James grew uneasy as he headed for the exit, following Menotti's stride. "*I don't know if I should join either side,*" he mused. *"Both could say that the other party is bad and join them."* James sighed. *"I'll just watch from the sidelines... see what happens."*

Upon exiting outdoors, he heard a car horn beep and waved when he saw the small compact car flash its headlights. "Leila!" James called and ran up to her vehicle. "How long were you out there?" he asked, opening the door. "It's freezing out here!"

"It's okay," Leila replied. "With you here, you can keep me warm." James flushed and clamored inside then shut the door. "So where to?"

"I'm going by Roxy's. I'm telling her it's over."

"It's not because of me, is it?"

"Nah, not because of you." James pat Leila on the thigh. "It's because of me..."

"Are you going to tell her your secret?" Leila shifted gears and pulled out of the parking lot.

"I have to..." James sighed heavily, looking away. "I just hope she accepts..."

"What if she doesn't?"

James grunted and looked out the window of the passing scenery while Leila drove.

CHAPTER TWENTY-EIGHT

"Okay, Jim, you can do this," James berated himself as he stepped out the compact car and made his way up the stoop. *"All right, just relax and don't panic. Just keep cool and use your head... Don't waste any time going in circles. Just up and tell her flat out."* James knocked on the door. *"Don't chicken out and make up some lame excuse or tell a lie like that you're some kinda junkie or a drunk..."*

The door opened, revealing Roxanne. James swallowed hard, taking in her hot pink blazer, tight red blouse, slim-fitting black slacks, scarlet flats and a pink bandana over her long red hair.

"Damn," James murmured.

"Oh!" Roxanne said, mildly surprised. "I wasn't expecting you."

"I *did* call you earlier," James replied.

"Yes," Roxanne said flatly, narrowing her eyes, "how considerate of you."

"Please don't argue with me, Roxy," James pleaded.

"You give me such a headache sometimes..." Roxanne blew a short sigh. "You act one way and then the next...! I just don't know what to do with you!"

"Please." James put up his hands.

"I just finished getting the children to bed, so they won't make too much noise."

"I, um, have to talk to you, Roxy," James said somberly. "Can I come in?"

"Of course," Roxanne murmured and opened the door wider. "It must be important... you look so serious!"

"I don't know how to tell you this..."

"Do you want to sit down?" Roxanne asked as James entered the house. "Would you like coffee?" She shut the door and headed into the kitchen.

"Sure, four scoops."

"That's strong!"

"And toss in a shot of liquor if you got it..."

"What kind?"

"Whiskey, rum, vodka, gin... whatever you have!"

"I have all that and more..."

"Then put in everything!"

James pulled out of his overcoat and slipped it over the arm of the couch. He sank into the cushions and leaned back, draping his arms on the top edge.

"*I need to hurry this up,*" James considered. "*Leila's waiting out there in the cold and I've got that fight at the mall tonight!*"

Roxanne returned moments later with a mug of coffee and handed it to James. James took the mug and Roxanne sat on the couch, curling up next to him.

"Hold me, James," she murmured and James put his free arm around her as she leaned against him, sighing. He sipped his coffee, contemplating. "You know," said Roxanne after several moments of silence, "I don't understand my children anymore, especially Darlene... I just can't figure what's gotten into her. I'm so tense since she's such a problem these days."

"It's probably just a phase," James muttered and shrugged his shoulders.

"But she used to be such an angel, and now lately she's been a brat... a total monster!" Roxanne reached up and gently squeezed James's free hand that draped over her shoulder. "I talked to my friends about it and they said I'm worrying too much!"

"It's not because of me, is it?"

"Why do you ask?"

"Well, I just thought maybe I'd scared her that one night when she had that toy gun and maybe that's why she's behaving badly..."

"No... I took her to the school psychologist and they said they think something happened to her, something traumatic that might have caused this sudden change."

James gulped the rest of his coffee that cooled and moaned softly when the liquor hit him hard. "*I shouldn't have asked her to make it so strong,*" he realized, cringing.

"Are you okay?" Roxanne asked.

"What did you put in this?" James inquired.

"Just some brandy and twenty-year-old scotch..." Roxanne placed a hand on James's chest. "Why, is that too strong?"

"It's fine."

Roxanne blew a disconcerted sigh. "I can't figure what happened to her to make her that way," she continued. "When I ask her, she won't tell me!"

James handed her his empty mug. "One more please."

"Where's the party?" Roxanne said wryly, gently teasing. James gasped when she grabbed for his crotch. "Is it in your pants?"

"Roxy...!" James mewed, flushing darkly.

"So let's fool around, what do you say?"

"*No*," thought James, struggling for the words he wanted to say as Roxanne set the mug aside on the nearby end table and kissed him softly on the cheek. James found it hard to breathe, frozen in place and unable to resist his body's response when she sat in his lap and loosened his tie.

"What are you thinking of?" Roxanne asked, running a hand through his hair.

"Nothing now..." James said softly.

Roxanne giggled. "I'll give you something worth thinking about..." she murmured. "Tonight and every little chance I get from now on, I'm going to be more of a lover than you ever dreamed of." Roxanne began unbuttoning James's shirt. "You're going to want to rush home to me and be with me every minute; you'll forget about everything else and won't even notice that there are other women out there."

"What about other men?" James asked, grinning.

"I'm going to blow your mind so that *nobody else* but *me* will occupy your thoughts!" Roxanne pulled away James's shirt and blazer at his shoulders, exposing his chest. She paused, running a hand over the tattoo on his right pectoral. "James, are you a Diabolist or something…?"

James frowned, raising an eyebrow. "Why do you ask?"

"That strange tattoo you used to have on your hand, now you have one on your chest!"

"I, um…" James cleared his throat. "I forgot all about that fake dumb tattoo. I, well, got it at a party a while back. It'll come off with lacquer thinner or something…"

"I thought it came off with a special soap!" Roxanne pulled away. "What is it with that thing; why do you keep putting them on?"

"*Damn,*" James thought, wincing. "*I moved the Signet there so she wouldn't see it until I was ready!*" He shut his eyes and leaned back, groaning. "Roxy, baby…" he started.

"Weren't you going to tell me something?" Roxanne snapped irritably.

"I was?"

"Some big secret…"

"Give me another drink and I'll let you know."

"If you have to develop liquid courage to just tell me…" James gasped when she grabbed his tie and yanked forward. His eyes snapped open, facing Roxanne who glared at him. "You're in a gang, aren't you," she spat, "or are you with some faction of The Syndicate?"

"No, it's not that!" James put his hands on Roxanne's shoulders. "Okay, I should've been straight with you from the beginning. Just let me explain and don't freak out, okay?"

"I can't promise you that."

"The truth is, that, you know, I was acting pretty weird for a while there because something happened to me. It's strange, so bear with me..."

"I'm listening."

"This is the reason why I've been acting strange lately, why I've been sneaking around and how I got that weird tattoo." James gave Roxanne a gentle squeeze. "You see... somebody, a man... he gave me something I don't fully understand. He gave me this tattoo..."

"Oh, no!" Roxanne wailed and pushed his hands off her shoulders. "So you're gay and with the Syndicate too?"

"No, no!" James yelped and grunted once punched in the chest. "Let me finish!"

"Damn it, James; out with it already!"

"He wasn't just a man. I mean, it seemed like he wasn't from Earth, you know?"

"So you're a junkie?" Roxanne pulled away and rose to her feet.

"Roxy let me finish!" James snapped.

"You've got five minutes and I'm throwing you out."

"Not until I try to explain."

"So stop stalling and just *say* so!"

"There's been a lot of weird stuff going on with me lately. The tattoo... it's not just *any* tattoo. It's called a Signet and it makes me stronger, a *lot* stronger than normal people and I can fly..."

"Get out of my house," Roxanne snarled.

James stood and approached her, only to have his head whipped back from a hard slap. "Roxy, listen," he growled and grabbed her hand before she swung again. "That's just the beginning of what I can do. I am a one-man world power - I could level whole countries if I wanted to."

"You're crazy!" Roxanne cried and yanked out of his grip. "And to think I wanted to marry you!"

"I'm not crazy." James stepped back as pale gold light surrounded his body and he levitated several inches off the floor. "See? It's not a trick or a gimmick... it's real!"

"Oh...!" Roxanne's face blanched when James released golden flames from his hands.

"I also control fire," James said, "though it's not just in my hands... I can light my whole body, but if I showed you without the special suit, I'd burn through my clothes!" Roxanne shook her head, terrified and James stepped down gently to the floor.

Roxanne immediately backed away, shuddering in fear when James approached her. "You're a demon!" she cried. "Get away from me!"

"You know I don't believe in that stuff!" James snapped, killing the flames in his hands. He grabbed Roxanne by the waist, pulling her to him and she banged her fists on his chest. James said nothing, holding her close as she broke down into tears, sobbing against him. "Are you afraid of me?" James asked softly and ran a gentle hand through her hair. "It's okay... who wouldn't be?" He lifted her chin and wiped away her tears with his thumb. "That's why I've kept this secret. Only you and, well, a couple friends know."

"I don't know what to say…" Roxanne moaned.

"You've got to promise me," James said seriously. "Don't ever tell *anyone*, no matter what. If I get found out or if the wrong people knew about the things I can do, there can be trouble, not for me but for the *both* of us!" James let go of his hold.

"What does this mean for us?" Roxanne cried.

"I can't stay with you anymore…"

"Will you still come see me every now and then…?"

"I don't want to endanger you or the kids…"

"Oh, James!" Roxanne bawled, sobbing into her hands. James led her over to the couch and they both sat down. She leaned forward, crying.

"I can't see you anymore," James murmured. "It's just not right…"

"No!" Roxanne wailed. "This can't be over! You're the only one that understands and is good with the children…"

"Roxy, please," James said gently, rubbing at her back. "I thought you'd understand… you're the most understanding person I know."

"James, if you won't see me, I don't know what I'll do."

"You can date other men like you did before!"

"I only did that to make you jealous!"

"You'll be okay, Roxy. You'll survive, you see."

Roxanne sat up and grabbed James by the lapels. "No, I won't!" she screeched. "Listen to me, I won't!" Roxanne shook him. "Do you hear me?"

"Roxy, baby, calm down!" James cried, gripping her wrists. "You'll wake up those little monsters!"

"I want to do whatever makes you happy..." Roxanne said quickly, "or if you want to do whatever makes you happy, then I'll put up with it. I don't care if you have other women or men in your life. I don't care if you even get married! Just, please, come see me sometimes, once in a while or you'll kill me, I mean it! Please, James, see me once in a while!"

"Okay," James said reassuringly. "Look, I'll see you once in a while, yeah?"

"Promise me!"

"I... I promise." James released his hold. "I'm sorry, just right now is a bad time to try the committed thing and settling down..."

"I understand..." Roxanne wrapped her arms firmly around James's neck. "Oh, James, I'm so happy. I love you so much!"

"I love you too," James muttered halfheartedly. Roxanne let him go and held her hands in her lap, smiling sadly. "So, what time is it?"

"A little after nine... why, are you in a hurry?"

"Not really..."

Roxanne rose to her feet and ran a hand through her hair. "So, would you like for me to show you that bikini you bought me last summer?" she asked. "Come upstairs and I'll show it to you. I can finally fit into it."

"*Yes*," James thought. "No," he said, standing. "No, Roxy... I have to go home. Now, like *right* now." Roxanne stepped over and stood close to James, stroking his chest. He grunted and clenched his teeth when she grabbed him by the waistband and loosened his belt.

"Or never..." James mused and sighed. *"Man, I can't understand it!"* He ground his teeth as Roxanne unzipped his slacks. *"I just don't understand! Every time I think I know anything, something happens and <u>everything</u> changes!"*

Suddenly the phone rang, killing the tension between them.

"Who would that be, calling this late?" Roxanne griped, growing annoyed.

"Hurry and answer before it wakes the kids," James urged.

Roxanne nodded and hurried for the kitchen, quickly picking up the line. "Hello?" she greeted. "Who is this?" She stood in the doorway, holding the receiver. "James, it's for you."

"For me?" James asked, incredulous. "Who else would know I was here?" He held up his slacks that threatened to fall past his hips and stepped across the room, taking the phone from Roxanne's hand. "Who is this?" he demanded into the mouthpiece.

"Hello, Russell," said a familiar voice.

"You!" James snarled.

"I've been following you, Russell."

"What do you want?"

"I'm with your pretty little friend... You come out within ten minutes or she dies."

"Adnan," James roared, "you son of a bitch...!"

"She shouldn't have gotten involved with you... Is it her eyes you're into, or is it her smokin' body?" Adnan cackled darkly. "Well, that's the one sure thing to change once I'm through with her."

"If you touch her, I swear...!"

"I just can't help myself, Russell," Adnan vaunted. "I'll tell the pretty lady that her boyfriend's coming to see her soon. If you take too long and make me wait, I'll pick her apart and debone her..."

The line cut off and James threw the receiver back on the cradle, heaving for breath. His clothing began smoking as his rage grew.

"What was that about?" Roxanne cried. "Don't get loud, please! The children--!"

"It's okay," James said quickly, taking in an even breath. "Just give me a minute to calm down..."

"James, you're smoldering!"

"I know... I know." James staggered over to the kitchen table and pulled out a chair, slumping into it.

"What's going on?" Roxanne insisted.

"It's getting too complicated..." The phone rang again and James rose out of his seat.

Roxanne immediately touched him by the shoulder. "I'll take care of it," she said. "If they ask for you, I'll take a message."

"Fine."

James stalked out the kitchen as Roxanne spoke on the phone in hushed tones. He heard a crash from outside and quickly pulled into his belt. Yanking on his shirt and blazer back over his shoulders after hearing a scream, James rushed for the door and flung it open.

"Leila!" he called, running for the car. James paused when he found the windows smashed in and one of the doors torn off, lying on the ground as twisted metal. "Leila!" James screamed and ran around the car, finding no one inside. He held in a weak breath when he saw blood staining the front seat and dashboard.

Coming around to the trunk, James noticed a bloody hand print on the end and his hands blazed in golden light. Ripping open the trunk, he gasped, finding Leila's unconscious body thrown inside, with her clothing bloodied and torn and her arms and legs twisted in unnatural positions.

"Oh, Leila!" James moaned and stroked her crimson-stained face with trembling fingers. "Oh no..." He scooped up Leila's body, cradling her close and slipped to his knees as tears ran down his face. "I'll kill whoever did this, I swear...!" James rocked slowly, burying his head into her shoulder. "I'm so sorry, Leila," he mewed, "I feel like shit, risking your life like that..."

Hearing the TEK DEK chirp, James pulled out the microcomputer from his pocket with his free hand and flipped it open, finding the cyan text scrolling on the screen.

UNKNOWN SIGNET IN RANGE

"What the--?" James hissed. "How can I fight this if I don't know what it is?" Hearing another scream, he set Leila's body gingerly down on the ground and tucked the TEK DEK in his pocket. "Roxy!" James called and raced across the yard. "Hold on!" Jumping the porch steps, he came through the door and received a hard rap to the face that corkscrewed him, darkening his world completely.

CHAPTER TWENTY-NINE

James moaned as he came to, blinded by bright white light and inundated by the scent of antiseptic that filtered into his nose. Hearing a chirp, he quickly sat up and cried out in agony when sudden pain engulfed him, forcing him to slip back, dazed.

"Hey there," a voice cried, "Easy now; take it easy!"

James gripped his head in pain, sucking in a shallow breath through his teeth as he sat up on his elbows. He grunted, finding his arms and chest taped with bandages, including around his head.

"Where am I?" James moaned.

"You're in General Hospital," answered the kind voice. James turned, spotting a middle-aged woman with cordial gray eyes and long brown hair pinned up into a loose bun, who wore a white uniform under a pale blue cardigan draped over her shoulders. "I'm Nurse Geller."

"How did I get here?"

"Someone found you," she said. "You were badly broken up when you came in..."

Suddenly everything struck James at once. "The house...!" he cried.

"Yes, you were found near a house that had burned down in Pomaderris," Geller said kindly. "You're very lucky to be alive!"

James groaned, recalling the events that led up to his demise. "I wish I wasn't alive..." he muttered. "I should've died with them!"

"You have a name, Sport?" Geller asked. "You weren't carrying any I.D."

James gave his name and she suddenly giggled as her face flushed. "What is it?" he demanded, narrowing his eyes.

"You had no clothes on either when you were found." James blushed darkly. "It's one thing to find you in a burned-out house after a blaze, but another thing to find you nearly frozen as an ice lolly in the dead of night..."

"How long have I been here?" James asked instead.

"You've been here three days."

"Holy shit!" James cried. "I have to find Leila. Where is she?"

"Who is that?" Geller asked. "Is she your sister or your wife...?"

"She's my friend..."

"Tell me her name and I'll see if we can track her down."

"She was hurt by that madman - he damn near killed her!" James struggled to sit up. "I have to find her! I can't waste time staying in here..."

"Don't try to move!" Geller grabbed James by the arm and let out a distressed cry as he flinched when a strong shock coursed through him. "Ouch! Your arm - there must be a lot of static in the air..."

"*Does she have a Signet?*" James wondered when Geller withdrew her grip. "*I can't find the TEK DEK with all these machines beeping around me!*"

"You've been horribly beaten, James," Geller said gently, "You need to rest and let the doctors help you get better."

James groaned and clutched his chest. "Look, Lady, hospitals creep me out," he grumbled. "Just get me some clothes so I can get outta here."

"You have broken ribs and a severe concussion! Until the doctor gives you the okay, you're staying here for a week!"

"That's it?" James asked incredulously, giving her a wary glance. "I thought I was worse off than this..."

"Like I said, you've been *extremely* lucky..."

James blew a disconcerted sigh. "*If she healed me or something,*" he wondered, "*I don't know whether to freak out or thank her!*"

James grunted. "I'm a sitting duck if I stay here like this!" he protested. "I have a lot of enemies!"

"I'll see to it that the doctor knows about this, okay?" Geller rose from her seat. "Sit tight."

"Like I've got anywhere else to go," James groused.

"Look, don't worry, Sport. I'll be here and I won't let anybody do anything to you."

"Yeah, sure."

Geller left the room and James blew a heavy sigh as he laid back. "*If I see that jerk Adnan again,*" he mused, shutting his eyes, "*He's going to burn so badly, he'll pray to get sent to Hell after I get done with him!*" James clenched his teeth. "*Since I don't have any I.D. on me, the Feds can't track me down...*

With two big explosions several weeks apart, they'll start to get suspicious!"

"Mind if I join you?" inquired a familiar voice.

"Huh?" James murmured and opened his eyes.

"Glad to see you're alive."

Sitting up, James faced a tall young man with broad shoulders and long copper hair standing over him. The mysterious stranger wore reflective silver glasses and a brown uniform that had a blue stripe going down the side, along with navy calf-length boots and matching elbow-length gloves. In his arms, he held a brown helmet that had a blue visor and around his narrow hips, he wore three belts, two that held a small case and the other a pack of metallic cards. Strapped to his thigh was an empty gun harness.

"Are you related to that Space Guy...?" James inquired.

"There are many of us Relayers..." answered the stranger.

"Wait, that term...!" James gasped and crawled back, forcing the machines hooked to him beeping wildly. "One of you tried to *kill* me!"

"There are some Relayers who have defected from the Resistance and left the Protectorate, joining with the Directorate."

"So I guess that's supposed to be mildly reassuring..."

"I am content that you are alive and well and not dead," said the star fighter. "We have a lot to cover in a short amount of time."

"Did you know about what happened?"

"Our scanners alerted us of Signet activity, so I came to investigate."

"Why did you save me?"

"You are quite important."

"There's something I want to know and it's been gnawing at me..." James blew a disgruntled sigh. "Why was this weapon *forced* on me?"

"It was not forced, it was *given*," the stranger corrected. "You could have easily refused."

"I didn't have much of a choice...!" James shook his head. "Besides, he planned to take it back. After I got it, I had plenty of people wanting to take it off my hands by force."

"I gather the burden has become wearisome and the Signet has caused you some inconvenience as well..."

"You call almost getting *killed* some kind of inconvenience?" James barked. "You call having my best friend broken to bits like some piece of plywood inconvenient?"

"I cannot take it back... since the original owner has died; it is not mine to take."

"But is it possible?"

"I cannot take an incompatible Signet..."

"Then what are you here for?"

"I came to check on your progress, as well as to honor demands..."

"So someone *sent* you to check me out?" James thrust out a faintly glowing hand. "Now hold it, buster! I'm not playing along anymore!"

"I must inform you of some important data, as the bearer of the most powerful weapon of the Resistance should attend to."

James lowered his hand. "Like what?"

"This isn't the place in which to discuss it." The young man turned on his heel. "I shall see you again."

"Hey, Space Guy, wait!" James called, reaching out. "Before you go, can you give me any practical advice dealing with this thing?"

"When you move the Signet to another part of your body, don't put it in peculiar locations," the star fighter answered. "Keep it on the outside, for it's not designed for mucous membranes, understand?"

"I think so..."

The young man left the room then moments later, the nurse named Geller returned with a doctor.

"How are we today?" asked the doctor.

James didn't answer, his head swimming in foggy perplexity as the doctor spoke to him and gave him a limited examination.

"*I don't get it,*" James said to himself. "*I don't know what to make of this...*"

"Do you hear me?" the doctor called and waved a hand in front of James.

"Yeah?" James murmured, snapping to attention. "What is it, Doc?"

"Maybe painkillers are in order?"

"No... don't dull me, please?" James pleaded. "I need to be able to feel... I won't let the pain master me."

"Just take it easy..." said the doctor. "If it gets worse, just let us know."

James nodded and the nurse Geller approached his bed once the doctor left the room.

"The doctor said you'll have to stay here for another two weeks," Geller replied.

James shook his head in return. "No can do." He gave Geller a weak smile. "Hey, would you make it two days?"

Geller raised an eyebrow. "What do you want to happen in two days?"

"I know you've been checking me out." Geller flushed slightly. "I don't mind... it's a nice change of pace."

"Okay, but if you get me in trouble, I know all sorts of tricks to kill a man."

James's face flushed scarlet in response. "Right that."

Two days later, Geller returned with clothing for James. She set the bags aside in the nearby chair then turned off the machines and pulled out the various intravenous tubes and wires connected to him.

"I'm sorry if they don't fit very well," Geller said apologetically. "They belonged to my twin brother..."

"It's all right..." James murmured, smiling faintly.

"Well, I do think that you'll be more comfortable at my place than at General. You seem so tense here..."

"I told you, I've got enemies."

"You're not part of the Syndicate, are you?"

James let out a strained laugh. "Why does everyone assume that?" he asked.

"Well, are you?"

"No, no, not at all!"

"Then what's with people trying to kill you?"

"It's not the Syndicate, okay?"

Geller nodded. "Whatever you say…"

"It's something completely different, if you catch my drift…"

"I think so." Geller took out the articles she brought and helped James put them on.

James pulled into blue jeans, a loose green button-down shirt, a dark blue windbreaker and a pair of gray socks with white slip-on shoes.

"How do I look?" he asked. "I won't win any fashion contests for sure!"

Geller smiled, giving James a long once-over. "You're still handsome in any shape or form," she purred.

James chuckled. "Look at me!" he protested. "I'm totally scarred up from that fire!"

"You seem fine to me." Geller held out a hand. "Now let's get you out of here."

"Why are you doing all this," James pressed, taking her hand into his, "even risking your job for me?"

Geller shrugged her shoulders. "Because I like you."

"But weren't they talking about doing tests on me…?"

"They know where they can stick those tests," Geller replied and gave James's hand a firm squeeze. "Besides, I can do more for you than whatever those nurses could… and then some!"

James blushed darkly in response and Geller led him out the room, making their way down the corridor to the elevators at the end.

"Are you planning to hold me hostage or something?" James asked as they stepped on the cable car.

"Why, would you want me to?" Geller responded.

"I don't know," James murmured, growing tense as the doors hushed close and the elevator descended into the bottom depths.

"I have a few things in mind..."

"Like doing freaky experiments on me?"

Geller smiled. "Possibly..."

"Well...!"

The doors opened moments later and they entered the parking garage.

"Why do you hate hospitals so much?" Geller asked, letting go of James's hand. He shuddered and zipped up the windbreaker once the brittle November wind blew through the lot.

"Hospitals are where you go to die," James answered and Geller nodded.

James followed the nurse to her compact sedan parked at the far end of the lot and waited as she unlocked the door for him. He carefully stepped in and Geller shut the door for him then went around, entering the vehicle.

"Yet you live," murmured Geller, starting the engine. "Either you have a strong sheer force of will, or..."

"Or maybe someone thought that much of me to keep me hanging on." James sighed and leaned back in his seat, rolling his eyes to the ceiling.

"I'll find your friend... Leila you said?"

"Leila Gibson."

"I'll find her, okay?"

"Thanks..." James grunted when patted on the thigh. "What is it?"

Geller chuckled and withdrew her hand, then pulled out the lot.

James looked away, growing increasingly uncomfortable.

Geller drove to Westside Petoria, eventually pulling up to a small yellow house with red trim in a quiet neighborhood and cut the engine. James made careful exit out the car and Geller quickly clamored out, immediately aiding him up the walkway.

"This is my house," she said. "It's not big, but it's mine, and it's all I have."

"It's pretty nice," James replied. "Nice and warm..."

Opening the front door for James, Geller led him into the parlor and set James on the couch. She passed the floor television and flipped it on, then made her way for the door.

"There's the couch and telly," Geller said as she shut the front entranceway. "Would you like something to drink?"

"Soda's fine." James answered and unzipped the windbreaker as he leaned back into the couch.

"Do you drink liquor?"

"Sometimes..."

Geller left the parlor and headed into the kitchen. Upon return, she handed James a can of diet soda, holding a light beer for herself. "Here you go," she said. "All I have is light beer and diet soda... got to watch the figure, you know."

James grinned wolfishly. "You've got a nice body," he said. "So tell me, why are you doing all this for me? I'm a total stranger..."

"Until a few days ago," Geller interjected.

"I'm not just a stray dog," James grumbled and struggled to pop the tab. Geller set aside her beer and reached over, opening it for him. "Thanks," he muttered.

"Oh, I don't know," Geller murmured and took a seat across from James in a reclining chair. "Certain people bring out the maternal instinct in me, I guess."

"How old are you?" James asked.

"How old do you think I am?"

James shook his head and took a sip of soda. "I'm bad at guessing ages."

"So, what's your age?" Geller questioned.

"Twenty-five," James answered and Geller blushed.

"You're ten years younger than me."

"Is that a problem?"

"Unless you have a problem with it."

"It's fine by me," James replied, smiling. "I like older women." Geller giggled and undid the pins in her hair, letting it down.

"*She may not be totally hot,*" James mused, "*but she's definitely stuck on me.*" He smiled warmly. "*Maybe if I play my cards right...*"

"I guess I've always been attracted to people who are needy in some way," Geller continued. "My last four husbands, my various boyfriends... they were all the hurt puppy types." She sighed heavily. "I gave them all the love I possibly could... but still..." Geller shook her head and opened her beer then took a long swallow. "Eventually they left me." She shrugged. "It's the story of my life."

"Why is she telling me this?" James wondered as he drank his soda. *"Is she <u>daring</u> me to walk out on her like everybody else?"* He studied Geller, admiring her beauty. Her hair was a rich shade of mahogany, flowing in loose waves that adorned her shoulders. Geller's skin, a smooth tawny color, offset her warm gray eyes that had golden flecks and framed by long lashes. She had a small nose and full lips and a curvaceous body – she seemed the picture of cuteness. *"Still I can use a place to stay and a little mothering until I can get around a little better..."*

"What are you thinking about?" Geller interjected.

"I don't want to hurt you," James said softly, looking down at his can of soda. "You know once I heal, I'll have to go."

"I know," Geller murmured. "Let me enjoy what time we have, okay? I want to keep the fantasy alive."

"Fine by me."

"Now get some rest and make yourself at home. We can talk some more once I get back."

"Where are you going?"

"I have another shift tonight... they're short-staffed today." James nodded and set his can of soda aside on the nearby cocktail table. "Would you like a massage before I go?"

"If you're offering."

"It might help you heal that much faster."

"Go easy on me, okay?"

Geller gave a gentle smile as she set her beer aside and stood. "I won't hurt you, I promise."

Geller left the room and James reclined back on the couch. Moments later, she returned with towels and a bottle of massage oil.

"Do you want me to move?" James asked, sitting up on his elbows.

"No, stay on your back. You're probably too sore and tired to move right now." Geller pushed him back gently by the chest. James blew a hard sigh and reluctantly lay back as Geller placed the towels and bottle of oil aside on the nearby cocktail table. "I'll go gently for now, and later when you're less broken, I'll rub deeper."

"Whatever you say," James replied. "You're the nurse." He relaxed slightly when Geller ran her hands through his hair, massaging his scalp with a deft touch. "This feels nice," James murmured, relishing the fading tension.

His arms eventually slackened when Geller started on his shoulders and he hung one arm off the side of the couch, while the other draped across his body.

"Feels good, hm?" Geller murmured and James looked up, smiling back.

"I never had a massage before," he admitted.

"Well don't worry if you get too relaxed and start drooling."

James chuckled. "I'll keep that in mind."

He closed his eyes once his mind began to wander and he grew warmer as Geller loosened his shirt. Her hands stroked his exposed chest, slowly moving down to his stomach.

Suddenly James felt disoriented when Geller's hands left him and he began to drift. He came back to the present, sensing her move his legs and weight descended on the couch on the other side of him. James felt her remove his shoes and socks with careful hands and moaned when she massaged his feet.

"I assume that you like having your feet rubbed," Geller teased as she focused on one foot, "Am I right?"

"I never had it done before," James drawled, "but it's awesome what you're doing!"

"It's a good feeling, I can tell."

"I can see why people pay for this..." James sighed contentedly once she massaged his other foot.

He tensed when Geller loosened his jeans. "It's all right," she crooned. "You're in safe, capable hands..."

"Don't hurt me," James mumbled.

"Don't you worry about a thing... Mama will take care of you." Geller's hands worked on his calves. "Enjoy the good feeling. You deserve it."

"If this is supposed to be gentle," James slurred, "I might melt if you go deeper."

"We'll see..."

James felt embarrassed when he moaned in response to Geller's hands moving up to his thighs. He shuddered intensely when she rubbed the inside of his thighs, her fingers snaking their way up and moved his legs to accommodate her hands. James gasped when he felt her hand at his hip and his eyes snapped open.

"What are you doing?" he asked, sitting up on his elbows.

Geller quickly pressed a hand against his chest in response. "Nothing out of the ordinary," she said gently. "Just relax and let me finish."

"Don't you have to go to work soon?"

"In a bit, but right now, you're my priority."

James settled back and draped his free arm over his eyes while the other lingered over the side of the couch, his fingers brushing against the carpet. Warmth coursed through James and he quickly drifted off to sleep.

CHAPTER THIRTY

For the next three weeks, James led a life of leisure, waited on hand and foot by the nurse who took interest in him. Geller would offer massages that James never turned down and his burns, sprains, cuts, bruises and broken bones healed quickly.

On a night when Geller had a day off, she sat with James on the couch, watching television.

"I'm pretty excited," said Geller. "It's not every Friday that I get a night off from General."

"So would you like to watch a movie?" James asked.

"Sure, what would you like?"

"Something with action and adventure perhaps..."

"What about romance?" Geller asked. "Something with a little glamour and fantasy thrown in...?"

"Some like watching that," James replied, "and some like doing that sort of thing..."

"I like doing too."

James flushed as Geller leaned in closer. "Oh really?" he teased. "You can't prove it by me."

"It wouldn't be nice to take advantage of someone who's still recovering from extensive injuries."

James ran a hand on her thigh. "I'm all recovered now," he said, grinning.

"Is that so?" Geller reached over James, grabbing for the remote and turned off the television. "Well, maybe your private nurse had better give you a thorough physical examination!" James felt the breath leave his body as Geller leaned over him, trapping his body beneath hers. "Would you like for me to see?"

"See what?" James asked faintly.

Geller chuckled. "You're too cute!" She quipped and unbuttoned her blouse, revealing a black lace brassiere.

James blew a hard sigh, his skin immediately growing prickly once she reached over his head and shut off the lamp. "You've got a smoking body," he muttered and took in a thin breath as Geller as sat on his thighs, barring him to move.

"Here, let me help you with that," she murmured and deftly unbuttoned his shirt then undid the fly of his jeans. "You know, I really, really like you, Sport. It's been really fun having you around."

"But I haven't done anything but loaf around, eat your food and watch your television!" James protested. "How is that fun?"

"Then you haven't felt what I do to you in your sleep, do you?"

James slackened and broke out in cold sweat. "What?"

"As far as I'm concerned," Geller said softly, caressing his chest, "you can stay here as long as you like!" James gasped, startled as her hands went lower down his body, forcing a freezing rush through him. "Feels good, huh?"

"Please," James moaned.

"Let me show you how a real woman kisses." Geller kissed James deeply on the lips and he cried out when his energy flared suddenly. Geller screamed and pulled back. "What did you do to me?" she wailed, quickly scrambling away. The light flickered on, revealing the woman clutching her scorched arm. "You burned me... how?"

"I can explain!" James stammered and immediately sat upright. "Please, just...!"

"You're like acid," Geller cried, "or poison!"

"I didn't mean to!"

"Get out of here!"

Unable to further reason with her, James grunted and rose to his feet, tucking in his shirt and buttoned his jeans. He stepped into his shoes and left the couch, storming for the front door. Opening it wide, James stepped back in shock when the mysterious star fighter who wore the brown and blue suit and silver glasses entered, holding a small hand-held scanner that beeped.

"Space Guy," James spat, "what are you doing here?"

"Who are you?" Geller demanded.

"My scanners indicate you're part of the Directorate," the stranger snapped. "You're trying to interfere with the weapon of the Resistance."

"Wait, wait!" James cried as the young man put away his scanner and withdrew a golden pistol. Geller backed away, forming a green staff in hand that buzzed in yellow electricity.

"We have to try all means," Geller said. "If force didn't work, then we had to try a softer tactic!"

"You have two options: either arrest or death!"

"Put down your weapon first!"

James stood between them with dimly glowing hands. "Both of you stop," he shouted as his hands blazed in pale blue flames, "or I'll blow all our butts sky high!"

Geller lowered her weapon and made it vanish once the stranger put away his golden pistol. Geller grunted and stormed out the room. James watched her go, stunned.

"So that's why she didn't freak out when she saw the tattoo on my chest," he thought. *"She was one of them..."*

"I've come to talk to you about important matters," said the star fighter seriously, breaking James's thoughts. "You must know in which you are embarking."

"So tell me," James grumbled, turning to face him.

"On the other side of the universe where this power originated, a war is being fought on a scale unimaginable to you. It is a war against oppression and the oppressors are winning. You must go there with me at once and use the power of the Luminis Signet to turn the tide."

"That sounds like that could take a while..."

"Decades, certainly."

James took a step back, clenching his hands. "Wait a minute," he growled. "I didn't sign up for that - I'm not going anywhere, Space Guy!"

"So you refuse?"

"Damn right, I refuse!"

"Will you be able to rest easy at night, knowing that your planet may be conquered?"

"Hey, going with you might as well be suicide!" James shouted.

"That's right... I cannot force you." The young man sighed and folded his arms across his chest.

"Look, I just can't go off running into space to fight some war I never heard of!" James protested. "You've lost your damn mind thinking I'll just drop everything right now!"

"Do not worry... eventually, inevitably, the war will come to you and then it will be far too late."

"I'll worry about it when it happens," James muttered.

"Then you would wish you had accompanied me and learned the full extent of the power of the weapon in which you hold." The stranger turned on his heel. "You would have wished to save your home world and know the victory of crushing the utmost evil this multiverse has seen at its source."

"Hold on," James snapped and grabbed the young man by the shoulder. "Tell me, what *is* the full extent of the Signet's power? Tell me how it works or you're toast!"

"Sorry," the star fighter said, brushing aside James's hand. "You are already dangerous enough. If you are not going to live up to your obligations, then why should I tell you anything?"

"Because I insist!" James shouted and the pale blue flames that flared around his hands turned black, growing in intensity. "Now tell me, what can it do that I don't know about?"

"Save it," the stranger snapped. "Let me go peacefully, for I am needed at home - with or without you... or the Signet."

"Why am I given the strongest one?" James yelled after the young man who walked down the steps. "Why hadn't anyone else been given this one? Why just others?"

The star fighter paused and turned to James. "Because they destroyed themselves when it became too much," he said simply. James blanched and stepped back. "Now, before I go, let me caution you: sooner or later, you too will need a respite from the burden. Do not try putting it on an inanimate object or lower life form. Unchecked by a high-order sentience, it'll explode like a supernova." The young man gestured to James. "If you die, certain safeguards will kick in, forestalling an explosion for a few hours... perhaps long enough for a second to remove the weapon from your corpse." The stranger shrugged his shoulders. "Provided you plan ahead, of course."

"You're lying to me!" James hollered. "You're just trying to frighten me to get me to go with you!"

"I still won't reveal the greatest secret of this power... though you'll probably figure them out after a while." The young man turned away. "It's a matter of principle."

"Hold on, Space Guy!" James ran down the stairs and the young man paused in step. "Just wait a minute..."

James met up along the stranger's side and grabbed him by the arm, turning him around. The young man pulled out of James's grip and folded his arms across his chest, frowning in disapproval. James stood there overwhelmed by the many thoughts swirling through his mind as he considered all his options.

"*Maybe I should give up this thing,*" James mused. "*It got me hurt, it got Leila broken to bits and it got Roxanne and her little monsters killed!*" The power that blazed around his hands dimmed slightly. "*What good did it do against that nutcase whack job Adnan who damn near wrecked me? Not a thing! Nothing at all!*" He sighed heavily and beckoned to the stranger to come closer. "*I'm not deserving of this power...*"

"What do you want?" the star fighter asked.

"Look," James muttered, "I was just thinking... how about I just give you back this thing?"

"Why the change of heart?"

"It's been nothing but trouble for me." James blew a hard sigh. "Once I got it from one of you guys, my life had turned to trash. Things were fine *before* I met you and your crew!"

"Do you know how to transfer the power?"

"Yeah, I did it once..." James touched his chest and his hand warmed as the brand burned into his palm. The young man pushed up his sleeves and held out an arm as James presented his hand.

"You're a fine and noble being, Russell," said the stranger. "My race and all the peaceful races will forever be in your debt."

James quickly paused and withdrew his hand. "Hold it..." he snapped. "What did you call me?"

"What?"

"What did you just call me?" James demanded.

"What's wrong?"

"Prove to me you're part of the Protectorate!"

"This is not the time for foolishness, Russell! Just give me the weapon!"

"Only a few people call me by that name..." James growled. "But only one who I hate calls me that exclusively!" He shoved the young man back by the chest and the flames around his hands burned brighter. "You're probably under his control somehow!" The star fighter stepped back, growing tense as the flames changed from black to dark red. "Besides, didn't you tell me before that my Signet was *incompatible* with yours?"

The young man grunted. "Very well," he said sourly, "for now..."

James turned away and stormed back inside the house. Slamming shut the door, he took in a deep breath and the flames died from around his hands.

"Now to ask that nurse some questions," James grumbled and made his way for the bedroom. "Hey, Nurse!" he called as he opened the door.

Finding the bedroom darkened, he flipped the nearby light switch and sucked in a shallow breath once the room became illuminated, finding blood, hacked remains, and viscera staining the walls, carpet and ceiling.

"Holy shit!" James cried and staggered back into the opposite wall, clasping a hand over his mouth. He heard the toilet flush and the bathroom door opened, revealing Adnan wearing a dark navy turtleneck, black jeans and boots. His short frizzy strawberry blond hair was wet, which he dried off with a towel.

"Oh," said Adnan cheerfully, tossing the towel aside. "Well, well, what do we have here?" He clenched his hands, forming the onyx spiked whip in one hand while the other turned to stone. Adnan immediately crossed the floor and James quickly righted his stance as reddish-orange flames erupted around his fists.

"You stay the hell away from me," James growled and Adnan came to a stop, smiling maliciously. "Why did you kill her?"

"Her use ran out, simply put," Adnan replied.

"I thought I burned your ass to a crisp!" James shouted. "What did you do?"

"Granite can't burn, silly boy," Adnan teased and let out a short laugh. "Besides, you just didn't run hot enough for me."

"Shut up!" James roared and rushed at Adnan, throwing a flaming punch.

Adnan swiftly turned out the way, slamming a heavy fist in the back of James's head that knocked him down. James grunted from the blow and staggered forward then quickly regained his footing. He took a small leap, levitating slightly over the floor as Adnan turned around, facing him.

"I thought controlling that pretty nurse would get you to give up your power willingly," Adnan said, winding the whip in hand, "but since she had an Earth Signet, whenever she touched you, either you burned her or she healed you..."

"You mean she had the same powers as you do?" James spat, dubious.

"Not quite..." Adnan grinned, grasping the onyx whip taut in hand. "So I tried it again with that Relayer. You almost gave up that power to him, but you're tougher than I thought..."

"I may be blond, but I'm not stupid!" James yelled as Adnan chortled. "I knew you were controlling him somehow!"

"Oh, so you've grown smarter since I've turned you out, eh?"

"You made a big mistake messing with me!" James thundered and the reddish-orange flames burning around his hands flared brighter, fading to yellow.

"Perhaps."

"Die already!" James screamed and lunged forward with a flaring fist.

Adnan quickly ducked out the way and cracked his whip, wrapping the end around James's arm and flipped him over onto the floor. "Oh it felt good to hear her scream," Adnan taunted over James. "You should've heard it! And the way her soft flesh felt between my fingers when I ripped her apart, piece by piece..."

James grabbed onto the whip, yanking Adnan forward, forcing him to stumble. Adnan retracted the whip once James pulled back his arm that blazed in yellow-orange flame and the binds holding him eradicated into ash.

"You're not hurting anyone else, you freaky psycho bastard!" James sneered and thrust forward his inflamed hand. "I meant it when I said I was sending you to Hell! I *will* destroy you!"

"Oh, there's something *deadly special* about you, isn't there?" Adnan snarled and rushed forward with his stone-covered fist held high. James immediately reversed him, ducking out a wild punch and picked up Adnan, hurling him through the wall. Adnan's body became metallic for a moment once he struck the partition before slumping forward onto the floor, returning to normal.

"Get up!" James bellowed, hovering over him as the burning fires swarming about his hands turned yellow-white.

Adnan looked up and snorted. "I can *feel* it from here," he said and cracked his neck. Standing to his feet with ease, Adnan formed a brown sphere of light in each hand. "You should've given up that Signet when you had the chance!" he shouted. "Now I'll just have to break you again!"

"No chance, sucker!"

"Ha!" Adnan thrust down his hands, releasing stone darts.

James quickly jumped back and grunted when several darts tore into his shoulder, arm and leg, forcing him staggering rearward. James clutched his bleeding arm and released a flaming sphere with his good hand at Adnan as he threw another salvo.

The darts pierced James, throwing him onto the floor on his back as the fireball slammed Adnan in the face, catching his clothing on fire. Adnan screamed from the consuming inferno, clawing at his face.

James stumbled to his feet and a sudden blast of force struck him from behind, tossing him head over heels. Landing sprawled on his face, James struggled to stand and whirled around, spotting the mysterious young man with the silver visor, generating a sphere of flame in both hands.

"What are you doing here?" James demanded.

"I've come to take back the Signet," said the stranger.

"I'm keeping it, Space Guy," James snapped. "It's to keep crazy killers like him from murdering everyone!"

"You do not understand... You must do this for your best interest."

"Back off!" James shouted.

"I too have a weapon, though a pale shadow of the one you wield; I control *all* of its power..." The star fighter thrust forward both hands, releasing a strong stream of bright red flame. James screamed when struck in the chest and thrown back into the wall by the force, burning away his clothing. "Whereas you can only control a fraction of yours!"

"Why are you fighting me?" James cried. "Unless that madman's controlling you again...!"

The stranger let out a demented laugh. "That's right," he sneered. "I also have no compunctions about devastating everyone here, including the entire planet!"

James peeled himself from the wall and rushed forward with lightning speed. He jammed his shoulder into the young man, sending him crashing through the other side. They both struck the pavement and James straddled the star fighter, throwing charged punches into his face. "Why?" he yelled. "Why are you doing this?"

The silver sunglasses fell off, revealing blind white eyes. "Because," the stranger hissed, grinning deviously, "Savoy promised me the utmost power!" He grabbed James by the face and a strong blast of light blinded him, surging his body full of sharp agony.

James pushed off the star fighter and bulleted skyward and the young man below took a jumping leap, generating a transonic wave. The star fighter swiftly gained ground, closing the gap between them as he propelled toward James with a burst of speed.

Racing forward, the star fighter caught up and grabbed hold of James by the waist, wrestling with James as they continued their ascent to the heavens. The air around them thinned and grew cold, with ice developing on their skin.

James hurled the stranger off and thrust both hands forward, releasing a strong blast of white flame that incinerated his opponent's clothing completely. James fell away, completely weakened once his power burned out and careened back to earth.

On his fiery descent, James's energy kicked into high gear and he swooped down before blazing toward the young man who hovered near the edge of the stratosphere. The star fighter grinned and beckoned to James, forming a sword three feet in length crafted entirely of flame in his hand.

The star fighter clasped his free hand around the handle of the blade, forcing the flames turning from red to black and slashed James once he approached, hurtling him rearwards.

James released a fireball, slamming into the star fighter and in retaliation, the stranger plunged the fiery sword into James's chest. James slackened once his heart stopped beating for a second and the young man swooped in, kicking him off by the shoulder. James dropped through the sky with wide eyes, dead to the world.

CHAPTER THIRTY-ONE

James found himself in total darkness once his eyes snapped open and his limbs refused to respond when he tried to move.

"*Where am I?*" he thought. "*Why can't I move...?*" He attempted to vocalize, only to have his mouth produce no sound. "*Why can't I speak?*" Growing frightened, unchecked tears streamed down his face. "*Is this how it ends, stranded somewhere between Death and Limbo?*" The pain crept through his joints, penetrating through his head. "*So, I'm not dead... I am alive, I think... I pushed myself over my limit.*" The agony rushed through his body and James shut his eyes as red light flashed behind them. "*But what's the point? Leila could be dead now, killed by that crazy son of a bitch...!*"

"Are you all right?" a vaguely recognizable kind voice called gently from afar.

James opened his eyes again, this time finding he resided in an unfamiliar bedroom. "How did I get here?" he muttered and sat up, holding his throbbing head in hand. "What a monster headache..." James pushed back the bedspreads and planted his feet on the floor. Standing, the sheets fell away, revealing his nude body.

"Where are my clothes?" James muttered and yawned. After stretching, he then headed for the door, trying the handle. It clicked open and James peered down the dark corridor. "Anybody here?" he called tentatively.

Seeing nothing but swirling shadows, James clenched his hands and they glowed slightly, illuminating the hall. In the dim lighting, he spotted another door at the end.

James sprinted for the exit and once he reached it, he pushed against the door. It creaked open and James reached in, feeling around for a switch. His fingers brushed against a toggle and the light came on, illuminating a simple bathroom with toilet, sink and shower stall with a glass door.

James blew a sigh of relief and headed for the stall. Stepping in, he turned on the water and stood under the stream, relaxing as the hot water pelted at his back. James put his forehead against the cool tile, sighing heavily and the power around his hands died.

A sudden draft entered the room and he looked up, noticing Nadine standing near the door, wearing a black silk bathrobe. James took in a weak breath, growing lightheaded as his body grew warm in response to the sight of her.

"I'm glad I found you," Nadine said gratefully. "You worried me there for a minute!"

"I'm fine," James said slowly. "How did I get here...?"

"Don't worry about that." Nadine approached, smiling seductively and slipped part of the fabric off her shoulder as she neared the shower stall. James broke out in cold sweat despite the heat of the shower, flushing darkly in return. "Didn't you say I had a smoking body?"

"Yeah, I did..." James sucked in a thin breath once Nadine closed the gap between them. "I think..."

"So take off my clothes," she murmured.

"But you'll get wet..."

"That's the point, silly!"

"*I must be dreaming!*" James thought. "*I haven't touched Nadine in years...*" He sucked in a shallow breath when Nadine stroked his face with a slender hand.

"What's the matter?" she asked.

"I..." James grasped at the robe's ties with burning hands.

"It's okay," Nadine said softly.

James let go and the robe fell at her feet. "*This feeling...*" he mused as Nadine stepped into the stall with him, "*it's familiar... But why does this feel so wrong?*" James backed away when Nadine put a hand to his chest. "*But it feels so right...*" Nadine stroked his chest and James grunted when pain shocked through him.

"Well, aren't you going to kiss me?" Nadine asked mildly.

"But when I kissed you the first time..."

"You just bit me by accident, is all..."

James leaned forward, cupping his free hand on the back of Nadine's head while his other hand wrapped around her waist. Kissing her deeply, James felt his breath thin when a strong sensation of dread coursed through him and his energy abruptly drained from his body.

"*That same fear,*" he thought. "*I felt it before...!*" James pulled away, gasping for breath.

"What's the matter?" Nadine inquired, growing concerned.

James shook his head, growing dizzy when he heard faint screams in his head and heaved for breath.

"*Calm down, Jim*," he told himself, slumping against the stall wall. "*There's nothing to freak out about...*"

"Is something wrong...?"

"Please, don't worry!" James carped. "I'm fine, really!"

"Maybe I can help?" Nadine reached out and James arched back as instant agony ripped through his body.

"Don't touch me!" he cried, pushing her away.

"You act like I'm trying to hurt you!" Nadine protested as James slipped to his knees.

"Just stay back!" He moaned and clutched his head, overwhelmed by a sensation of intrusion. "Just leave me alone!"

"*Just relax,*" a faint voice said in his head. "*Relax and the pain will pass...*"

"Who is that?" James cried. "Who's talking to me?"

"Hey, hey," Nadine said tenderly. She perched beside him and stroked a gentle hand through his wet hair.

"What's wrong with me?" James mewed.

"There's nothing wrong..."

"*You belong here,*" said the echoing ominous voice. "*You're safe with her... Forget everything, just enjoy yourself...*"

"Enjoy..." James murmured.

"*Just sleep, sleep deeply...*"

Nadine kissed James on the back of the neck and he stiffened. "*This fear... am I making it up?*" James wondered, "*Is it unreasonable?*" He whimpered and Nadine took his hand, holding it to her cheek.

"You need to sleep," said the faint voice. *"Sleep deeply and dream..."*

The hot water turned cold and Nadine began to melt, turning into blood and bones. James immediately rose to his feet, terrified. *"Don't lose it, Jim!"* he yelled inside his mind, watching in horror as Nadine became ground beef and giblets before his eyes, her discombobulated parts swirling down the drain. Hearing demented laughter from behind, James turned around and let out a surprised yelp when kicked in the face by a heavy boot.

"You're so easy to manipulate," snarled a familiar voice.

"You...!" James crawled back as Adnan hovered over him nude with bat-like wings, wearing only heavy combat boots. He had a spiked tail that wagged behind him and two large horns protruded from his head through his long frizzy pale reddish-blond hair that cascaded down his shoulders and back. In each of his clawed hands, he held a leather whip with knots braided throughout and stone chips tied on the ends while the other held a large stone knife with serrated teeth.

"Keep awake, wannabe!" Adnan howled.

"You sick demon," James wailed, "stay back!"

"You're going to stay awake for all the torture I'm going to put you through!"

"No!"

The demonic Adnan lashed out with his whip and it wrapped around James, barring movement. James sucked in a pained breath as the chips dug into his skin, slicing into his flesh. Adnan yanked back, hurling James through the glass door and sent him crashing through the transparent panel.

James bowled over onto the floor, screaming in the agony from the shards of glass that penetrated his skin, forcing black blood weeping through the cuts. Adnan retracted the whip and threw the knife before James could get up, piercing him in his left shoulder. James let out another cry in anguish.

"Yes," Adnan howled, "scream for me!" He flew over to James and wrenched out the blade embedded in his shoulder. "Scream louder as I take you apart piece by piece!"

James clenched his left hand that had the tattoo, forcing it blazing brightly. Adnan brought down the knife and James rolled out the way then thrust forward his left hand, releasing a fireball. Adnan immediately dodged the attack and James staggered to his feet, clutching his bleeding shoulder.

"You'll burn for hurting me like this!" he thundered.

"You can't defeat me, wannabe," Adnan taunted as he levitated over to James. "So just suck it up and turn over for me. I promise the pain will be long lasting!"

"You know, I'm pretty much fed up with you," James snarled. "I know you're obviously a fragment of my dream or maybe a part of my fear, but either way, I'm not giving up this power or the fight." The flames quickly spread around his body, forcing steam to appear from the water on his skin. "Ever since I got this damn thing, someone's been trying to take it away or control me and I'm *sick* of getting pushed around!"

"Then push back!"

The devil Adnan rushed forward, slashing down with the knife. James grabbed it with his flaming hand and struggled against Adnan's strength, losing the fight once the knife tore through his hand and down his arm. James screamed and thrust forward his other hand, unleashing a forceful blast of flame.

Adnan dropped the knife to the floor and it shattered on impact as he somersaulted out the way behind James. Swiftly turning around, Adnan hurled forth several stone darts, jamming them into James's back. James roared in pain, falling forward on his knees and the demonic Adnan landed softly on his feet. He stormed up to James, forming another leather whip in his free hand with many strips that held lacquered wooden hooks on the ends.

"You'll pay for that," James growled beneath him.

"Oh, you haven't had enough," Adnan snarled, kicking James forward on his face. "Are you beginning to understand?" James screamed when Adnan lashed into his back with both whips, tearing open skin. "This will not turn out like you expected!" Adnan roared, throwing blood against the walls and floor as he slashed into James again. "Keep awake!" James ground his teeth from the pain and everything flashed in red from the continued whipping. "Wake up!" James fell into the darkness, embracing the fierce pain that assaulted his flesh.

James sat up screaming and gentle arms embraced him at once.

"Oh, James!" a voice cried. "James..."

James gasped for breath, frantically taking in his surroundings once the tinted red world faded away, replaced by white sterile walls and bright blue-white lights shining down on him.

He looked around, finding machines nearby that chirped and whooshed, drowning out the haunting manic laughter that rang in his head. The strong scent of antiseptic filtered in the room, dousing out the smell of blood. He pulled away, noticing that many bandages covered his torso and arms.

"James..."

James looked up, facing a young woman who had bobbed sandy hair and hazel eyes, wearing an oversized dark green shirt and flared brown pants.

"Nadine...?" James inquired.

"Yes, it's me."

James reached out with a hesitant hand and stroked her cheek. She took his hand and squeezed gently. "I thought I heard your voice..." he murmured.

"I'm here," she said softly.

"How... why...?"

"I heard about the gas explosion in the paper," Nadine said. "I called Allen and he said you were supposedly picked up by your friend Leila, but when neither one of you showed up to your jobs, we looked for you in the hospital."

"Leila...!" James squeezed her hand tightly. "Is she alive?"

"Yes, but she's in traction." Nadine shook her head. "The house that blew up, torn her pretty badly..."

James shuddered and looked away. "*If only you knew!*" he thought.

"But when we came looking for you, you were reported missing - you were gone for almost a month!"

"How did I get back here?" James asked.

"I don't know who found you or who brought you here," Nadine murmured. "I just kept calling every day, hoping you'd be here. I was afraid you died, James!"

James gave a tight smile. "Why do you care so much about me?"

"I never stopped caring..."

"Even when you dropped out of Central?"

"Even then..."

"But you never kept in touch."

"Life got in the way..." Nadine sighed heavily. "Even after I let you live with me for a while when your parents died, I still cared and worried about you."

"But you know I haven't seen you in almost three years!"

"My feelings haven't changed."

"Please, don't hold a torch for me."

"Don't worry." Nadine smiled faintly.

"I want to see Leila... I have to see her!"

"Once you heal up some more, okay?"

"So you know where she is?"

Nadine nodded and let go of James's hand. "Just rest." She sat across from him, taking a seat in the padded chair situated on the other side of the bed.

James groaned as he laid back and shut his eyes. "*I shouldn't be here,*" he thought. "*I shouldn't be <u>here</u> at all. I should be <u>out there</u>...*" James blew an unsettled sigh. "*With all this fighting over a measly tattoo, I'm surprised no one's set off a basic nuclear winter and started World War Three...*"

Unable to rest, his eyes fluttered open and James grunted as he struggled to sit upright. "*I wish I could have trashed*

Adnan." He looked down at his scarred bandaged hands. *"Twice he handed my ass to me and twice, he nearly wrecked me."* James ran his hands through his hair. *"Even without this supposedly powerful Signet, I can't keep it together!"* He glanced at Nadine who dozed off in the chair across from him. *"I can't be sure if Allen's safe, or if Nadine will be safe since I know for sure she's going to be in my business."*

James ripped out the cords, cables and tubes attached to him and the machines pinged in response. He slipped out of bed and wrapped the sheets around his waist, then approached Nadine who began to rouse.

"James..." she murmured.

James reached over and kissed her on the forehead. "I'm here," he whispered, stroking her cheek. "Go back to sleep. The machines... they're just hating on me."

"Okay," she muttered.

James let her go and carefully made his way out the room, stepping silently down the hall. *"If she's in traction like they said,"* he mused, *"then she shouldn't be too far..."*

Checking several rooms down the corridor, he then came back around and headed in the opposite direction. Moments later, he came across Leila's name card outside one room and opened the door, entering the dimly lit space.

James stood silently before her bed, watching her breathe evenly. The sight of her, from her head to her torso, to her arms and legs bound in plaster casting, while the remaining parts of her body had stitches and bandages. He gripped the railing to keep his footing as his knees grew weak and the sheet around his waist fluttered to the floor.

"Oh, Leila!" James cried out and slipped to his knees. Overcome with grief, sobs wracked his body.

"James?" a voice croaked. "Jamie... that you?"

James sniffled and wiped his eyes with the palms of his hands. "Yeah," he murmured and stood. James stroked a weak hand down Leila's cheek and she winced from his touch.

"Jamie... he just... he touched me," Leila rasped. "It was like... it was fire... I was on fire..."

"I know," James whispered, stroking her hair. "Take it easy. Don't try to talk now."

"He... he came that day..." Leila looked away, her green eyes distant. "When you lost... Lost your clothes, your keys..."

"You mean to say Adnan met you before?" James cried, aghast. "That early?" He bit his fist and turned away, contemplating.

"That could explain why she was acting all weird after I got the Signet! He somehow saw in my head and tried to manipulate her to get to me..."

"You shouldn't be..." Leila's hoarse voice cracked and she took in a weak breath. "Shouldn't be afraid... I'm the one..."

"What are you saying?" James murmured.

"I should be afraid..."

"Why?"

"I love you... but you hurt... You hurt me..." Leila shuddered. "He hurt me bad... I can't face it..."

"I'm sorry," lamented James. "Please, forgive me. I swear; I'll kill that bastard for doing this to you!"

"He hurt me so bad... I can't face you... face anything... that tries to hurt you... even me..."

"What do you want me to do?"

"There's nothing... nothing to talk about..."

"What are you trying to say?"

"I should've read..." Leila shut her eyes. "...read the handwriting... on the wall..."

"What do you mean?" James took her bandaged hand, squeezing firmly. "Leila, speak to me!"

Her eyes fluttered open and she glanced up at him. "I should've known," she said faintly. "Once you got that mark... bad stuff happens..."

"What?"

"I got involved..." She hacked a weak laugh. "I guess I got what I deserved..."

"Don't say that!" James wailed. "Don't say things like that!"

"Don't... don't talk me out of this..." Leila took in a shallow breath and exhaled slowly. "I want you to leave..."

"Please!" James moaned and held her hand to his face. "Please, don't do this to me!"

"I'll be safer... without you around..." Leila slipped out of his grip and James backed away, shaking in fear. He picked up the fallen sheet and held it around his waist.

"Leila, listen," James said as tears ran down his face full force. "The whole world is at stake, and so are you. You're a part of this. *We're* a part of this!" James stroked Leila's cheek with his free hand. "I'll come back once I get rid of this mess and get our lives back to normal, okay?" James kissed Leila gently on the lips. "I promise you that, okay? I promise you that with my life!"

Leaving the room, James bumped into Nadine and dropped the sheet as he quickly whirled her around, clasping a hand around her mouth.

"Don't scream," he murmured in her ear as he pressed against her. Nadine looked up at him with frightened eyes. "Listen to me, get me out of here." James released his hold and Nadine grabbed him gingerly by the arm.

"James," she hissed, "why are you up and around?"

"Get me out of here!" he whispered. "I can't stay here!"

"Why?"

"I have the Syndicate after me!" Nadine gasped and let go, taking a step back. "If you don't want to get involved, I understand!"

Nadine ran away and James picked up his fallen sheet. Padding back to his room, he got into bed and immediately fainted from exhaustion.

CHAPTER THIRTY-TWO

A gentle hand shook James awake and he opened his eyes. Nadine stood over him, holding a shopping bag. She wore a simple pale yellow blouse over green slacks and black flat shoes.

James sat up on his elbows, intrigued. "What's that for?" he murmured.

"It's clothes," Nadine said simply. "I'm getting you out of here."

"Why?" James demanded. "I don't want to put you and Tony in trouble!"

"I still love you, though everyone's telling me I shouldn't," Nadine replied. "I'll stick with you and face anything you face, even if someone tries to hurt you."

"You won't be safe," James said seriously. "No one will be safe as long as anyone hangs around me, including yours truly!"

"Are you going to sit here and talk," Nadine interrupted, "or change and get out of here before the doctors finish their rounds?"

James grunted and took the bag out of Nadine's hands. "Persistent, aren't you?" he grumbled and pulled out the clothing, examining them. The articles consisted of all black:

turtleneck, jeans, trench coat, gloves, and socks. The pair of flat-soled sneakers was the only items of color: red and white. James swallowed hard and broke out in cold sweat. "What--?" he started.

"I didn't forget your size," Nadine interjected and James glanced up at her. "I doubt you grew any taller or gained any weight since our college days." She smiled sheepishly. "You've always been pretty active."

"No underwear?" James carped.

Nadine shrugged her shoulders. "You never wore any around me."

James nodded and started the task of pulling into the clothing. After changing with Nadine's help, James took her hand and she led him out the room.

Following Nadine's stride, James grew nervous as she made her way around the various corridors. Taking the stairway out the hospital, they exited into the parking lot in the rear and his apprehension worsened once they approached Nadine's car.

"I don't want to cause you any trouble," he murmured.

"It'll be okay," Nadine said in assurance. "If you're worried about Tony, I can have him sent to camp somewhere."

"You're not serious!" James blustered.

Nadine laughed and opened the door for him. "Really, if something happens, Tony will be safe," she said in a firm tone. "I know some people who are willing to take care of him."

"What about you?" James entered the car and Nadine leaned against the door, smiling at him.

"I'll worry about you and you worry about you."

"I don't think Tony should be the only one to worry about you."

Nadine ran a hand through James's hair. "We'll get to that problem when we get there."

James said nothing once Nadine shut the door, disturbed as he watched her come around the driver's side. She calmly entered the car and started the engine and he clenched his hands. "Nadine..." James said softly.

Nadine glanced at him, concerned. "Hm?" James shook his head, unable to say what he wanted and looked away. Nadine patted at his thigh. "It'll be alright," she said. "I promise."

"I hope so," James murmured.

His tension worsened while Nadine drove for her house in the darkness of the early morning.

Pulling into the driveway of a small brown house with dark shutters, Nadine turned to James and touched him lightly on the arm.

"Yeah?" James murmured.

"You look awful," she said.

"It's almost light soon," James muttered. "You'll soon have to get Tony up for school."

"It's okay. Do you want a pot of coffee?"

"Later... I just need someplace to sleep without letting my guard down."

"That's why you're welcome to crash here any time."

Nadine left James's side and exited the car, hurrying up the walk. She entered her house then departed moments later, returning to the vehicle. She opened the door and pulled gently at James's arm to get him up. He groaned as he stepped out and she shut the door for him.

"My legs feel like lead," James moaned as he shuffled up the walkway.

"Once you get into a nice soft bed," said Nadine, "you'll feel much better." She led James to her couch and he slumped down over on his side once his body met the firm cushioning.

"I know this will sound crazy," James mumbled, "but I want you to wake me if anybody comes to the door."

"But I have to work today..."

"Let me know if anybody or anything unusual happens, okay?"

"I guess I can take a day off..."

"Just promise you'll wake me."

"Are you expecting someone?"

"Let's hope not..."

"If that's what you really want..."

James dozed off immediately.

James drifted, alternating between sensations of pain and pleasure. He later sensed warmth beside him and quickly sat up, panting for breath. Glancing over, James found Nadine curled beside him with her arms draped over his waist.

Pushing her gently away, James carefully unhooked her arms from around his midsection and deftly peeled himself out from beneath Nadine. He left the couch and wandered around the house, checking into various rooms only to find nothing of particular interest. He then set his intentions on searching for the bathroom.

Finding it down the main hall, he flipped on the switch and ran the cold water on the tap in the sink. Splashing water on his face, James looked up at his reflection in the mirror, staring back at a haggard young man with tired blue eyes, shaggy blond hair, large and broken thin nose and sunken cheeks.

"What the hell is wrong with you, Jim?" he muttered to his reflection. "You're better than this; get it together!"

James stiffened when he heard a knock on the front door and raced out to answer it. Flinging open the entrance, he found a note tacked to the wall and ripped it out. Glancing over the paper, James swallowed hard, struck with the intense sensation as if a ball of ice generated in his stomach.

"*The power you hold is too dangerous to fool around with,*" he read. "*Give up the Signet or people die.*"

"James?" Nadine called. "You left the water running in the bath." James clenched his flaring hand and the paper burned to ash. "Is there something wrong?"

"Let's go out to eat," James called back. "I'm starving!"

"Let me change clothes." Nadine said.

James growled under his breath, glaring skyward at the cold morning sunshine. "*Who am I kidding?*" he thought. "*I must be out of my mind thinking I'm safe here!*" James clenched his teeth as his hands warmed in response, releasing pale blue flames. "*Adnan must have a way to read my mind and control people - he probably saw all my friends and those close to me and looked them up so he can torture them later!*"

Nadine came out moments later and touched James gently on the arm, bringing him out of his thoughts. She smiled brightly at him and he smiled faintly back as they stood out on the porch.

"You look cute," James noted.

"Oh, this outfit is nothing," Nadine replied. "I just changed out of slacks and trouser socks to skirt and pantyhose!"

Scarlet flushed on James's face as he watched her lock the door and walked past for her car. "Isn't a little cold without your coat?" he called after Nadine.

"It's in the car," she answered. A strong cold breeze suddenly whipped up, forcing Nadine to drop her keys. Cursing under her breath, she bent to retrieve them and the wind blew back her skirt, showing off her hosiery and garters. James cleared his throat as the flush on his face spread to his ears.

"*Keep it together, Jim,*" he thought and hurried to join her.

Nadine opened the car door and pulled into her coat left on the seat then grinned at James once he entered the car.

"Have a good look?" she teased as she got in and shut the door.

"You did that on purpose!" James fussed.

"Right, like I have the power to ask the winds to do that!"

"You said pantyhose, not stockings!"

"Well, at least I know all your faculties are still functioning! I was starting to get worried..."

James snorted, looking out the window and Nadine laughed in response.

"*Nadine and Tony will not suffer the same way Roxy and her kids did...*" He contemplated as Nadine started the car and put it in drive. *"I'll kill him a thousand ways from Sunday before he gets another chance!"*

Later at the restaurant, James downed cup after cup of coffee as Nadine ate her meal with careful consideration. After getting another cup of coffee served, Nadine poked at James with her fork, tapping against his hand.

"Your food's getting cold," she noted. "Is the soup no good?"

"My stomach is still bothering me," James muttered.

"So coffee is the worst thing you ought to put down your gullet right now!"

James gave a tight-lipped smile, picking up his spoon. He took a slurp of the cold soup and Nadine smiled slyly in return. She then slipped off her shoe, pressing a stocking-covered toe up his leg. James grunted, tensing as Nadine's foot traveled higher up his thigh.

"What are you doing?" James hissed, hunching over his bowl of soup.

"I'm trying to get you to relax," Nadine purred. "You're way too tense!"

"Please don't do that..."

"Nobody can see us."

"Nadine, please!"

James sucked in a shallow breath as a freezing rush coursed through him and quickly scoot his chair back. The hairs on the back of his neck suddenly rose and he glanced over his shoulder, searching for his source of unease. Instead, he only found other patrons dotting the small diner for breakfast, either reading the morning newspaper or talking softly amongst themselves.

"See, nobody's paying us any attention," Nadine said calmly. "Now get back here or I'll have to crawl under the table!"

"Don't make a scene!"

"Then come over."

James tentatively moved his chair back in place and picked up his cup of coffee with a shaking hand while the other bent the spoon between his fingers. He clenched his teeth, trying to ignore Nadine's foot that pressed against him in his lap.

"*That bastard's toying with me,*" James thought, grinding his teeth. "*He could've struck at any time, easily taking hostages or making Tony a target at school, or taking down Nadine if he wanted to... But no, he's playing a waiting game to drive me nuts, wearing me down...*"

James took in a weak breath and broke out in cold sweat when he felt Nadine's foot press against his groin. "Please Nadine!" he pleaded.

"Come on," Nadine goaded. "Don't make me unzip your pants with my toes!"

Great heat rushed through James and he set down his cup with a firm bang. "Not now!" he snapped.

"You need to relax!" Nadine complained. "I'm only trying to help!"

"*This girl isn't going to quit,*" James considered, grinding his teeth harder as he vainly tried to ignore his growing interest. "*Either I'm giving her mixed signals or she doesn't care!*"

"James?" Nadine suddenly piped up, interrupting his thoughts.

"Huh?" James murmured.

"The spoon...!"

James glanced at the spoon; noticing knots in the metal and his flushed face immediately blanched. "Neat trick, huh?" he quipped and quickly straightened it. "Look, I'll be back. You know, input food, output crap." James stood and pulled the trench coat in front of him.

Nadine giggled. "You're fine," she said, smiling warmly. "Don't be so self-conscious!"

"I didn't know you were this freaky Nadine!" James complained.

"There's a lot about me that you don't know!" Nadine leaned forward, seductively unbuttoning the collar of her blouse. "You get to find all that out once we get home later."

James clenched his hands and blew a hard sigh as the flush returned to his face, rising to his ears.

"*Don't push me*," he prayed and immediately left the table. On his way to the restrooms in the rear, the payphone tucked in the corner began ringing. James glanced around and finding no one nearby to answer, he walked over.

"Hello?" he greeted after picking up the receiver.

"Give up the Signet," a mechanical voice sneered. "If not, there will be a massacre!"

"Where are you?" James barked. "Show yourself, you rotten piece of shit!" Cold laughter came from the other end of the line. "Where are you hiding, huh?" James roared, growing incensed. "From now on, you stop coming to me and tell me where you are so that I come to you and wipe your face off the planet!"

"You shall come to me," snarled the unfamiliar voice. "Tonight, you will know this is a war you cannot win!"

James slammed the receiver into the cradle and leaned against the wall, heaving for breath.

"James?" Nadine called and James turned around. She ran up to him and took his hands. "James, I heard you yell…"

"Just a phone call…" he moaned, giving her hands a firm squeeze.

"It was the Syndicate, right?"

"In a way…"

Nadine let loose her grip. "I heard that there's no way to truly leave, unless you die." James stiffened when she embraced him firmly. "Please, don't die!"

"I'll try not to," James murmured and stroked her hair. "Come on; let's go out for a drive. I need to get my mind off these things…"

"I know of a really good place to get your mind off everything!"

"Oh?"

Nadine pulled away, grinning mischievously. "With no one around, maybe we can do some interesting stuff together…"

James raised an eyebrow. "Like what?"

"Doing some dirty work at the crossroads, perhaps?"

James groaned. "Spare me!"

"You know I won't!"

James blew an annoyed sigh and pulled out of her grip. Nadine swatted his bottom and James whirled around, his face burning scarlet. He watched her walk away.

"This girl is nothing but trouble, Jim," James thought as he followed her outside. *"She'll eat you alive and completely destroy you!"*

CHAPTER THIRTY-THREE

Nadine pulled up onto a large park and stopped on a little-used road. James took in a shallow breath when he realized it was the rear of the office park belonging to Parsons and Parker.

"Why are we here?" he asked, growing tense once Nadine cut the engine.

"It's a nice quiet place," she replied. "Besides, no one can see us." Nadine leaned over, stroking his thigh.

James swallowed hard and gripped the seat in his hands. "What are you doing to me?" he moaned. "Why are you doing this?"

"What are you going on about?"

James sighed heavily and grabbed Nadine's hand before it traveled elsewhere. "I might as well tell you, show you, *warn* you before things get too heavy..."

"What would that be?"

"Follow me." James released his hold and clamored out the car then waved at Nadine to follow.

Light snow began to fall around them from the dark gray sky and James shuddered, flipping up the collar of his trench coat. When Nadine proved too slow to catch up to James's strides, he took her by the wrist and pulled her along through the woods.

"Where are we going?" Nadine cried. "Slow down; you're going too fast!"

"You'll see!" Approaching the area of downed charred trees and stubby grassland, James walked to the edge of the crater and waved a hand in its general direction. "See that devastation?" he asked. Nadine nodded, unable to answer. "It's related to a lot of things, a lot that might just blow your mind!"

"Like what?" James let go of her hand and took a small jump, hovering in the air above her. Nadine gasped and took a step back. "James...!" she cried. "What does this mean?"

"It means..." A sudden flash of light flared from behind and James pushed her back. Nadine let out a mild cry as she fell back on her rear, stunned and he turned, clenching his hands that burned in golden flame. "Stay back," James ordered.

"What's going on?" Nadine whimpered and clutched her chest, wincing in pain.

"Who's there?" James barked. "Are you another Relayer or a Corpii or something?" He hovered higher over the ground, scanning the area for signs of activity. "Come on, Space Guy, come out!"

"James, who are you calling out?"

"I've had plenty of time to think about your offer," James went on, "and you know what? I don't care what you do! I've been lied to so much since the first Space Guy showed up and stuck me with this curse that I don't believe *anything* anymore!" The bright golden light spread from his hands and surrounded his body. "I got dumped with some weird tattoo that makes me super strong, lets me fly and blow stuff up, though I have a feeling I was tricked into accepting it, you know? The Space Guy ditched it on some sucker because he knew that what was gonna happen, was gonna happen anyway. We don't have the technology to prevent you aliens from wasting our planet. So come on; get it over with already!"

"What are you going on about?' Nadine wailed.

"So you understand what I'm about to do, huh, Space Guy?" James ranted. "I've got to kill you, even if it means you'll kill me."

"James, no!" Nadine howled.

"You're nothing but a mad dog, am I right?" James yelled. "You can't be ignored; you can't be reasoned with. So I've got to try and kill you before you kill everyone else around me." The flames surrounding James began smoldering the clothes he wore. "Go on and do it, Space Guy - get it over with! Come out and kill me, otherwise, the fight is *on* and I'm *coming* for you, no matter what!"

"You won't stay alive for long," a dark voice hissed in return. "You've got your weapon and I've got mine... and this is the day we get to find out what else you're capable of!"

A sudden blast of frigid air slammed into James's chest, hurtling him head over heels. He slammed into the earth, forming deep cracks beneath his fallen smoking form.

"James!" Nadine screeched.

James groaned and held his head as he sat upright. Hovering before James levitated a young man with large dark violet-feathered wings that twitched lazily at his back.

James noticed the winged stranger had long silver hair and a well-conditioned athletic body, wearing navy calf-high boots, black slacks with a white stripe on the side, a form-fitting white shirt that buttoned halfway, exposing his narrow chest, and golden wraparound sunglasses.

"Do you think you've outsmarted me?" the mysterious young man snarled. "You didn't leave yourself any choices..."

"Who are you?" James uttered in a grating voice.

"The name is Spira Savoy..." Savoy landed softly on his feet, drawing frosted light in his hands. "I am a corpse collector and the destroyer of worlds."

"Why do you want to destroy my world?" James shouted. "What have we ever done to you?"

"Your race will destroy each other anyway, so I might as well beat you to it!"

"There's another reason." James's body lifted in the air by invisible forces. "Until you kill me, I'm not letting you destroy the only planet I know!"

"Fair enough." Savoy thrust forward his hands and James leaped out the way as a blast of ice formed on the ground. James fired off a shot of flame and Savoy dodged it with ease. "Don't you see?" Savoy crowed. "You're outmatched! Fire is weak against Water!"

"*Damn it,*" James thought and fired off round after round of flaming spheres, only to get them dodged or negated by blasts of ice. Savoy suddenly turned out and thrust forward his hands, releasing crystal darts. Struck in the side and back, James screamed and hurtled into the earth.

"Why are you here?" he moaned as Savoy touched down to the ground.

Savoy stepped up to James and planted his foot firmly on his face. "I came to annihilate..." he answered.

James shoved the foot out of the way. "No, there's another reason."

Savoy tried to stomp on James's face and James grabbed the alien by the foot, throwing him back. James swiftly rose to his feet before the alien corpse collector could regain his balance and ran to Savoy as he got up. James slammed a furious blazing punch into Savoy's face, knocking him rearward. The power of the punch sent Savoy hurtling through the forest, splitting trees as he slammed into them and his body crashed into the deepest part of the woods.

James took off and hovered over the ground, watching the fallen timber icing over. He held out a charged hand, drawing energy into large sphere of flame, forming the largest fireball he ever created.

James released the flare with such force that knocked him back and screamed when crystal spears suddenly blasted through him in retaliation, striking him at various points of his body.

His flaming body struck the ground hard, burning through the grasslands and the fireball struck the trees, lighting them on fire instantly.

"Ah, I thought that might flush you out," Savoy boasted as he emerged through the rubble, unhurt. "I knew at once I turned my back, you'd attack." James grunted when Savoy swooped down and picked him up, locking his arms behind his back. "I'm through playing by the rules with you," Savoy snarled. "There's too much at stake."

"*He's planning to kill me, I know it,*" thought James as he gave no resistance. "*If I want to take him out, then maybe I should build up my power and go supernova on him...*" The ice cold penetrated his very being, seeping down into his bones.

"What are your last words?" Savoy sneered in his ear.

"You have no conception of the stakes," James growled back. "You don't know why I fight..."

"Spare me the details."

"Then here's the short version!"

Bright white light blinded James once he released the power from his body. A crystal saber suddenly jammed through his chest from his back and he slumped forward to his knees, gagging and choking for breath.

"Getting desperate, aren't we?" Savoy teased. "Next time you'll think twice before unleashing that Energy Burst against me!"

"That's okay," James wheezed, "I know a few tricks myself..."

Savoy withdrew his blade and laughed, shoving James to the ground. James looked down, seeing a pool of blood and realized to his horror he was bleeding from the puncture.

"*I thought I could heal quickly!*" he thought wildly, grasping his chest. "*I'm bleeding out! Just don't panic--!*"

Savoy chuckled. "This is much too easy! If I had known you can die so readily I would have gotten rid of you sooner!"

James staggered to his feet and turned to face Savoy. "I'm not going down that quickly, punk!" he snarled. "You're gonna have to try harder than that!"

"Let's have at it! Come on, I'll let you strike first." Savoy beckoned to James. "You can't kill me anyway!" He grinned, showing fangs. "I want to see you try!"

James let loose a strong force of flame. A sphere of frosted light surrounded the alien and the embers faded on contact as the ice shield melted. Savoy smirked. "That would have hurt," he sauntered. "Is that the best you have?"

"Shut up!" James roared and sprinted forward, throwing another hard punch. Savoy's head whipped back from the force and he laughed darkly, flicking James back with a blast of crystal. James grunted once thrown down again and Savoy nonchalantly spat blood on the ground above him, grinning as his busted lip healed quickly.

"Since I have Fast Healing," retorted the alien, "it'll take more than a few taps to damage me." James struggled to breathe and Savoy grabbed him by the throat, lifting him into the air. "Listen to me," the corpse collector growled. "Join me and you won't have to die... you can live forever! Imagine that: immortality, power, everything beyond all that you've ever known!"

"No!" James rasped.

"James!" Nadine's voice shrieked. "James! Help me!"

The flames erupted around James and he kicked Savoy back before blasting off for the crater. "Where are you?" James called.

"Here, in the cave!"

James sped down into the crater and entered through a crevice carved into the earth on the side of the wall. Slowing to a stop, he noticed a support beam and gasped when the shadows inside moved.

"Nadine!" James bellowed.

Pale blue fluorescent plate lights abruptly flickered to life, humming softly around him from an unknown energy source. James found himself in a narrow corridor inside the caverns and ahead a harsh golden light flashed at the end of the hallway, pulsating crazily. A horrified scream echoed through the hall and James rushed toward the sound.

Coming onto an opening, he gasped when he saw numerous bodies hanging from the walls, connected by wires between the brilliant plate lights that illuminated the caverns.

"All these bodies!" James thought as he hovered over near Nadine's unconscious form lying on the floor of the cave. *"I recognize some of them... like the first Space Guy and that Space Cop...! He killed them, he killed <u>every</u> last one of them!"*

As an unexpected explosion rocked the cavern, James quickly touched down, throwing up his arms over his face to shield from the flying debris that came sailing his way, and using his body to protect Nadine.

Hearing footsteps crunch across the gravel, James relaxed his stance and turned toward the entrance, only to get a charred body wearing a uniform and helmet with polarized visor tossed in, rolling over at his feet.

"Oh no," James murmured and swallowed hard, kneeling down over the badly burned officer. He examined the mysterious young man and took off his helmet.

"That's the Space Guy that Adnan took over!" James realized, immediately disturbed. *"He tried to help me after Adnan got ejected..."*

"I see you found my secret laboratory," Savoy's voice called.

James glanced up, watching the corpse collector enter and noticed his hands were burned and bloodied and his wings partially shredded and broken.

"What have you done?" James thundered. "Why have you killed them all?"

"To put it simply: they fought me back."

The bright golden flames around James flashed as he became consumed with rage, fading the initial pain that crept into his joints. "I'm sick of all the killing!" he shouted.

"Then stop me."

The energy around James blazed brighter. "Why?" he screamed and rushed forward. Savoy swiftly dodged the attacks and James grew enraged, striking harder, faster, using stronger punches and kicks as he sped up to keep pace of the alien fighter. "I'll break your face! I'll make you bleed!" James boomed. "I'll *kill* you, hear me? You want me to fight you; you *will* get it! You want intergalactic war, you'll get it!"

Savoy continued to laugh as James burned his skin and broke his bones. "You'll never learn the secrets of the Signet in time," he rasped.

"No more lies!" James bellowed and grabbed Savoy's collar, shaking him.

"Then know this... no one will live to save you!" Savoy spat in his face. "Mark my words!"

James hurled Savoy's body through the cavern wall, blasting a crater through it and flew off through the hole in the sidewall. He grabbed for Savoy's downed body by the throat and lifted him up off the ground.

"Whatever you are," James snarled, "I want you to stay off my planet!"

Savoy let out a weak hacking laugh. "That is unlikely," he said faintly.

"I know I've been lied to before, but you're not going to fake me out again," James sneered. "You came from the stars, then return back to it!"

"Your power will be mine to keep," Savoy hissed. "You will be drained entirely, leaving behind nothing but an empty shell, just like all the others!"

"I will bury you!" James slammed Savoy into the ground headfirst and released an intense fiery blast that incinerated the entire forest around him in a flash of white heat. Collapsing to his knees, James gasped for breath and shivered from the cold as snow began to fall heavier around him.

"*Man, I need to stop blowing off my clothes,*" he reprimanded himself as his teeth chattered and the last shreds of his clothing burned away, "*or I'll freeze to death!*"

James rose to his feet and looked down at the smoldering husk of Savoy that lay at his feet. "Heh," James murmured. "Look at who's the empty shell!" He hoisted up Savoy's body and hurled it skyward with all his might. "Go back to where you came!" James hollered. "Stay there and never come back!" Totally drained, he panted hard for breath that came out as frosty puffs and ran a hand through his hair, looking up at the dark sky.

Hearing footsteps crunching across the charred vegetation, James quickly turned around, facing Menotti who carried Nadine's unconscious body slung over his shoulder.

"What are you going to do now?" Menotti asked.

"I just hope that everyone is *wrong*," James muttered, "and that this war out *there* somewhere doesn't eventually find its way *here*."

"Your actions today only delayed it."

"For how much longer?"

"A day, a week, a month, a year... We don't know."

James shuddered. "I can't dwell on that now," he groused. "Right now, I need to check on my friend Allen and see if he's okay."

"First let's stop by my place for some clothes," Menotti offered. "The longer you stay our here, more of your body parts are going to freeze and fall off."

James chuckled. "You must get this often..."

"I'm used to it." Menotti started walking ahead. "Come on, my car isn't far from here..."

"Is Nadine okay?" James asked as he followed in step behind Menotti. "She doesn't look so great..."

"She's broken some ribs, so we should drop her off at the hospital before we get into any heavy matters."

"*I must've pushed her too hard*," James thought sullenly. "*Now she's in deep with me! What am I going to do? How am I going to protect my friends?*"

Approaching a clearing that had a large dark gray sedan with black plush interior, Menotti set Nadine inside on the rear seat and reached into the driver's side, withdrawing a trench coat. He passed it to James and James pulled into it.

"It's open," Menotti said and James took a seat in the rear with Nadine, placing her head in his lap as he gently stroked her hair.

"Nadine, I'm so sorry," James murmured as Menotti gave a dismissive shrug, shut the door after him then got in the car.

Menotti successfully started the engine then shifted gears and pulled away from the office park. Nadine's eyes fluttered open and she smiled faintly at James. James took her by the hand, holding it at her waist.

"James..." she said faintly and winced in pain.

"Don't try to talk," James said softly. "We'll take care of you. I'll take care of you. It's okay now, you're safe..."

"I love you," Nadine murmured.

James gave a gentle smile and firmly squeezed her hand.

CONTINUED IN...

Enter A Shadowy Figure

Book Two of the Signet Saga

James Russell is a brilliant computer programmer... too bad he's not getting paid for it, since he's nothing more than a desk jockey at a dead end job!

While working his way up the company ladder and trying to destroy the gears of the corporate machine, James finds himself drawn into the struggle between creatures of another world and other earthly fighters with Signets.

Knowing he has a crucial role to play in the conflict, James unfortunately meets up with a sinister new threat: a power-hungry alien who wants him wiped out off the face of the Earth!

Trapped in what seems to be a losing battle, James must make a choice: stay on Earth and risk death by fighting to protect it from outside forces or joining the alien warlord and his army by aiding them in destroying other worlds... or is there a third option?

Name: James Russell
Age: 25
Hair/Eye: Blond/Blue
Height/Weight: 6 feet, 180 pounds
Skills: high school gymnastics, some karate
and boxing
Hobbies: running, roller skating, dancing at
the disco, and lifting weights
Job: programmer, clerical processing at
Parsons and Parker's (Employee ID: JR703 in
Dept 387)
Signet: Luminis (appears as a solar cross
tattoo)
Element: Fire/Light
Nickname: Jamie (by close friends), Jim (to
himself)

SIGNET: Luminis

Element: Fire/Light

Mind Powers: NONE

Hand Powers:

Fire Ball - a sphere of flame generated in one hand.

Flame Thrower - a blast of flame generated in both hands.

Flaming Shield - a flaring shield of flame projected at the front of the body

Body Powers:

Bullet Shield - a protective force of psychic energy surrounds the owner of The Signet to deflect bullets and other small projectiles. Anything bigger than a bullet (such as arrows or darts) can't be deflected unless using one of the elemental shields.

Frenzy - both *Super Speed* and *Super Strength* combined; The wielder's base speed is doubled and they can carry double their weight (their weight x 2).

Flaming Aura - the body is surrounded by flames.

Energy Burst - a blast of light that blinds opponents, up to 5 feet; derived from Flaming Aura (Sunburst), Electric Aura (Starburst), or Neon Aura (Irradiated Burst).

Nova - a blast of destructive flame or light, up to 20 feet; derived from Flaming Aura, Electric Aura, or Neon Aura.

Super Nova - a blast of destructive flame or light, up to 50 feet, derived from Flaming Aura, Electric Aura, or Neon Aura

Barrier - a field of psychic energy that absorbs most attacks.

Flight - the body is lifted into the air by will alone.

Weapon Powers:

Flaming Sword - a psychic blade that burns intensely hot, resembling flames. It is about 1 foot long from the hand and grows longer in response to base strength (up to 3 feet).

Energy Level Power Colors:

Low/Turned On - yellow

Medium/Annoyed - orange

High/Angry - red

Weakness:

Namoras (Water/Ice)

www.ingramcontent.com/pod-product-compliance
Lightning Source LLC
Chambersburg PA
CBHW070758180626
46818CB00001B/9